DEGREES
OF
SEPARATION

A Jessie Arnold Mystery

SUE
HENRY

AN OBSIDIAN MYSTERY

OBSIDIAN
Published by New American Library, a division of
Penguin Group (USA) Inc., 375 Hudson Street,
New York, New York 10014, USA
Penguin Group (Canada), 90 Eglinton Avenue East, Suite 700, Toronto,
Ontario M4P 2Y3, Canada (a division of Pearson Penguin Canada Inc.)
Penguin Books Ltd., 80 Strand, London WC2R 0RL, England
Penguin Ireland, 25 St. Stephen's Green, Dublin 2,
Ireland (a division of Penguin Books Ltd.)
Penguin Group (Australia), 250 Camberwell Road, Camberwell, Victoria 3124,
Australia (a division of Pearson Australia Group Pty. Ltd.)
Penguin Books India Pvt. Ltd., 11 Community Centre, Panchsheel Park,
New Delhi - 110 017, India
Penguin Group (NZ), 67 Apollo Drive, Rosedale, North Shore 0632,
New Zealand (a division of Pearson New Zealand Ltd.)
Penguin Books (South Africa) (Pty.) Ltd., 24 Sturdee Avenue,
Rosebank, Johannesburg 2196, South Africa

Penguin Books Ltd., Registered Offices:
80 Strand, London WC2R 0RL, England

Published by Obsidian, an imprint of New American Library, a division of Penguin
Group (USA) Inc. Previously published in an Obsidian hardcover edition.

First Obsidian Mass Market Printing, April 2009
10 9 8 7 6 5 4 3 2 1

Copyright © Sue Henry, 2008
Map copyright © Eric Henry, Art Forge Unlimited, 2008
All rights reserved

This one's for
Tom Colgan—
accessible, patient, and encouraging
editor and friend,
through more years and manuscripts
than I care to count.
And for his terrific assistant,
Sandy Harding.
Thanks, guys!
Whatever would I do without you?

ACKNOWLEDGMENTS

SINCERE THANKS ARE DUE TO:

Dr. Justin Ferris, Oceanographer and Senior Watchstander of NOAA's West Coast and Alaska Tsunami Warning Center (WCATWC) in Palmer, Alaska, for his kind assistance, both in person and in print, providing information concerning earthquakes.

The center, a fascinating place at 910 South Felton Street in Palmer, is open to visitors for tours on Friday afternoon at 1, 2, and 3 p.m. (groups of more than six people should call ahead to 907-745-4212) and is an excellent source of information, especially for all of us who live in earthquake country and need to know how to be prepared for the shakers we take too much for granted.

The WCATWC can be accessed online at wcatwc.arh.noaa.gov/watcher/tsunamiwatcher.php.

ALSO TO:

Bruce Merrell, Alaska Bibliographer at the Loussac Public Library in Anchorage, for his knowledgeable assistance in researching the history of earthquakes in Alaska, most especially the major quake of Good Friday 1964.

Captain Dennis Casanovas, for information concerning the Alaska State Troopers' detachment in Palmer with posts at Big Lake, Talkeetna, and Glennallen.

And, as always, to my son, Eric, for creating the map for this book.

INTRODUCTION

An earthquake is the vibration, sometimes violent, of the Earth's surface that follows a release of energy in the Earth's crust. This energy can be generated by a sudden dislocation of segments of the crust, by a volcanic eruption, or even by man-made explosions. Most destructive quakes, however, are caused by dislocations of the crust. The crust may first bend and then, when the stress exceeds the strength of the rocks, break and "snap" to a new position. In the process of breaking, vibrations called "seismic waves" are generated. These waves travel outward from the source of the earthquake along the surface and through the Earth at varying speeds depending on the material through which they move. Some of the vibrations are of high enough frequency to be audible, while others are of very low frequency. These vibrations cause the entire planet to quiver or ring like a bell or a tuning fork.

EARTHQUAKES, U.S. DEPARTMENT OF THE INTERIOR/U.S. GEOLOGICAL SURVEY, U.S. GOVERNMENT PRINTING OFFICE: 1996—421–205

"If You Build Your House on a Crack in the Earth, It's Your Own Fault."

ANONYMOUS; USED AS THE TITLE OF A SCIENTIFIC PAPER ON EARTHQUAKES IN LAURENCE J. PETER, *PETER'S PEOPLE*, 1979

ONE OF THE MOST FRIGHTENING AND DESTRUCTIVE PHE-nomena of nature is a severe earthquake and its terrible aftereffects. An earthquake is a sudden movement of the earth, caused by the abrupt release of pressure that has accumulated over a long time. For hundreds of millions of years, the forces of plate tectonics have shaped the earth as the huge plates that form its surface slowly move over, under, and past one another. Sometimes the movement is gradual. At other times, the plates are locked together, unable to release the accumulating energy. When that energy grows strong enough, the plates abruptly break free. If the earthquake occurs in a populated area, it may cause many deaths and injuries and extensive property damage.

People who have lived in Alaska for any real length of time have learned to take earthquakes pretty much for granted, as they do periodic volcanic eruptions, spring breakup flooding, avalanches along the Seward Highway, and that the price of their groceries is going to be higher there than in the Lower Forty-eight. They may not be particularly fond of any of these things, but accept them as facts of life, the price of living in the far north, which is usually balanced by their appreciation of the northern lights, the beauty of the wilderness that surrounds them, a general hardy sense of humor and individuality, and that by the summer solstice in June daylight will last from eighteen to twenty-four hours, depending on which part of the largest state in the union, Barrow to Ketchikan, they call home—though it will reverse itself and be dark that long by the winter solstice on December 21.

Alaska, at the northern edge of the "ring of fire" (which includes the volcanoes along the Pacific coasts of North and South America, the Aleutians, Japan, Southeast Asia, and Australasia), is in a region of frequent earthquakes that are usually minor and short-lived, but not always. Far beneath the west coast of the United States and Canada, miles underground, the Pacific Plate slides under and lifts the North American Plate, building up enormous tension that eventually overcomes resistance and is released as it slips and creates a shock with often far-reaching and ruinous results from both the ensuing quake and, at times, depending on location, tsunamis—powerful ocean waves that *can* travel at up to 600 miles per hour and crest at more than a hundred feet as they reach land.

On Good Friday, March 27, 1964, at 5:36 p.m., an earthquake struck southern Alaska registering a magnitude of 8.2 to 8.7 on the Richter scale (though some seismographs recorded readings up to 9.2). It was the most intense quake ever recorded in North America to that date and time.

The epicenter (the point on the earth's surface twenty to fifty kilometers directly above the underground disturbance) of the Alaska quake lay in the northern part of Prince William Sound and the event violently shook a number of communities for three to five minutes.

The tsunamis that resulted in the Pacific wiped out several Alaskan communities, including one complete native village. The quake and tsunamis left devastation in their wake and killed more than 130 people, several as far away as Crescent City, California.

There are Alaskans who tend to ignore the facts of living in earthquake country, pretending a big quake couldn't possibly happen to them. But many of us take the possibility more seriously.

At a minimum, in an area that can be accessed safely if the structure we live in is dangerously damaged:

We keep wrenches for turning off gas and water mains.

We have fire extinguishers handy.

We keep a supply of batteries and flashlights within reach, along with a battery-operated radio.

Our first-aid kits are comprehensive and kept up-to-date, along with any necessary medication for individual family members.

Enough nonperishable food and water for each family member for a week is available and replenished a couple of times a year as necessary.

Warm clothing, blankets, and sleeping bags are also available.

We know and teach our children what to do during and after a quake.

Most of all, we know that it is not a matter of *if* the next big quake will come—for it *will* come—but *when*.

DEGREES
OF
SEPARATION

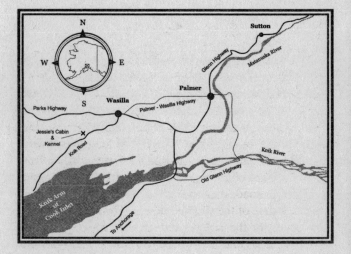

CHAPTER ONE

Late on a Friday afternoon toward the end of October, Jessie Arnold stood at a front window of her log home, frowning out at the sky full of heavy gray clouds that for three days had almost unceasingly poured rain onto her house and dog yard. Significant ponds of water had collected in every low spot in the long gravel drive that led to the cabin, and the amount of water falling from the sky almost obscured the vehicles frequently passing along Knik Road, their drivers on their way home from work. Because of the weather, it was growing dark earlier than usual for the season and all that was now visible were headlights and the blurred red glow of taillights that quickly disappeared.

From the window she could see that the majority of her sled dogs were curled up inside their individual square wooden boxes, staying dry and snoozing away the hours on their comfortable straw beds. Only three of them had braved the rain to go outside, though the noses of a few could be discerned through the square openings that provided access to the boxes. Most lay, muzzles on paws, snoozing or staring out at the rain like their mistress, preferring to stay as dry as possible. As Jessie watched, one of the three outside shook itself vigorously and vanished once again into its shelter.

Turning, she glanced across the room at her lead dog, Tank, who was dozing comfortable and dry on the braided rag rug that lay before the large sofa a short distance from the potbellied stove that radiated heat. Somehow it didn't seem quite fair that he should be allowed indoors while the rest remained relegated to the yard. All the same, his company was welcome and the rest were used to all kinds of weather.

As she looked across at him, his ears suddenly pricked up and, as he raised his head to look attentively at the front door, Jessie heard a splash of water in the drive and the growl of an automotive engine approaching. Turning back to look out, she watched Alex Jensen's pickup truck rock and roll its way through the puddles toward the house and come to a stop. The tall, long-legged Alaska state trooper climbed out and came loping up the steps to the shelter of the roof over the wide front porch, holding a newspaper over his head to little effect.

Tank scrambled to his feet and trotted across the room to be at the door when it opened and Alex came in, shaking water off his Western-style hat and stomping his feet on the outside mat to rid them of as much of the downpour as possible.

"Hey, lady," he said, removing and hanging his wet raincoat on a hook between the door and window, where it dripped water onto the rubber mat placed there for that reason. "What a day out, yes? Is this stuff ever going to quit? Did you call the weather people and complain?" he asked, bending to remove his boots and set them on the mat as well.

"Sorry." Jessie smiled in answer to his teasing. "All the

lines were busy and they wouldn't have paid attention anyway."

Alex turned, his stocking feet leaving damp tracks on the polished wood floor, and reached to enfold and greet her properly. But, as quickly as she moved forward into his embrace, she stepped back again.

"Ugh! You're cold and wet, Trooper—even your hair and mustache! What have you been doing to get soaked through?"

"Last run of the day for Becker and me was our third fender bender since this morning—this one out on the Parks Highway. People just don't seem to realize that, even with wipers going full tilt, you can't see well with rain pouring on the windshield in front of you, obscuring visibility. Nobody hurt in that one, but we had to stand outside and direct traffic until a tow truck showed up to haul one of them out of the ditch."

"Poor babe. You'll be as glad as I will when this rain stops, won't you? Why don't you take a hot shower before you change into dry clothes?"

"I've been planning just that—all the way home. This can't last much longer, can it?"

"I certainly hope not. I've already got a bad case of cabin fever and the dogs need to be run. They're getting fat and lazy out there with no exercise, but at least I don't have to water them. It's frustrating that just when the doc finally agrees that my knee is well enough to get back to training runs with the mutts on the four-wheeler, someone evidently wants Noah to build another ark. Snow I could have used, not this constant, miserable drizzle."

Before heading for the shower, Alex hunkered down to greet Tank with a few pats and rub his ears.

"Hey, buddy. You're lucky to be in here where it's warm and dry."

Halfway across the room to the stairs that led to the bedroom and shower on the second floor, he hesitated, then turned back to nod in the direction of the kitchen.

"What's for dinner? I'm not just soaked—I'm starved, woman. And I don't smell anything that leads me to believe you've been slaving over a hot stove all afternoon."

"Well," she told him, with a grin. "You're right. I haven't been. But don't ever say I don't make plans with you in mind. I had a call from Oscar earlier. He said that he's got a huge pot of his infamous chili and suggested that we hustle over to the Other Place soon, before it's gone. And it'll go quick, considering that it's Friday night and there'll be a lot of rain-frustrated local mushers with empty stomachs and time on their hands heading for their favorite watering hole."

"Good idea," Alex agreed. "Give me half an hour and we'll go join them."

In just under that amount of time, clad in rain slickers, they had dashed to the truck under a large umbrella and were heading back down the long drive to make a right turn onto Knik Road, aiming for Oscar's Other Place, Jessie in the middle between a clean and dry Alex, who drove, and Tank, who was watching the scenery go by through the rain that ran down the passenger-side window.

In just a few miles they were pulling into the large parking lot in front of Oscar's popular pub, which was already occupied by a number of other vehicles, and again had to splash through puddles to reach the front door. Once through the double doors of the arctic entrance, however, they found the place warm and already well over half full of the crowd that even a rumor of chili at Oscar's was bound to attract, especially on a rainy Friday night.

"Hey, thanks for the phone call." Jessie leaned across

the bar to greet Oscar, who was pulling the tap handle to fill three glasses with amber brew.

"Glad you made it while there's some chili left," he told her. "It's half gone already and vanishing like the last of the snow in spring. Hey there, Alex. Haven't seen you in a while. How're you keeping?"

"Just fine, when I can stay dry," the trooper told him.

"Not much chance of that recently. Where's my canine buddy? You leave him at home?" Oscar questioned.

"No, he's right here, as usual." Jessie nodded to Tank, who, hearing Oscar's familiar voice, was waiting with expectant dignity beside her.

Setting up the beer for a waiting customer, Oscar wiped his hands on the apron he had tied around his considerable middle, reached into a large glass jar, and came around the end of the bar to lean down and give Tank a friendly pat along with a sizable chunk of the homemade moose jerky he kept stashed for his four-legged friends.

"I'd swear that mutt smiles," the bar owner told Jessie, who had thanked him and ordered Killian's Red Lager for herself and Alex, who had turned to speak to an acquaintance at a nearby table. "Bottles or glasses?"

"Bottles are fine. And run a tab for us, will you, Oscar?" Jessie asked, taking the bottles and turning away at his "Can do."

Handing them both to Alex, she crossed to the huge slow cooker on a table against one wall and filled two bowls with chili, topping both with diced onions and shredded cheddar.

"Thanks, love." He smiled, pulling two empty chairs up to an empty table. "This may just about make up for the lack of home cooking."

"Don't push your luck," she told him with a mock scowl. "Today was actually your turn to cook, remember."

"So it was. I'll make up for it tomorrow, okay?"

"Sure."

For a minute she stood looking around to see who was there, knowing most of the crowd from the racing community, or past visits to this pub, and responding to greetings from several.

Waiting across the room for his turn at a pool table, Hank Peterson, an old friend, signaled a hello with the cue he held in one hand, beer in the other. "Wanna play when I win?" he called.

She laughed. "That's optimistic when you're playing Bill. When I'm through eating, I'll bring over quarters on the off chance that you do."

"Stay where you are. I'll put 'em up for you until then."

While she savored the chili and lager, half listening to conversations going on around her, Jessie found herself remembering how the original Other Place had looked a couple of years earlier, before it was destroyed by an arsonist.

It was much the same in most respects, as Oscar had been determined to renew the place that before the fire had grown familiar and comfortable to the residents of Knik Road, many of them sled dog racers or their handling crews and fans. So, with the remaining cement footprint of the original still solid and useable, he had put the insurance payment straight back into a new building—with a few improvements and a lot of unexpected help from many of his patrons.

"They kept showing up in droves," she remembered Oscar saying. And they had. Bringing their own tools and enthusiasm, they had worked together to rebuild the Other Place in record time, refusing any kind of remuneration beyond the beer, food, and thanks he had gratefully provided.

Oscar had originally intended to call the pub that had burned the Double Dozen, for it had stood approximately twelve miles from the main highway that ran from the middle of the nearby town of Wasilla and continued close to another twelve to where he lived, farther out Knik Road. The name, however, had never worked for the simple reason that most of his local customers were already familiar with "Oscar's"—the bar he had opened years before in town. With the possessiveness of regulars, they had referred to the new pub as Oscar's other place, ignoring anything to do with double pubs or dozens of miles. So it hadn't been long before he cheerfully bowed to the inevitable, replaced the sign out front, and made it official. Oscar's Other Place it had become and remained.

Year-round, before and after the fire, something was always happening there. Dart and pool tournaments were popular. Three or four tables of bridge players usually collected on Sunday afternoons. A large television set above the bar was tuned to a variety of sports in their seasons, often accompanied by potluck dinners and, always, many friendly wagers. A pig roast became traditional on Super Bowl Sunday. Every summer the Other Place sponsored a softball team that carefully kept its error count just high enough to remain solidly in the B league but too low for the A, where the game was more intense and less fun.

From the day it opened, located in the center of an area popular with racing aficionados, where there were possibly more sled dogs per square mile than people, Oscar's Other Place had quickly become a haunt for local mushers, handlers, and their followers. So many of them stopped by to warm up during training runs that during the winter Oscar provided straw for their dogs to curl up on in back of the pub.

Leaving Alex to finish his second bowl of chili, Jessie

took what was left of her lager and made her way across the room and, sliding the promised challenge quarters onto the edge of the pool table to replace Hank's, stood watching as Bill Monroe came close to finishing the game, but missed on the next-to-last ball—a tricky double-bank shot. His leave allowed Hank to easily sink the last two for the win.

He swung around with a grin. "Next victim!"

"Don't get greedy," Jessie told him, lifting balls back onto the table and racking them neatly in preparation for the break. "You won't be so lucky this time."

"Don't count on it. I'm on a roll tonight."

"Pride and a fall often *roll* up together, don't they?"

Easy needling was usually part of the play, and knowing she and Hank were pretty well matched in skill, she assumed they would both win about as many games as they lost.

Four shots after the break, Hank missed one. Leaning over the table to take careful aim, keeping one foot on the floor to be legal, Jessie considered the angles, then carefully hit the cue ball and sent it rolling toward the other end of the table with what she hoped was just enough force to sink the yellow-striped eleven ball, which she wanted to drop into a corner pocket, but not to send the cue ball in after it. Holding the position in which she had taken the shot, totally focused on the result of her action, she watched the ball roll away.

Then an odd thing happened. Instead of continuing straight, at the speed she expected, the ball began to curve to the right, away from the path it should have maintained, and, arriving at the table's end, missed the eleven completely.

"What the . . . ?"

Standing up, one hand on the rail, one holding her cue, she realized that the floor was vibrating beneath her feet. As she watched the table, within the confines of its rails, all thirteen remaining balls began an erratic waltz over the green felt surface of the five-by-ten-foot table. Several collided with each other. Others bounced off the rails. The yellow eleven, at which Jessie had aimed, fell neatly into the corner pocket all by itself, with no encouragement from the meandering cue ball.

The rectangular light that illuminated the table was swinging back and forth on the chains that suspended it.

As the tremor grew stronger, conversation died. There was a gasp or two and empty chairs rattled their legs on the floor. In the startled and alert silence, Jessie could hear a low rumble like a distant train passing. Turning, she saw several people grab for the drinks and food that were dancing on the tables in front of them. A beer bottle crashed to the tiled cement floor and shattered. Across the room Alex lunged to keep the kettle of hot chili from walking off its heater and upending itself down the unsuspecting neck of a man sitting with his back to it.

Glancing at the bar, she noticed that, though Oscar was busy rescuing loose items along it, the liquor bottles behind him were safe enough, held in place by four- or five-inch retainers that kept them in place. She could, however, faintly hear beer bottles in the cooler clinking against each other musically.

As an ashtray, holding the smoldering cigarette of a woman who had abandoned her bar stool, began a clattering stroll off the edge of bar, he dived to rescue it and made the catch. "Hey, one fire in this place was enough, thank you."

"Good save, Oscar," someone called as, swiftly as it

had arrived, the minor earthquake lessened and was gone.

"Well, this wasn't the first rodeo today," he said. "There was another, smaller one this afternoon."

As everyone settled and began to talk again, Jessie turned back to the pool table.

"Hell of a shot, Jessie," Hank told her, looking down with a crooked grin at the ball with the yellow stripe, which was now resting securely in the corner pocket. "The quake gods must really know how and when to throw a pool game in your direction."

"Well-l-l," Jessie said with a grin. "We could either call it a draw, or try to set the balls back up the way they were before the quake and play it again."

"Naw." Hank shook his head and shrugged. "I'm not about to challenge fate. Let's just say that somebody up there likes you tonight and let it go at that."

CHAPTER TWO

ALMOST THREE HOURS LATER, ALEX AND JESSIE PULLED into the long drive, Tank once again riding shotgun by the window.

After fastening Tank's collar to the tether attached to his box, Jessie followed Alex up the steps and into the house.

"Want a cup of tea?" he asked, hanging both their coats by the door and joining Jessie in removing the rubber boots they had worn.

"Sounds good. Maybe a couple of those Double Stuf Oreos to go with it," she suggested, crossing sock-footed to the stove, where she added a log to the fire, then stood rubbing her hands together in the welcome heat. "It's stopped raining and the temperature's dropped a bit. I may be able to run the guys with the four-wheeler tomorrow, if it isn't too muddy."

"As long as you don't run late. I forgot to tell you that we're invited to dinner with Cass and Linda tomorrow night," Alex called from the kitchen, where he had put two mugs of water with tea bags into the microwave.

"We are?"

"You bet. Have you forgotten what tomorrow is—or are you trying to ignore it this year?"

She frowned for a second or two, then said, "Oh! It's my *birthday*!"

"Right!"

"I had totally spaced it. Where did October go?"

Coming back with both mugs in one hand, a package of cookies in the other, he gave a mug to Jessie, and they settled, one at each end of the sofa—purposely large enough so there was room for both to stretch out their legs—Oreos within reach of both.

"October," Alex answered, "probably went as usual, but you've been pretty focused on getting back out with the dogs, after a long, frustrating delay."

"Well, I *was*—until this rain made an appearance. Sure hope it's about over. We're all tired of being either cooped up or soaking wet."

"How's old Pete doing, by the way?" he asked with a frown of concern.

Pete, one of the oldest dogs in Jessie's yard, was a favorite, though he was no longer allowed in the teams of a dozen or more at a time that she trained for racing. He had sprained a foreleg badly about the same time she had torn a tendon in her knee over a year earlier in a fall down the side of a mountain. They had healed together through the winter, but she knew Pete would never be strong enough again to help pull any of her sleds over the hundreds of miles necessary for training and distance racing.

"The leg's okay," she said slowly, a sad and concerned expression on her face. "The vet says he's got heart and breathing problems that are only going to get worse. He's such a sweet old guy that I'd really miss having him around, but I may have to have him put down before spring.

Can't have him struggling just to get by. That's not fair, however much I hate it."

"Would it help to bring him inside to sleep?"

Jessie shook her head sadly. "He'd just want to go back out with the rest. I've been bringing him in with Tank during the day—especially with this rain—and I moved Jeep and put Pete in the box next to Tank. They're good buds. It'll be okay, if I watch him close. But every time I take a team out for a training run, it's all I can do to leave him behind, looking longingly after us with those sad eyes. He doesn't understand at all—just wants to be back where he thinks he belongs."

Alex was not surprised to see tears in Jessie's eyes, knowing that she loved all her sled dogs, but that Pete was special, for he had been with her as long as any in her kennel and had sired many good pups, some of which were now racing in what he felt was his place. Strong, even-tempered, and ready to do whatever was required of him, it was true that he was not at all happy to be left behind. Besides many shorter races, he had been a member of the teams that made the long, thousand-mile runs in both the longest and most famous races of all, the Iditarod and the Yukon Quest, more than once in the former.

"I'll help keep an eye on him," Alex said, setting his half-empty mug on the floor beside the sofa and swinging his legs to stand up. "Hey! You want your present now?"

"But tomorrow's the day."

"That's okay. I think you should have it now. Besides, maybe you'll want to use it—have it—maybe even wear it—tomorrow anyway," he called back, taking long strides to the bedroom. Jessie heard a drawer open and shut, then he came back with a kid's grin on his face that was so infectious it made her smile too, as she wiped her eyes. Stopping beside her, he handed her a box that was about a foot square, clumsily wrapped in bright yellow paper, with an excess of Scotch tape, and festooned with multicolored curly ribbons. "There ya go! Open it up, almost-a-birthday-girl!"

She examined the decorative object in her lap for a long minute, as he sat down again on the opposite end of the sofa, swung his stocking feet up, retrieved his tea, and sat waiting, eyes dancing in anticipation.

"Wrap this yourself, did you?" she asked.

"What could possibly have given you *that* impression?"

"Well—it's—ah—very artistic in design," she teased.

"Maybe I should advertise—make more and autograph them? Or, on second thought, maybe not. Just bear in mind that I considered the funny papers first, so this is first-class."

Under the paper was a box with a lid, which Jessie removed to find—another box with another lid. Three boxes later, each smaller than the last, the tears had vanished and she was giggling as she took the lid off what turned out to be the last—a black velvet–covered jewelry box. Inside was something she immediately expected and found.

"Oh, Alex! They're beautiful! You replaced the diamond earring I lost on Niqa Island. But—wait a minute—these two look different from those. Did you get *new* ones? You didn't need to do that."

"Well—yes, Jess. As it turns out, I did. What I learned in the attempt was that you can't just pick up a diamond post to match one you already have. They're matched in pairs for size and quality and color and who knows what else. It was easier to trade in the one you didn't lose and get a matched pair than it would have been to try to find one or have one made. These are almost exactly the same, but slightly larger and set a little differently—with screw-on backings, so you won't lose one this time. I hope you don't mind that I raided your jewelry box for the old one."

"Mind? Alex, I love them!" Jessie said, getting up to give him a huge hug and a kiss. "Thank you, dear man. And you're right. I'll definitely wear them tomorrow night to dinner. Linda will be green."

With a swallow that emptied his tea mug, still holding Jessie, Alex stood up and set her on her feet.

"I'm for bed. It's been a long, damp day, with an earthquake thrown in, so I'm ready to hit the hay." He gave her a sideways leer and twirled one end of his handlebar mustache suggestively. "I recommend that you come too and thank me properly."

Later, in the dark bedroom at the top of the stairs, Jessie lay with her head on his shoulder, his arm holding her close.

"You know," he said drowsily. "My mother has a poem she always said at bedtime on birthdays when I was a kid."

"What?" she whispered in his ear, knowing his penchant for poetry and quotations.

"'When your birthday is over, and you've wound up the clock, and put out the cat, and fastened the lock, may you say with a smile, that's contented and glad, this has been the best birthday that ever I had.'"

Jessie giggled.

"In my case, I think it should probably be changed to *put out the dog*! But since this isn't really my birthday, will you promise to say it again tomorrow night?"

"Sure thing."

Half an hour later both were slumbering soundly, lulled by the repetitive rhythm of rain on the roof overhead and drizzling from it to the ground below.

Familiar with living next to over forty dogs, neither heard the long howl of one that, disturbed from sleep by something moving in the nearby trees, had ventured into the downpour outside its box in the row farthest from the house and nearest the woods that lay to the west. As that wail slowly faded, another dog answered from the far corner of the lot with a similar cry that rose and fell into a series of yips and yowls.

There was a distant sound of movement in the trees as something crashed hurriedly downhill through the brush. The noise terminated upon reaching Knik Road and was heard no more.

Both dogs shook themselves free of much of the rainwater that had dampened their coats and disappeared once again into the shelter of their respective boxes.

CHAPTER THREE

WHEN ALEX WOKE THE NEXT MORNING THE SPACE next to him in Jessie's big brass bed was empty. Reaching out, he laid a hand on the sheet and found a faint bit of warmth remaining, so she hadn't been up long. It seemed very light in the room for some reason, despite the closed curtains, and he wondered if he had slept longer than usual. But his side was exactly his favorite morning temperature, so he rolled over, tucked the quilt more comfortably around his shoulders, closed his eyes, and prepared to snooze for just a bit longer.

Except for Jessie humming an upbeat tune in the kitchen below, it was very quiet, so it had evidently stopped raining. Soon the inviting scent of fresh coffee wafted its way up into the bedroom, challenging his reluctance to rise. Giving up the idea of further sleep, he got out of bed, found a pair of comfortable, well-worn jeans, and put them on, along with a wool shirt over a thermal undershirt, knowing there would undoubtedly be kennel work to be done today, rain or no rain.

"What's got you warbling first thing this morning, birthday girl?" he asked, padding down the stairs, his feet making little sound in a pair of heavy boot socks.

"Oh—you're up. Look out the window," Jessie said, grinning at him and waving a spatula in that direction before turning back to the eggs she was frying to go with bacon and toast.

Alex crossed the room and stood looking out into the dog yard with surprise. *"Snow!"*

"Yeah! There must be five or six inches of the beautiful stuff—white, fluffy, wonderful, beautiful *s-n-o-w*! Enough to run dogs with a *sled*."

"No wonder you're so cheerful." He joined her in the kitchen to pour mugs of coffee for both of them, which he took to the table. "It must have snowed hard all night just to give you a birthday present."

"Yes, and they're still coming down—big, fat, fabulous flakes. You can barely see the highway from here they're so thick. If it keeps up like this, and we don't get warmer weather and more rain, it'll stick."

"How about the woods trails? Will there be enough snow under the trees? We had that big wind a couple of weeks ago. Will there be fallen branches clogging them?"

Jessie brought plates of food to the table, set one in front of Alex and sat down with her own, pulling the sugar bowl across to spoon some into her coffee mug.

"Just about all the leaves are down, so the trails should be fine," she answered. "I went out on the four-wheeler after the blow and cleared branches and stuff from a couple of them—the one that runs across behind the Johnsons' place and the one that goes to the top of the hill and loops around. I think they're fine, but we'll take it slow for a while anyway, just to be sure."

As they ate, Alex noticed the pleasure on her face, as she glanced often at the white flakes drifting down outside the window, and considered the enthusiasm with which Jessie was welcoming the arrival of winter.

It had been a difficult and frustrating year for her. First, in the spring of the previous year, there had been the fall that tore a tendon in her knee enough to require surgery. It had taken her off a sled behind her dog teams for months, as she waited for it to heal, so there had been no training or racing—a frustrating situation for a dedicated musher. Along with it came many hours of therapy to rehabilitate the knee.

The majority of her dogs had been moved to another kennel, where a friend had cared for and run them, allowing them to continue what they loved and lived for, trotting happily in a team in front of a sled. Two or three times a week, for the past year, Jessie had gone to visit this kennel, keeping her contact strong with the dogs that she would be running again this year.

The dozen or so that had been left in Jessie's yard were either older dogs like Pete, ready to be retired, or females pregnant with puppies that would need both their mothers' care and feeding. It was also important that the pups be socialized—learning to recognize and imprint with a person who would eventually add them to racing teams, or sell them to other mushers. A few of them would, for one reason or other, be unsuitable as racing sled dogs, and would likely wind up in good homes as pets.

Then there was Tank, her leader, from whom she refused to be separated, knowing they would both be unhappy and dissatisfied apart.

In June, when her doctor finally allowed it, her dogs had been returned to their home yard, where she trained them during the summer months by letting the teams pull the four-wheeler on dry, local trails. Now she was not only ready but anxious to get back into the real game—on the back of a sled—on snow.

"After all the rain we've had, it wouldn't hurt to take

another look at those trails," Alex suggested. "Why don't you run them once on the snow machine? I'll feed and water the dogs while you're gone, and get out whichever sled you want to use."

"Good idea. That'll pack the trails enough to make better running for the mutts. But I can help with their breakfast before I go."

"Naw. You go ahead. I really don't mind doing it. Which ones do you want to take out first? I'll feed them before the others."

As Jessie named the dozen dogs she wanted to put into harness for the initial run, she and Alex took their dishes to the kitchen, where they quickly washed and left them to dry in a rack by the sink. Then, both dressed warmly against the cold, they headed outside and were soon busy at their respective jobs.

Good sled dogs are agile, strong, love to run, and most are highly intelligent. Aware—perhaps from some non-verbal communication of Jessie's elated intention for the day—that some of them were about to be taken on a training run, they leaped onto their boxes or pulled against their tethers. Their excited barking was loud, eager, and demanding: "Take me! Take me! Take me!"

She grinned at their antics and crossed to a shed, where she kept equipment, supplies, and a couple of snow machines, one of which she drove out, intending to make a quick run to assess the trails through the woods.

Though she would have preferred a dog team, as she drove into the trees and away from the cabin and dog yard, Jessie was pleased just to be outdoors, knowing that a run with one of her teams, and a sled, was finally about to become reality.

Deciding to check the shortest trail first, she headed north through the woods and was soon passing behind the Johnsons' place, just over half a mile away. It was so fine to be out on such a day, even on the snow machine, that she drove with a smile of appreciation on her face. Several inches of snow had buried all the bright brassy gold of fallen birch leaves under a white blanket several inches deep that matched the sky and the flakes that were still drifting down. The green of the spruce was so dark in contrast that she felt as if she were traveling through a black-and-white photograph.

The trail was good, without fallen branches or other obstacles, so she soon took a side road west to Knik Road, where she followed along a trail beside it until she came to her own drive. There, she found Alex finished with the food and water chores, but still in the yard.

"How's it look out there?" he called, straightening from where he had been bending over Pete with a frown.

"Great. No troubles. I'll leave the other, longer trail for the dogs to break. They can use the exercise and experience."

"Before you hitch them up, come here a minute and have a look at Pete. I think he may have a bigger problem than you thought."

Turning off the snow machine engine, Jessie came quickly and fell to her knees in the snow beside the older dog, who had come out of his box and was lapping half-heartedly at the water Alex had poured into his bowl. Between laps, he was panting and there was a wheeze accompanying each breath.

"That really doesn't sound good," Alex said, shaking his head. "And he's not too steady on his feet—had trouble getting up. Hasn't touched his food, just wanted a drink."

He watched as Jessie took a long careful look at her dog and ran knowledgeable hands over him. Laying an

ear to his chest, she listened closely, after which she pet-
ted him sadly, crooning fondness. "Good old Pete. Not
feeling so good, are you? Poor guy. It'll be all right, good
dog. I love you."

He leaned against her and gave one side of her face an
affectionate lick.

She looked up at Alex, and in her clear gray eyes
were tears that overflowed and ran down her face.

"He was like this once a couple of weeks ago," she told
him. "I took him in and the vet said that if it happened
again, and didn't get better fairly soon, I should bring him
back and consider putting him down before his suffering
got worse."

"What did he say to do while you waited for *fairly
soon*?"

"Just keep him warm, give him plenty of water, and
wait an hour or two to see how he does."

"Then that's what we should do. I'll take him inside
and make him comfortable, if you want to run that other
trail."

Jessie shook her head as she stood up, unhooked Pete's
tether, and lifted him carefully off the ground into her
arms. "No. I can do that trail later, or tomorrow. It'll keep.
There's always another day for training, snow or no snow.
Bring his water bowl—and Tank, will you? Having him
along may make Pete more comfortable."

Once inside, she put Pete on the rug near the stove,
where he lay down immediately, muzzle on paws. She
could hear him wheeze all the way to the kitchen, where
she put water in his bowl and took it back to him. Tank
had followed Alex in the door and gone immediately to
lie down next to Pete. In a few minutes they were both
napping.

Jessie settled close by on the sofa with the latest *Mush-*

ing magazine, where she could monitor the older dog's condition, but soon found herself unable to concentrate and tossed the periodical aside.

"I think I'll call the vet," she said, getting up and heading for the phone.

Alex, who had also been listening closely, nodded agreement.

"That's a good idea."

A sick dog was Jessie's responsibility, he knew. She was more familiar with and knowledgeable about the health and temperament of each of her animals, so he hesitated to give advice or involve himself in their care unless invited to do so. Still, Pete was a favorite of his, as well as hers, and he knew without asking that she would welcome his support.

After a few minutes on the phone, Jessie put it down and turned to say, "He says not to wait to see how he does, but to bring him in now. Will you come with us?"

"Of course. I'll take Tank to the yard and start my truck."

"Good. I'll get a blanket to keep Pete warm and bring him out in just a minute."

He watched her leave the room as he moved to the door to put his coat and boots back on, assessing her mood. There had been no more tears. She was a practical woman who took life as it came, good or bad, with composure and little complaint. Dogs grew old, or got sick, and sometimes died. It was part of what owning and driving so many of them meant. She knew and accepted that as part of the game. It didn't mean she took it lightly or didn't care. That Pete was special in their history together made it harder, but she had a way of appreciating the good stuff and not allowing herself to dwell on the bad. He admired her for it.

"Come on, Tank," he called quietly.

Pete raised his head at the words and watched his buddy get up and cross the room to Alex, but stayed where he was on the rug.

They went out the door together without looking back, knowing Jessie would be quick to follow.

Two hours later they were back. Jessie had said little on the way home, just stared out the window at whatever they were passing. Pete's limp body lay in the bed behind the cab, wrapped in the blanket Jessie had taken along to keep him warm.

"He's a lot worse, isn't he?" Jessie had asked, as the vet examined the old dog, listening carefully through his stethoscope to Pete's breathing and heart.

"I'm afraid so. And he's not going to get better, Jessie. I'm sorry to say it, because I know he's special to you, but you won't be doing him a favor by keeping him around this way. I can put him to sleep, then give him another shot to put him down humanely now, without the painful struggle to breathe that he'll have if you take him home to die slowly in the next day or two."

Stepping close to the table to lay gentle hands on Pete, she had given him a long, thoughtful look. Then she nodded sadly.

"Yes," she said. "I know you're right. I'll hold him while you do that."

So the three of them had come home again, for Jessie wanted Pete buried in an open space back in the woods behind the cabin, with the few other dogs she had lost from her kennel over the years.

And so he was. Alex managed to scrape out enough of a hole in the cold ground for Pete and she had laid him carefully down in it, blanket and all. When it was filled in and the ground leveled again, she stood looking down sadly.

"He was a sweet old guy, with a huge heart," she said quietly. "Patient, hardworking, even-tempered, he never picked fights. He was good with puppies and there wasn't a lazy bone in him. He may not have been the smartest, or the best runner of the pack, but he was always willing to try to do what you wanted of him—asking little, giving much. I'll miss him—a lot."

CHAPTER FOUR

Mᴏʀᴇ sɴᴏᴡ ꜰᴇʟʟ ᴅᴜʀɪɴɢ ᴛʜᴇ ɴɪɢʜᴛ ᴀɴᴅ ᴡᴀs sᴛɪʟʟ falling thinly the next morning. Jessie was up early. While Alex made breakfast, she fed and watered the dogs, and readied herself to take a team and sled out for a run over the trail she had checked the day before on the four-wheeler. After choosing a sled from several in the storage shed, she attached a gang line to the front of it and brought out harnesses for eleven dogs.

Familiarity with the activity set almost all of the dogs to barking enthusiastically and yanking at their tethers, eager to be chosen for the training run.

Like many of the others, Digger, a regular team member, leaped excitedly at the end of his tether in the third row, wild with the desire to be selected.

"Okay, okay! Take it easy. You can go," she told him, laughing and giving him a pat of reassurance. "You too, Taffy. But I want food first, so settle down."

She came back inside, smiling at their antics.

"All it takes is a little snow," she said, pouring herself a mug of coffee. "After all these days of rain and no exercise they're raring to go and it'll take miles to calm them down. I'm going to have to watch it out there or they'll have us ricocheting off trees on the turns."

"Well," Alex answered with a grin, handing her a bowl of oatmeal. "I'd say the musher is just about as eager to hit the trail, wouldn't you?"

"Yeah, you're right. I'm sick of being stuck indoors. Even with an evening at the Other Place night before last and bridge with Cass and Linda last night, it's been too long indoors."

They had gone, as planned, for dinner with Ben and Linda Caswell, complete with a candle-laden cake for Jessie's birthday, and had played several hands of bridge afterward in an ongoing casual competition begun years earlier. Though she had been a little quieter than usual, Alex knew the evening had lifted her spirits.

"We really got lucky with all those good cards last night. And those new earrings looked great on you."

"Thanks to you." Jessie lifted the last spoonful of her oatmeal, but held it balanced over the bowl as she nodded agreement. "We should get together with them more often—our turn next time."

Ben Caswell, a pilot who worked with Alex frequently, flew his small plane for the Alaska state troopers on contract. Jessie and Linda shared gardening and canning the results on a seasonal basis, exchanged recipes, and generally helped each other out with whatever needed doing by more than one person. The four had enjoyed each other's company for years.

"Well," said Jessie, rising from the table with her empty bowl and coffee mug in hand. "I'd better get out there before the guys drag their boxes into the driveway or break their tethers."

"Not much chance of either, I suspect. You've got those

boxes pretty well staked down and the tether cables are unbreakable."

"Thanks be!" She crossed to the door and began to put her warm outdoor clothing and boots back on. "Leave the dishes. I'll clean up the kitchen when I come back."

"Naw, I'll do it. As promised, I'm going to make a batch of beef stew and put it on the back burner to simmer. Seems appropriate for the first snow of the season."

"Sounds great! Just the thing after a day with the mutts," Jessie called back over a shoulder, as she went out the door.

Ignoring the kitchen for the moment, Alex took his coffee across to the window and watched as she put a harness on one dog at a time, took each to the gang line, and attached it securely in its place before going back for the next animal. In just a few minutes ten of them were matched up in pairs, still excitedly barking, and ready to go. Tank made eleven, in front, where he stood looking back for her signal, ready to lead the team out of the yard.

After walking the length of the harnessed team and sled, giving each dog a pat or a word as she passed, Jessie swung herself onto the back runners of the sled, pulled out the snow hook that held it back, took a firm grip on the handles, and called to her lead dog.

"Okay, Tank. Let's *go*. Take 'em out."

He sprang forward and the team followed eagerly, jerking the sled into motion, all of them eager and pulling hard. In a very short time they were into the woods, vanishing from Alex's sight like some kind of magic through the veil of gently falling snow.

The dogs left behind in the kennel gradually quieted their yapping disappointment and went to their water pans or back into their boxes. Some, ignoring the weather, leaped to the top of them to watch, knowing the vanished team would eventually be back and they might get lucky next time.

Alex turned back to the kitchen, where he quickly cleaned the few dishes from breakfast, poured himself another mug of coffee, and began to chop carrots, onions, and celery, while the cubed beef browned in a heavy cast-iron skillet. As he worked, he cheerfully whistled his way through a repertoire of golden oldies from the sixties and seventies, and decided that later a batch of biscuits would complete the dinner menu.

As they followed the trail through the woods, Jessie let her dogs run until their enthusiasm calmed a bit and they slowed, content to drop into a familiar and comfortable, steady, ground-covering trot. As always, she was pleased with their desire to run. It was what they were born to, trained for, and wanted more than anything to do. But on this first of the snow season training runs she was just as pleased to finally be back in her own chosen element—the white silence of a winter trail, with the scrape and swish of runners on snow and the intermittent creak of a flexible sled almost the only sounds, the feel and soft whisper of tiny icy crystals on her face and clothing, the rhythmic motion of the team and sled crossing over uneven ground and around trees.

She caught a whiff of smoke in the air as they passed above the Johnsons' unseen cabin and heard the sharp sounds of her neighbor chopping firewood.

With a startled and seemingly resentful croak at her passing, in a flurry of feathers a raven seemed to leap into flight from its perch on the bare limb of a birch and soared swiftly out of sight in sharp, black contrast to the surrounding white world.

Though covered with several additional inches of new snow that had fallen during the night, the familiar trail they followed was easily discernible and Tank led the team confidently along it, as he and other leaders had many times in the past.

When they came to the side road that she had followed west to Knik Road the day before, instead of turning down it, she took the team across onto a trail that headed more uphill, which she knew would swing around in a large loop to where another branched off and would eventually take them home. With so many kennels in the area, it was not surprising that there was a maze of trails and tracks that linked together and provided a good local training ground for many mushers and their dogs. She could see that at least one team, possibly more than one, had already traveled this second trail. From the new snow now covering it, they had evidently passed along it the day before, but everyone who ran dogs would be as anxious as she had been to be out, so someone might have passed very early, as soon as it was light enough to see the track.

In unspoken and unorganized effort, all those who ran teams helped to keep the trails in good order, cutting brush when necessary, clearing them of obstacles. Jessie stopped once to toss aside a branch that had broken and fallen, overloaded with heavy wet snow.

Headed south, she came at length to the trail that would take her west and downhill to the house and dog yard. It was a cutoff she had made years before and was almost never used by others unless they intended to wind up at her kennel. Directing Tank to take it, she began to watch more carefully, for this trail had not been used after the snow and was more crooked as it ran through the trees.

The dogs, trotting quickly, rounded a curve and disappeared behind a stand of spruce and brush that hid the front half of the team from their driver. As the sled followed, bearing right, she was startled when, though they were still moving forward, Tank slowed the team to half speed. Her response was a quick, heavy stomp on the brake, a device that jammed itself into the snow and kept the sled bow from hitting the wheel dogs that ran closest to the sled—brothers, Darryl One and Darryl Two, named for characters in the long-gone Bob Newhart television show. As they moved on, she felt the sled pass over some snow-covered thing in the trail that pitched the bow up, over, and down, then the rear.

"Whoa, Tank," she called, keeping pressure on the brake and tossing out the snow hook on its line attached to the sled.

"Whoa, guys."

The team came to a stop a few yards beyond what, looking back, she could see was a significant bump of something in the otherwise clear track.

Whatever it was, it did not belong there and had better be cleared, or they, or someone else, would run over it again next time they used the track.

"Hold 'em, Tank," she instructed, as he turned to look back at her for instructions.

He sat down and watched her toss down and stomp in the snow hook, leave the sled, and walk back toward whatever it was they had run over. Several other dogs either sat or lay down to wait.

Good thing I'm not running rookies, Jessie thought with a grin as she moved away, knowing Tank would make sure the team stayed put, though the other ten veterans of many runs were almost as trustworthy.

Halfway there, she could see something dark in the tracks the dogs' feet and sled runners had made as they passed over and drug snow from the obstacle. There was something else, pieces of something red, not just in the tracks but in the snow that had been disturbed by the passing team.

Within a yard of the thing in the snow, Jessie stopped cold, staring. It was not pieces of something in the snow. Part of the disturbed snow itself was red with something she recognized and refused. It couldn't be blood, could it?

If it was, maybe a yearling moose had been hit on the road and moved away, uphill far enough to fall and die there.

But it wasn't large enough to be a moose.

Before she stepped forward and dropped to her knees next to the partially uncovered thing, she knew what it was—that it was no moose—and that he was clearly dead.

Brushing aside the icy red and white snow that still hid much of it, she exposed a blue plaid shirt under a half-zipped jacket, then the face of the man whose body the sled's passing had turned over in the trail, caught by the edge of the brake she had stepped on to slow it. The ground where he had lain, facedown, was bare of snow and covered with soggy gold birch leaves that had fallen from the surrounding trees. He lay stiff and cold, eyes half closed, skin pale and a little bluish, the shoulder and front of his shirt and jacket stained with the blood that seemed to have mostly seeped into the birch leaves. But enough had colored some of the snow to dye what the team's passing had scattered around him.

Dead. And not by accident. The bullet hole in the side of his head was either his own doing or someone else's.

If it was suicide, there would be a gun somewhere

nearby, for his hands were empty, but Jessie had no intention of looking for it. Frowning, she sat back on her heels, looking down at him in confusion and shock.

Leaving him where he was, she slowly stood up, backed away as carefully as possible, and, turning, jogged back to her waiting team.

All the dogs came to their feet as she stepped onto the back of the sled.

"Okay, guys. Take us home, Tank."

Pulling the snow hook, she let them trot on down the twisting trail toward home, trusting her good leader to guide them without incident.

Twenty minutes later they were pulling into the yard.

Leaving the dogs in harness, snow hook down again and Tank to be trusted, she walked to the house, up the stairs, and threw open the front door.

Alex glanced up from where he was reading the Sunday paper at the table, having hiked to the box at the end of the driveway to retrieve it.

"Hey. You're back ear—" he started. Then, seeing her pale face and serious expression, he stood up, eyes wide. "What's wrong, Jess?"

Closing the door, she leaned against it and took a deep breath.

"There's a dead man on the trail up there," she told him, waving a hand in the direction of the hill she had just come down. "We ran over his body. From the look of it, he's been there since before it snowed."

CHAPTER FIVE

JUST OVER AN HOUR LATER, ALEX HAD TAKEN HIMSELF and fellow trooper Phil Becker up the hill on a snow machine on the track Jessie's team and sled had made coming down. An investigator from the crime lab had followed them on a second machine, having come in response to Jensen's phone call to report the circumstances and request assistance.

Alex stood looking down at what he could see of the body in the trail, having examined the area carefully before stepping into the depression created where Jessie had knelt earlier.

A small amount of light snow had fallen on the dead man, or drifted over him on the gentle breath of a light breeze. Cautiously, he reached a mittened hand to brush it away from the face, noticing that it had not melted in contact with the skin; therefore, the body was cold and not recently dead.

"Recognize him?" he asked Phil Becker, who was standing farther away.

"Shit yeah! As a matter of fact, I do. It's Bill Thompson's youngest boy, Donny. What the hell could he be doing up here?"

"He run dogs?"

Becker shook his head. "No mushers in that family. Bill and Helen have four boys and a girl. They're all into motorcycles and snow machines. Thompson's a mechanic. Has his own shop out at Sutton on the Glenn Highway. Donny and two of his brothers work with him off and on. The oldest, Carl, is bartending at that biker bar in Palmer."

"The Aces Wild?"

"Yeah."

Tall and lean, Jensen shook his head as he frowned down at the dead man, reached up with one hand to remove his Western hat, slapped it against his leg to rid it of the snow that was falling more thickly again, and put it back on.

Becker, younger, shorter, and stockier, shifted his weight from foot to foot and huffed, his breath creating a small cloud that quickly disappeared as it drifted off in the cold air. "This sucks. I guarantee you, Bill's not going to take it at all well."

The investigator, Raymond Calb, had stood back, leaning on the snow machine he had driven up the trail from Jessie's yard, silently awaiting his turn at the death scene. Behind the machine was a sled that would be used to carry the body down to the van he had left below.

"What do you think, Ray?" Jensen asked, waving him forward. "We're not gonna be able to find anything much under all this snow, are we?"

"Not much," came the expected answer. "There's no way to tell if it's a case of murder or suicide unless, and even if, we find a gun. That's going to mean a lot of careful work removing snow and the leaves under it in an area as wide as it could have been thrown. If he shot himself, the recoil would probably have forced a handgun away from his head. If it flew out of his hand it could have wound up several feet from where he was standing. If someone else shot him, it's unlikely there'll be a gun to find. But we won't know that until we've looked."

He hunkered down to carefully turn and take a long look at the dead man's head before continuing. "There's a little stippling on the skin around the entrance wound, so the gun wasn't held directly against the skin. The bullet went in at an upward angle and there's an exit wound on the other side toward the rear. We'll have to keep an eye out for that as well, but probably won't find it."

Jensen nodded. "From what I see, he was lying on leaves, so this occurred before it snowed—Friday evening at the latest. With all these leaves there won't be any tracks or prints to be found."

"Right. Ground's pretty well frozen, as well as our friend here. We'll have to check temperatures for the last two days and nights, and his internals, before we can begin to estimate a time of death. Don't expect much else, Alex. Any evidence we get will probably be found on the body itself. Let's start by getting him bagged and on the sled. We'd better tape off the area as well—help us see how much needs to be searched and keep anyone from driving a dog team or a snow machine through it for the time being."

About the same time, on a rise that allowed a view across Knik Arm toward the Fort Richardson and Peter's Creek area, Jessie sat on her sled, elbows on knees, chin in her cupped hands, and stared unseeing out across the saltwater inlet. The snow had all but ceased and the rugged, dominating wall of the Chugach Mountains rose sharply in black and white, stone and snow, to the south. Far to the west the horizon lay below a line of clear bright blue sky, but she had noticed little more. Having snacked her dogs, she was letting them rest for the moment and trying to sort out the turbulent feelings that had taken her swiftly away from the law enforcement response to what she had found earlier.

After relating what she had run over on the upper trail, she had gone back outside and, while Alex was on the phone to report it to headquarters, had driven the team out of her yard. They had run, not into the woods but along a track adjacent to the highway that was well used by both snow machines and dog teams. In just a few minutes she had turned south, crossed the highway at Settlers Bay, and taken the crooked road down over the bluff to the flats below.

Along that side of Knik Arm ran part of the original Iditarod Trail, established by gold seekers back around 1900, who had landed from ships near what ultimately became the city of Seward and taken the difficult and dangerous trails through both the Kenai and Chugach mountains, then north and west over endless hundreds of miles of untamed country that eventually, days later, led them to the small mining community of Iditarod. It owed its existence to gold, and when that inducement played out, it had become a ghost town as miners scattered elsewhere. Until then, far from the ocean, almost everything necessary, or desirable, to survival and the search for yellow metal came laboriously in over the rough trails by strings of packhorses in summer, or on huge freight sleds pulled by dogs in winter.

Jessie had run her team along several miles of the historic trail, as far as the old town on Knik Road, where it turned more to the north. Instead of following it, she had continued along the arm to Goose Bay, where she had stopped to snack and rest the team. There she sat, allowing herself time to sort through her feelings.

The man in the trail was not the first dead person she had ever seen, or even discovered. But combined with the stress of having Pete put down the day before, it had rocked her emotions harder than she expected. She thought back, recalling a friendly old man she had found drowned and washed up on a beach in Kachemak Bay years before.

But that was different—not violent—not bloody. This is too much death all at once, she thought, and shuddered, remembering the way the sled had rocked in passing over today's corpse. *If only we hadn't run over him. . . .*

It made her remember the body of a boy who had been dropped almost ninety feet from the historic Kiskatinaw Bridge on the Alaska Highway in British Columbia to his death on the stones of the shallow river below. That particular memory made her feel a little sick and she consciously pushed it away.

Her hands were cold. As she turned and reached for the heavy mittens she had removed to find the snacks for the dogs in the sled bag, she heard, then saw, another musher and team approaching from a trail that ran south from Nancy Lake and the Parks Highway, an area heavily populated with kennels.

Most of her dogs were immediately on their feet, some barking, tails wagging, as the other team drew closer. Standing up, she recognized the driver, who pulled up close by, set his own snow hook, and came across to give her a hug, then held her at arm's length and grinned.

"Hey, Jessie. Back on a sled must mean your knee is okay. Yes?"

She nodded as she said, *"Lynn Ehlers!* Haven't seen you in weeks. Thought maybe you'd gone back to Minnesota."

"Not likely. I'm afraid I'm well and truly hooked on Alaska. It's where most of the action is. How're *you*?"

"Oh . . . okay mostly. Not so good at the moment. Stay for a bit and I'll tell you about it."

A concerned frown replaced his grin. "Give me time to give these guys a bite and some water."

"Sure."

She sat back down on her sled and watched as Ehlers found snacks for the dogs in the string of ten he was driving. Both teams had calmed down quickly, used to parking next to other dogs in races and on other training runs. Most of hers were back to resting, several snoozing, as they would have in a race, where many teams came and went in close proximity at the checkpoints.

"There. They'll hold for a bit," Ehlers said, sitting down beside Jessie on her sled with a day pack in one hand, thermos in the other. "Sandwich?" he asked, setting the thermos down and pulling several from the pack. "Tea? Cookies?"

"Sandwich, thanks, if you're sure it's an extra. I came away without lunch. Too much going on at my house."

"Yeah?" he asked, handing her a tuna sandwich in a Ziploc bag and filling the cup from the thermos with hot tea that steamed in the cool air. "We'll have to share this. I didn't expect company, but there's lots of sandwiches and cookies. I always think I'm going to be hungrier than I am and wind up taking half of it home again. What's up at your place?"

"Well," Jessie said, with a sad frown. "To begin with, I had to have old Pete put down yesterday."

"Oh, Jess. I *am* sorry. He was a good old guy."

Ehlers knew most of her dogs, having cared for them while her injured knee was healing. This included Pete, though she had kept him at home.

"Yeah, me too. But even worse, I took the gang out for

a first run in the new snow—up on that trail that loops above and comes down at my place."

"I remember that one. Taken it a couple of times myself."

"Well, you probably didn't run over a dead man in the middle of it. We did—this morning."

Ehlers froze, sandwich halfway to his mouth, and gave her a startled look, eyes wide. "Good God, Jessie. What . . . ?"

"I don't know, Lynn. As soon as I knew what I'd found, and that he was dead, I went straight down to the house and turned it over to Alex. He was on the phone reporting it when I decided I just couldn't stick around with all of what was about to go on there. So I went out the door, pulled the hook, and just took off."

He gave her a long thoughtful look, combined with a puzzled frown. "No dogs? No team? That's a mushers' trail. Who was it? Did you recognize him? Anyone we know?"

Jessie shook her head. "I don't *think* I had ever seen him before. It was nobody I know who runs dogs and uses that trail—but I was more than a little shook up. The snow hook had caught and turned him over as I stepped it down to slow the sled. There was a fair amount of blood on his clothes and the leaves and snow from what looked like a gunshot wound in the right side of his head."

It was well after noon when the three officers finally finished their job and came down off the hill with, as predicted, little to show for it. The snow had slowed and finally stopped falling while they examined the crime scene, but clearing away snow had them all chilled and damp by the time they had finished and were ready to leave.

Alex and Becker followed Calb, the snow machine, and the body on the sled down the hill and into the yard, where they helped to load all three into the van he had driven from the crime lab.

"Come in and warm up before you go," Alex invited. "I've got homemade stew that must be ready by now."

Both men were more than willing to take advantage of dry heat laced with the stew's enticing aroma, and they were soon adding to the warmth with mugs of fresh coffee and bowls they emptied rapidly.

Alex had been a little surprised to find the house empty and Jessie evidently still out with her dogs. A glance at the kennel had told him none of the ones in the team she had originally taken out were back in their places in the yard.

Assuming she was okay and would be back sometime fairly soon, he turned the conversation to what they had found on the hill.

In moving the body, they had found in the back pocket of his jeans Donny Thompson's wallet containing several pieces of identification, a list of several phone numbers, and a small amount of cash. A front pocket yielded some small change and several keys on a ring, one evidently to a motorcycle. A red knit cap filled one jacket pocket. A well-used handkerchief lay in another.

There had been nothing else of significance to find but the frozen bloody leaves on which Thompson had fallen and lain facedown, and not many of those; no gun, no footprints, nothing to tell there had been anyone else there at all. But, with no sign of a gun, they had to assume that the man had not shot himself, so someone else had to have been responsible.

Jessie, her dogs, and the sled had made the only tracks in the snow in running over him, so it was clear that anyone else that might have been there had gone before the snow began to fall sometime shortly after midnight on Saturday.

As Ray Calb finished the last swallow of his coffee and rose to his feet to leave, thanking Alex for the food and shelter, there was a sudden uproar of welcoming barks from the dogs in the kennel, a sure announcement that Jessie had come home.

"Better get the van out of the way out there," he said, shrugging on his coat and heading for the door. "Time to get Thompson to the lab anyway."

After removing her dogs from their harnesses and taking them back to their boxes, Jessie watered them well before coming inside, where she was soon at the table with Jensen and Becker, warming her own hands on another mug.

"Jess, did you see anyone else on your run up the hill this morning?" Alex asked her.

She shook her head. "No. It was pretty quiet for the first day of decent sledding. I wouldn't have been surprised to see a couple of teams on the upper trail, but we had it all to ourselves. That won't last long."

Giving Alex a long look, she changed the subject before he could ask her anything more.

"You know I don't ask questions about your cases. You couldn't answer them if I did. But can you at least tell me if you know who it was? I've been afraid ever since I found that guy that it would turn out to be someone I've met and just didn't recognize."

The tall trooper gave a quick glance to the man still seated at the table, then nodded slowly, as he seemed okay with her request.

"She did find him after all, Alex," Becker commented.

"Yes, well . . . I guess, after the way you found him,

you have a right to that much, Jess," he told her finally. "But I doubt you knew him. His name's Donny Thompson, from out east of Palmer—a mechanic who works with his father, Bill Thompson. Ring any bells?"

She sighed in relief, and shook her head. "No. But I think I've heard the name somewhere from someone—maybe Hank Peterson. You know around here it's definitely less than the proverbial six degrees of separation. Everybody knows somebody. If you ask one or two people, you can usually find a connection to number three."

Alex nodded, but suspected that he would soon be asking a lot more than just one or two people before he discovered just how, and why, Donny Thompson had died on the hill, a long way from home.

CHAPTER SIX

AFTER SHARING HIS LUNCH WITH JESSIE, LYNN EHLERS turned his team north toward the kennel he shared with another sled dog racer on the Parks Highway between Wasilla and Talkeetna, a few miles from Nancy Lake. The snow had stopped falling for the time being, and the clouds had thinned enough to allow a hint of sun to fall through and brighten the day, creating purple-blue shadows that made the trail anomalies easier to read.

Running through the first snow of the season was always a pleasure to mushers, especially when it came early. Like kids let out of school, they enthusiastically hit the trails. Ehlers had passed half a dozen teams on his way to the Goose Lake area. He had not been surprised to find Jessie out with one as well and had been glad to hear that her knee was healed enough for it. It had saddened him to hear of the death of a favorite dog and he was astonished at her finding the dead man in the trail above her house. It had clearly taken the luster from her enjoyment of the day.

Somehow it seemed that trouble had followed Jessie like a specter in the past few years. It reminded him of the difficulties she had experienced during the Yukon Quest,

the race during which he had met her for the first time and
been immediately attracted. He recalled his concern when
she had vanished during the race, relief when she reappeared safely, and regret in realizing where her affections
lay when Alex Jensen had reappeared in Alaska. He and
Jessie had become good and lasting friends, however,
which pleased him.

Now it seemed another unwelcome problem had shown
up in her life. Who, he wondered, would the body in the
trail turn out to be? Possibly, as she had suggested, it was
not a Knik Road resident, as most of them had lived there
a long time and were well known to their neighbors. That
was not as true as it had been in the past, for in the pre-
ceding few years there had been a flood of newcomers
who, as Wasilla grew, were finding the Knik Road area
perfect for building new houses in small planned communities. Perhaps this guy was one of them, for, evidently,
from what she had described, he had probably not been a
musher. But why would he have been on that upper trail,
which was traveled mostly by those with dogs and sleds?
How long had he been there anyway? Not more than a
day or two, he guessed. Anxiously awaiting the first snow-
fall, frustrated mushers had been out cleaning up the
trails they planned to use soon.

Who was he? What had he been doing there? And who
had killed him, if he had not killed himself? Could a plan
for suicide have given him an inclination to hike off into
the forest?

Ehlers decided he would soon check with Jessie to see
what had been learned about the dead man.

Coming to a partially frozen creek that needed to be
crossed, he turned his attention to getting his team and
sled over without incident to dogs, sled, and himself.

"Come on, guys. We're almost home."

* * *

Leaving Alex and Jessie, Phil Becker was also thoughtful as he drove Knik Road back to Wasilla and took the connecting highway across to the Alaska State Troopers office on South Valley Way in Palmer. There he planned to write up his report on the morning's activity, while he waited for Jensen to show up and accompany him out the Glenn Highway to take what would certainly be shocking and highly unwelcome news to the Thompson family.

It was not a duty either of them was looking forward to, but one which should be done in person. The reaction of the family to the unpleasant news would be important, as would gathering as much information as possible concerning their youngest son. Perhaps they knew something, or could direct attention to someone who did, that would give the troopers a direction in which to focus the initial phases of their investigation.

It seemed odd to have found Donny Thompson's body in a location so unrelated to anything he knew about the young man, though he was not someone Becker knew well or pleasantly. He frowned as he drove and considered what he did know.

Donny hung out with a fast crowd, though mainly on the fringes, where he might have felt a need to prove himself. On two occasions Becker had pulled him over for driving his motorcycle erratically. In the second instance, late in the evening, after several hours at the pub where his brother was bartender and should have known better than to let him leave for home drunk, Donny had been arrested for driving under the influence. Convicted, he had spent three days in jail, besides paying a substantial fine along with the significant cost of retrieving his wheels from impound when it was at last released.

Unfortunately, he seemed to have learned little from

the experience, and Becker expected there would have
been a repeat of his performance in his future had he
lived. It could be there would be some kind of information to be gained through contact with the bikers he hung
with. So that too was worth putting on the list for inquiry.

Pulling up at the Alaska State Troopers office, Becker
got out, locked his car, and shook his head ruefully at the
idea as he headed inside to wait for Jensen. It was often
all but impossible to get any real information out of hard-
core bikers. They often tended to close ranks and play
stupid when confronted by *the law*. The ones who weren't
hard-core usually didn't know much that would help.

Hank Peterson, Jessie's Friday night pool opponent, was
not far away. Across the railroad tracks that ran through
the middle of town and west a block or two from Becker's
office, he had just lost a game of pool and returned to his
bar stool in the Aces Wild. Setting back his empty beer
bottle, he nodded to Carl Thompson's questioning look
and watched as the bartender retrieved the empty and set
a full one in its place, collecting the price from the small
pile of bills and change Hank had left on the bar for that
purpose.

"Where's Donny?" he asked the older Thompson
brother. "Thought I might catch him for a game this afternoon."

"Don't know," Carl answered with a frown and a shrug,
hands busy mixing a pair of screwdrivers for a couple at
the other side of the horseshoe-shaped bar. "Haven't seen
him since Friday. He was here early that night, but left
about seven with Jeff Malone. Hasn't been home since
then either. Must have tied one on and, when it started to
snow, decided to bunk with one of his buddies here in

town. He's probably nursing a two-night hangover and will show up later looking like death warmed over."

"Too bad I can't stay much longer," Hank said with a grin. "I'da had a better chance to beat him if he was hungover."

Carl took the screwdrivers around to the other side of the bar and came back to the till, where he entered the amount of the sale and made change from the cash drawer.

"Donny may not stay, if he comes in at all," he told Hank. "The old man was pretty pissed at him for not coming home yesterday. He was supposed to help fix a truck engine and didn't show."

Turning his head as Carl moved away to answer a request from the blonde in tight stretch pants who was waiting tables, Hank noticed that an older man sitting by himself at the bottom end of the U-shaped bar, two empty stools away, had been silently following his conversation with Carl.

"Hey, Stan," he asked, "you seen Donny in the last couple of days?"

"Nope. Haven't seen him in over a week. Maybe he's drinking somewhere else these days."

"Better not be," Carl commented with a grin, as he passed on his way to the cooler to retrieve three Budweisers to add to a vodka tonic already on the waitress's tray. "We need the business. Here you go, Jill."

"Change for a twenty," she reminded him, got it, and turned to deliver the drinks to a table across the room.

"You feel that shaker this morning?" Stan asked, changing the subject. "Woke me up just before five."

Hank shook his head. "I'm so used to 'em that I sleep right through the little ones. Takes a pretty significant quake to make me sit up in bed—like the one we got Friday night. I was playing pool with Jessie Arnold at the Other Place and it completely scrambled the balls on the table. Cue ball never touched the one she was aiming at, but it rolled right into the corner pocket anyway."

"Yeah, that was a good one. Seems like there've been more like that lately."

"Naw. You're just noticing 'em more for some reason. How long have you been up here, Stan?"

"All my life. Born in Kodiak, where my dad was a fisherman. Lived there till I got married and moved here thirty years ago, back when Palmer was just a stop on the railroad, before it got all citified."

"So you were here for the big one in sixty-four."

"Oh yeah. March twenty-seventh, Good Friday, just after five thirty in the afternoon. *Now that was a quake!* Biggest one ever recorded in North America—eight point seven on the Richter scale, but some people say it was over nine!

"Shook us pretty good, but it was worse in Anchorage than it was out here in the valley. The ground opened up and a whole block on one side of Fourth Avenue dropped down about ten feet. Took the second story of the businesses along the street right down to ground level, including the Denali Theater. The marquee looked like it was sitting on the sidewalk. Couple of blocks away the whole concrete front of the new Penney's building fell off on a car and killed the woman driver. A lot of the Turnagain area collapsed and a whole bunch of houses fell over the cliff or broke up."

"The control tower at the airport fell over, didn't it?"

"Yeah. Guy who didn't get out in time died inside."

In a rare free moment, Carl Thompson had stopped to listen to what Stan was saying. Turning toward a man sitting farther along the bar, he asked, "Hey, Hardy. You were in one of those bars in Anchorage that day, weren't you?"

"Yeah, I sure was. Won't ever forget it either!"

A tall man wearing a green baseball cap stood up shaking his head and moved to a stool next to Stan, bringing his drink with him.

"I was covering sports for the *Anchorage Daily News* and had finished my story, left the office, and gone to the Highland Fling on Fourth between D and E streets. A bunch of us from the paper usually showed up there on Friday nights for their twofers. Back then the *News* was an evening paper, but it was going to mornings that weekend to compete with the *Times*, which would change our working hours and pretty much end our weekly gettogethers.

"The Fling was a long, narrow place on the north side of the street with a restaurant on Fourth, a bar behind, and a parking lot out back on Third. There was a tremble that we felt, but thought was just the usual minor stuff, so nobody moved. Then seconds later the place got slammed so hard I thought the building would collapse. All the lights went out and it went on shaking for several minutes. Stuff in the bar started falling and breaking—bottles, glasses, the big mirror behind the bar. You could smell the spilled whiskey. People were yelling bloody murder and trying to get out, but you couldn't stay on your feet. I saw one woman crawling toward the back door.

"I just grabbed my two drinks and sat there hoping I wasn't going to die. Finally it stopped and I had to jump over a hole in the floor to get out the door, and when I got to my car out back it was right on the edge of a crevasse ten feet deep, so I wasn't going anywhere in it. Then I realized I was still holding the drinks I had grabbed on to in the bar so they wouldn't fall off the table.

"I heard later that the bartender at the 515 Club down the street had just served some drinks and was still carrying some empty glasses on a tray when the thing hit and he left in a hurry out the front door. So he turned around, went back inside, and put them where they wouldn't get broken. Then he got out again."

There was laughter and Hank noticed that several other people in the room had moved close to listen. As he turned back to the bar, a man on the other side stood up frowning and went out the door, leaving most of the beer he had just ordered where it sat.

Hank gave Carl a questioning look.

Carl shook his head. "He lost his wife and child when the Turnagain bluff fell into the inlet."

CHAPTER SEVEN

"JESSIE OKAY?" BECKER ASKED WHEN JENSEN ARRIVED at the office. "She seemed a little upset."

"She was, but she'll be all right. It's been a bad weekend for her all around. Yesterday she had to have one of her oldest and favorite dogs put down. Finding a dead guy practically in her backyard this morning shook her up some more, but she's tough and she'll be fine in a day or two."

"Good. You think we ought to check with Timmons at the crime lab before we go out to Thompson's?"

Alex considered calling the medical examiner, then shook his head. "John won't have anything for us until tomorrow at the earliest, maybe Tuesday. We might as well get on out to Sutton, like it or not."

"You want to stop at the Aces and tell his brother before we go?"

"No, we'd better go out and tell his parents first. But Carl may know who Donny was with Friday night, before it snowed, so I want to talk to him too."

Ten minutes later the two had left the office and were heading out of Palmer in Jensen's pickup, rather than a patrol car.

From the junction of the Palmer-Wasilla Highway, the

Glenn Highway runs almost 140 miles northeast to Glennallen. Fifteen miles along it, on the north side of the Matanuska River between the scenic peaks of the Chugach and Talkeetna mountain ranges, lay the small community of Sutton, which was founded around 1918 as a station on the Matanuska branch of the Alaska Railroad, which transported coal from its mine to Anchorage. Throughout World War Two Anchorage was heated with Sutton coal.

On the outskirts of the town, Becker directed Jensen to a cluster of buildings including a two-story frame house, white with gray trim. The other two or three buildings were built of concrete block with metal roofs. The largest of these had two huge roll-up doors to allow access for large vehicles and bore a hand-painted sign: THOMPSON'S AUTOMOTIVE. A fenced area toward the rear of the yard held what appeared to be the owner's personal junkyard, full of a variety of vehicles—cars, trucks, motorcycles, whole or in pieces, some rusty with time spent in the elements of Alaskan winters. Many appeared to have been cannibalized for parts.

The doors to the shop were shut and no one seemed to be around.

"Must have finished his work for the day," Becker said, peering through a window into the dark shop.

He followed Jensen up the steps onto the wide porch of the house next door and the two waited for an answer to their knock.

It took a minute or two, but a woman wearing an apron over jeans and a brown plaid flannel shirt finally opened the door and gave them an apologetic smile. She was wiping her flour-covered hands on a handful of damp paper towels that she had obviously carried along from the kitchen. "Sorry, I was making bread. Can I help you with something?"

"Mrs. Thompson?" Jensen questioned.

"Yes, but everyone just calls me Helen."

Jensen showed her his identification and badge. "Is your husband here, Mrs. Thompson?" he asked.

"No," she said, shaking her head, the smile gone. "Bill doesn't usually work on Sunday. He and Garth went down to the Alpine Inn for a beer. Should I call him? He could be here in five minutes."

"Yes, please. We need to see you both."

Her expression changed to anxiety as she asked, "What is it? Is it one of my kids? What?"

"Please, Mrs. Thompson. Call your husband."

She stared at Jensen without moving, fear and confusion written on her face.

"Please . . . ," she began, then stopped. "Oh, God," she said, now wringing her hands together as the paper towels fell to the floor at her feet unnoticed.

"Call your husband, Mrs. Thompson."

Leaving the door wide open, she whirled and they watched her cross the room to a telephone on the wall by the kitchen, dial a number, and wait for someone to answer.

"Pete, this is Helen Thompson. I have to speak to my husband—right now, quick. Yes." There was a short wait, then, "Bill, there are two state troopers at the door that want to see us both. I don't know. They won't tell me. Come on home—right now. I'd say so, yes."

She hung up and turned back to face Jensen and Becker.

"Please," she said, "come in and close the door. It's cold. He'll be right here."

He was.

Pulling off the highway that had been recently plowed of snow, Thompson slid the motorcycle he was riding to a stop in the semi-icy parking area in front of the house and came hurrying up the steps.

"What is it?" he asked brusquely, closing the door behind him. "Something wrong? One of my boys in some kind of trouble?"

Though Helen had sat down on the sofa and invited the two troopers to take chairs, they had remained standing. She stood up again as Bill Thompson turned away from them to address her. "Where's Sally?"

"She went up to Julie's. Said she'd be back for dinner."

"Well, Carl's working at the bar today. Garth was at the Alpine, so he's on his way right behind me. Lee went into town to see if he could find Donny. So that leaves the two of them. Which one is it?" he demanded. "Lee or—Donny?"

The sound of another motorcycle engine, then boots on the porch, announced the arrival of Garth Thompson, who came hurriedly into the room with a frown on his face at the sight of the troopers.

"What's up?" he asked, stripping off the leather gloves he was wearing. "Lee go off the road on his way to Palmer? Damn it! I told him to take the truck, not his bike. He just won't listen to . . ." The sentence died as he took in the serious expression on the faces of the law enforcement officers. "Oh, shit," he said. "It's bad, isn't it?"

Jensen once again took out his identification and showed it to the two waiting men, before proceeding to tell the three family members present about the death of their son and brother, Donny—a part of the job he had always hated.

"I regret to have to inform you," he said slowly, formally, "that your son, Donny, was found dead near Knik Road the other side of Wasilla this morning. As near as we can tell, he was shot, or shot himself, sometime before it snowed Friday night."

They stared at him in silent shock as he paused, as if they didn't understand what he had just told them.

"Oh, God! Oh, God! Oh, God!" Helen Thompson breathed softly, as the color drained completely from her already pale face and she swayed perilously on her feet.

Garth caught his mother before she fell and sat down with her on the sofa, an arm around her. She buried her face in his shoulder and began to sob.

Bill Thompson, all but expressionless, simply, slowly, turned away and walked like a man twice his age to stare out the window at the snowy yard between the house and his shop next door, though Becker doubted he was seeing any of it.

Though the afternoon was cloudy with the threat of more snow, it had not started to fall close to an hour later, as Jensen and Becker headed back toward Palmer.

Before leaving Sutton, they had stopped at the Alpine Inn, where Bill and Garth Thompson had been before heading home.

"This is a small town," Becker had told Alex in suggesting the stop. "Everyone who lives here knows everybody else. They're good folks for the most part and take care of each other. We might find out who Donny hung out with.

"Besides being a watering hole, the Alpine is a community center of sorts. Lot of things go on there—potluck dinners to music nights. It's a local package store and restaurant as well. Some of the old miners are still around and the Alpine is full of memorabilia from those early days. During World War Two they supplied a lot of the coal that heated and supplied electricity in Anchorage.

"I come out here once in a while to see my hunting buddy Kyle."

Half a dozen people were sitting at the near end of a bar long enough to seat at least twenty on the left side of the large room when the troopers walked in. The rest of the room was in shadows where the light from the two front windows didn't penetrate. The bartender had just set up a pair of beers for two men farthest from the door and looked up with a smile.

"Hey, Phil. Haven't seen you lately. I'd guess you're here on business, considering how fast Bill and Garth Thompson went out the door a while ago. Something wrong at home?"

"'Fraid so," Becker answered. "You got a couple of minutes?"

"Yeah, sure. Let me build another drink for Judy and I'll be right there. Get you anything while I'm at it?"

"Killian's?" Becker asked Alex, who nodded.

"Sure. We're not in uniform on regular duty."

They took two stools a few seats away from the line of drinkers already bellied up to the bar, and Alex leaned back to look at the collection of historic photographs of miners that were hung over the bar. Other pictures and antique bits of mining equipment decorated the walls around the room. "I see what you mean about the memorabilia."

"Yeah. The old mine is out of sight up on the hill, along with most of the town. Some of the company houses built for the miners still have people living in them. There's a preschool, a library, grocery, post office, airstrip, even a volunteer fire department and an ambulance service up there—just about everything they need—you just don't see it from the highway. What isn't here, they go to Palmer for."

In a few minutes the bartender, Pete, was back with the lagers they had ordered. He set them up, leaned on the bar with both hands, and asked quietly, "What can I help with? What's going on?"

Becker introduced Jensen, who shook hands and gave the tall, thin man a thoughtful look of assessment before he spoke. "How long have you been tending bar here, Pete?"

"Pretty close to twenty years, off and on—mostly on."

"So you know most everyone in Sutton?"

The bartender grinned. "Everyone knows everyone in Sutton."

"Probably not always as well as you do."

"Well, that's *possibly* true. But if I couldn't keep my own counsel I wouldn't keep customers or last long in a job like this."

"Tell me what you know that I should know about Donny Thompson."

Now the thoughtful look of assessment was directed at Jensen from the opposite side of the bar.

"Why would I forget to keep my own counsel and do that?"

Jensen's next words were low and to the point, clearly meant to startle.

"Donny Thompson was shot dead, or shot himself, night before last in the woods off Knik Road out of Wasilla. I'd like to be able to figure out who might have had reason to kill him and why."

Pete took his hands off the bar and stood up straight, mouth and eyes wide in surprise. He narrowed his eyes and took a deep breath.

"Well," he said. "I knew something was wrong, from

the way Bill reacted to that phone call. Helen isn't the sort to holler for help unless she really needs it. She's had a lot to do with raising those five kids, four of them boys and pretty wild at times with their motorcycle racing and such. But they've all turned out pretty much okay. So I knew something had happened, but I never figured it would be that bad. Jeez! Give me a minute, okay?"

He walked back to the group sitting at the bar and leaned across to speak to a woman who was part of it. She nodded, got up, and came around the bar to take his place behind it.

"Thanks, Sharon."

"Not a problem. You ready for another, Bob?" she asked a heavyset man in overalls, who had pushed back his empty beer bottle.

"Let's go to the far end of the bar," Pete suggested to Jensen and Becker, when he came back. "I better sit down for this one, I think."

Taking their lagers, they moved farther away from the group to the end of the bar, next to where it dropped off and became a counter behind which a glass-fronted cooler held an assortment of beers and other bottled drinks for sale. Pete pulled up a stool and sat facing them across the bar with a beer of his own.

"Now, what can I tell you that will help?"

"When was the last time you saw Donny Thompson?" Jensen asked.

"Friday. Midafternoon. He stopped in for a bottle of Beam before heading to Palmer."

"He said that's where he was going?"

"Yes. That's where he usually went on Friday lately."

"Anyone with him?"

"Jeff Malone. They only stayed long enough for one drink and to buy the bourbon."

"Malone's from Wasilla, right?" Becker asked.

Pete nodded. "I think so."

"Did Donny hang out with anyone from out here?" Jensen questioned.

"Not to speak of. Just his brothers—mostly Lee. I know he goes to the Aces in Palmer because it's where his brother Carl tends bar and a lot of bikers hang. They come in there from all over, even Anchorage, but mostly from the valley."

"You know of any particular trouble Donny's been involved in recently?"

"Nothing more serious than a DUI last spring that I'm sure you're aware of. But it wouldn't have surprised me if there was another in his future. I've had to cut him off on a pretty regular basis lately. He's okay when his brother Lee's riding with him, but tends to take off on his own."

"Anything else you can think of that might be of help in finding out who shot him?"

There wasn't.

The bartender was shaking his head and frowning as the two troopers left the Alpine, and Jensen knew that the news of Donny Thompson's death would reach just about all of Sutton before the end of the day and the community would gather and close ranks in support of the family.

"Jessie said the Palmer-Wasilla area is less than six degrees of separation—that it's more like two or three," he commented as they pulled out of the parking lot, heading for Palmer. "I think in a place like Sutton it's more like none."

They made it to town just in time to catch Carl Thompson coming out the door of the Aces Wild in a hurry as they pulled up in front.

CHAPTER EIGHT

Jᴇssɪᴇ ᴀɴᴅ Tᴀɴᴋ ᴡᴇʀᴇ ᴡᴀɪᴛɪɴɢ ᴀᴛ ᴛʜᴇ ᴅᴏᴏʀ ᴡʜᴇɴ Alex pulled into the yard early that evening, tired, frustrated, and slightly depressed after a day of learning little in terms of the death of Donny Thompson.

"You look tired," she said, taking his coat and hat to hang on the hooks beside the door while he removed his boots. "It's been a bad day, hasn't it? And this was supposed to be your weekend off."

He gave her a weary smile as he gathered her into his arms and rocked her close for a moment or two.

"Yeah, well, some days are like that and it wasn't so good for you either. We didn't find out much, but it wasn't all that bad, except for going out to Sutton to tell the Thompsons about their son. That kind of visit's always unpleasant."

"I'm sure it was. Good thing you don't have to do it often. Why don't you get a beer, sit down, relax, and tell me about it, if you want to? There's the rest of your stew for dinner and I'll make biscuits in a bit."

Alex nodded as he retrieved a Killian's from the refrigerator.

"Actually, if you're getting yourself one, I wouldn't mind

having a shot of that Jameson of yours. Might take a few of the kinks out of my mind as well as body."

"Coming right up."

As Jessie headed for the kitchen, Alex took his Killian's to the living room, where he laid a piece of firewood into the cast-iron stove that was putting out comforting heat, lowered himself onto the big sofa, and put his feet up on the coffee table with a sigh of relief.

In five minutes they were both comfortably ensconced at opposite ends of the sofa, Jensen sipping his whiskey gratefully.

"A-a-ah! That's the ticket. Now, before I tell you what I can of what transpired this afternoon, tell me what you've been up to. Did you take another team out or stay home?"

"I took another out. Wasn't going to at first. After you left I thought I'd just stay in for the rest of the day, but that began to seem silly after a while, when all I could do was feel bad and wonder about what happened to Donny Thompson and why. So I did what I knew would make me feel better—hooked up another bunch of the mutts and we went down the road to John Singleton's kennel. He and I spent over an hour talking about the races next spring. His daughter's going to run the Iditarod again, as she did this year.

"But the big news is that, next year being the hundred-year anniversary of the All Alaska Sweepstakes, the race they ran from Nome to Candle in the early years, they've finally decided that they *will* run it again next March and it *will* have a cash prize of a hundred thousand dollars— winner take all."

"You going to do it?"

"I don't know. It's going to be a tough one. You can't have more than twelve dogs and can't drop any of them— have to finish with the same ones you started with—even if they're riding in the sled. I've had the Iditarod in mind, but I'm not even sure about that until I know my knee will take it."

"Well, you've got time to think about it. Wait and see how your knee does now that you're back out there on a sled."

"That's what I thought I should do. Now, what happened for you and Phil today?"

Alex frowned and considered for a moment what to tell Jessie about the little he had learned in the past few hours. He didn't usually discuss his cases with anyone but law enforcement people, but this was a little different because she was peripherally involved.

"Jess," he said finally, giving her a straight look of assessment, "I really don't want you any more caught up in this one. You were pretty upset when you came down the hill after running over that guy in the trail. It seemed to hit you pretty hard, and should have. But I couldn't take time to get a reading on your feelings or reactions—I had to focus on investigating. Then, while the three of us were up there, you disappeared and I was worried when I came down and found you gone without even leaving a message as to where you were headed."

"I know," Jessie said, when he paused. "I should have left a note, I guess. But I decided to go ahead with my plan to spend the day with the dogs, so I went as far as Goose Lake, where I ran into Lynn Ehlers and shared his lunch. By the time I came back I was feeling much better, Ray Calb was leaving, and you and Becker were about to head for town."

"You're sure you want to hear about it?"

"Yes. I'm okay with it, Alex—really. It's not as if I'd never seen a dead person before. It was just so unexpected to actually *run over* him up there. I'm fine now. Truly.

And it's better to know about it than to wonder—you know? So tell me what you can. I don't want to get in your way or be involved. You know I try to stay out of your cases and work."

Alex remained thoughtful for another long minute. Then, finishing the whisky in one gulp, he picked up the bottle of lager Jessie had brought him and took a sip to chase it down, and nodded.

"Okay," he agreed. "On those usual terms, I'll tell you what I'm comfortable with, and I have a couple of questions you may be able to answer for me."

"Sure. If I can."

"Well, as I said, we went out to Sutton to tell the family, which wasn't pleasant for any of us. Then, at Becker's suggestion, we stopped in at the Alpine Inn to talk with the bartender, who seems to have a pretty close finger on the pulse of what goes on in the community. Spent about half an hour there, then came back to Palmer.

"We got to the Aces Wild just in time to meet Carl Thompson, Donny's older brother, who tends bar there. He'd had a call from his father to come home, but had to wait for a replacement before he could leave. Turns out Donny had been in there on Friday night and left sometime during the evening—about seven, Carl said—with a guy named Jeff Malone, who was also with him that afternoon in Sutton. He didn't know where they went, but Donny was supposed to be home to work with his dad on Saturday and didn't show. Of course, we know he was dead before it snowed Friday night, but his father didn't and was not happy with his unexplained absence.

"That's about all we got from Carl. Inside the Aces, we ran into Hank Peterson, who had stopped to see if Donny was there. Evidently Hank plays pool with him fairly often."

"Doesn't surprise me," Jessie said with a smile. "Hank plays pool with just about anyone above learner's level who's willing. I think I may have heard Donny's name from him, now that you mention it."

"Well, he didn't know where Donny had been on Friday night, except that Carl had told him that he had left the Aces with Malone. Do you know him?"

"Nope. But not many mushers hang out with the biker crowd. Totally different kind of transportation and attitude."

"Carl didn't tell the group in the bar why he had to leave in such a hurry—just that it was a family emergency. Hank asked if I knew anything about it, but I told him it was Carl's business. They'd been telling earthquake stories."

"I'd bet anything Hardy Larsen was part of *that* conversation. Did he tell his story about being in an Anchorage bar when it happened?"

"Not while we were there, but . . ."

As if conjured by the mention of earthquakes, every dog in the yard outside unexpectedly began to bark or howl, and there was suddenly a tremor that interrupted Alex and reminded Jessie of the one that had shaken the Other Place two days earlier. She sat up straight on the sofa, alert, eyes wide.

"They really hate quakes," she said, as the mild shaking decreased, disappeared, and the canine cacophony faded as well.

Leaning back, Jessie ask a question. "So you still have no idea how and why Donny's body would be up there?"

"No idea at all. Wish I did. It seems an odd place for him to have been. But here's a question for you. Who uses that trail besides the local mushers?"

Jessie frowned in thought as she considered the query.

"Hikers. Hunters, sometimes, though they're not supposed to hunt in populated areas. I know one guy who shot a moose up there somewhere a couple of years ago. I won't bother to tell you who.

"It used to be okay, but not anymore. Every year there are more and more small groups and communities of houses going up as more people move out here. I'm beginning to feel as if we live in town, not scattered rural cabins like the days when I first moved here. If I hadn't just built this house, I'd consider moving somewhere else. I could probably get a lot for this piece of land and the house. I'd be willing to bet it won't be long until the new people begin to complain about our kennels being so close to where they live.

"But that's not what you asked, is it?

"Some of the neighbors walk their pet dogs once in a while, if they don't want to use the trail that runs next to the road. I've seen a few kids on their bikes, though it's pretty rugged for that in some places. I don't think the majority of people who aren't mushers even know those trails exist."

"That's pretty much what I assumed," Alex said. "The other thing I'm considering is that it could be possible that Donny was with someone from the Big Lake area. Though I can't think what he would have been doing that far out. But if he was there for some reason and wanted to come here, it would be quick and easy to take Carmel Road or Sunset Avenue, both back roads that run through to Knik Road."

Jessie nodded agreement. "That's true. I wonder how many people use those roads. I've driven Sunset a few times this last winter to get to Lynn Ehlers's kennel off the Parks Highway, while he was keeping most of my dogs. It's shorter than going through Wasilla."

"Well," said Alex, finishing his lager, getting up from where he had been sitting, and stretching his tall, lean body to ease the ache in his back. "Time for some more of that stew, I think. It's been so long since lunch my stomach thinks my throat's cut. Let's forget the biscuits and go for crackers instead this time, okay?"

"Okay with me," Jessie said, nodding toward the kitchen, where the kettle of stew was keeping warm on a back burner of the stove. "There's still some of that Ben and Jerry's left for dessert, if you want to dig it out."

"Oh yeah?" Alex grinned. "So you're gonna force me to eat ice cream just to get rid of it, right?"

"No. I could share it with Tank, if that'd make you happier."

"Not a chance. Ice cream has gotta be terribly bad for dogs. Probably for you too. I think I can force myself to clean it up for you."

"You wish!"

CHAPTER NINE

BEFORE GOING TO BED THAT NIGHT, JESSIE WRAPPED A jacket around her shoulders, stepped outside, and stood on the front porch to assess the weather.

It had not snowed again. The temperature had risen to several degrees above freezing and she was not happy to hear snowmelt dripping from the roof of her house with an almost musical sound as it dribbled into the puddles that had formed on the ground below. Through a thin layer of high cloud, the moon hung almost full, a cold, pale circle that looked as if it were caught in the bare branches of a tall birch to the left of the driveway. She could see a heavy band of dark cloud moving slowly in from the west, which would be disappointing if it carried rain to melt off the new snow and make training dogs with a sled impossible again.

The kennel yard was very quiet, each dog in its box, curled nose to tail on the thick straw bed on which it slept.

Well, she thought, *no use crying over milk that isn't spilled yet. It could get colder and snow again before morning.*

But somehow she didn't really think it would. This time

of year the weather was frustrating, hovering unpredictably somewhere above or below freezing, as if attempting to adjust to whatever prevarication the weatherman had put forth in his guesstimate for the next twenty-four hours.

A car went by on the road at the end of the drive, its tires making a wet, slushy sound on the pavement. Some late-returning soul on his way home, she assumed.

Its passing drew her mind to Alex's idea of someone with Donny Thompson, coming on the back roads from Big Lake to Knik Road. It could have happened, but even if it hadn't, she realized, transportation would have been necessary no matter what route was taken to reach this out-of-town location—they would have had to park their vehicle and/or his motorcycle somewhere. If they had intended murder, they certainly wouldn't have parked it in the place closest to where she'd found his body—her driveway. Where, then? Could he—they—have ridden it up the hill?

It still made no sense to her that Donny had been left where she found him, on the hill behind her house. Why would someone kill and leave him *there*? Who—and why? Or had he gone up by himself, hidden his bike, then shot himself on the trail where someone would be sure to find him soon enough?

It was all speculation and questions, and she wasn't sure she really wanted answers.

With a frown and a shiver, no answers, and one last long look at the moon, hanging like a dim lantern in the birch, Jessie turned, went back inside, and, still uneasy, carefully locked the door behind her.

She was standing in the same place early the next morning, a mug of coffee steaming in one hand, a piece of toast in the other, another disappointed frown on her face as she once again listened to water from melting snow falling from the eves of the house. Though the rain that had fallen instead of snow in the night had stopped for the moment, everything was wet and a low mist seemed to cling to the brush beneath the trees. The snow she had enthused over two days before was now mostly slush where it lay on the ground, which was largely bare and totally unsuitable for sleds.

From the unwelcome sound of dripping water, her attention was caught by the low mutter of a motorcycle in low gear just before it appeared, turned in, and came slowly up her drive to stop in front of the house beside Alex's pickup.

Killing the engine, the driver swung himself off and lifted the helmet from his head, allowing her to see his face.

"Good morning," he said. "You Jessie Arnold?"

"I am."

"Trooper Jensen live here?"

"He does."

"Well, I'm Jeff Malone. And I understand he'd like to talk to me about Donny Thompson."

Less than an hour later, Jensen and Becker were sitting in an interview room at the office of the Alaska State Troopers in Palmer, taking a formal statement from Jeff Malone about what he knew concerning Donny Thompson's whereabouts and contacts on the previous Friday night.

"From what we've heard and you've told us, you and Donny were in the Aces Wild early in the evening."

"I met him there at six, like I said."

"His brother confirmed that the two of you went over to La Fiesta for Mexican food just before seven o'clock and were planning to go on to Oscar's in Wasilla—where you say he stayed another hour and a half, right?" Jensen asked.

Malone nodded. "About that. He left sometime between nine thirty and ten."

"Tell me about that. Any particular reason that he left?"

"Well, he said he was going home to Sutton, because he had to be there to do some work for his dad on Saturday."

"And you?"

"I stayed there. You can ask Cole Anders. Oscar was out at the Other Place, so, as usual, Cole was tending bar in town. He knows me and that I was there for another two and a half or three hours. The girl I've been dating came in just before Donny left and only stayed a few minutes. She was driving and I didn't want to leave my bike, so she went on home. I played another game or two of pool, then left to go to her place about eleven thirty and stayed the night."

"What's her name? And where does she live?"

"Robin Fenneli. She has a place on Bodenburg Loop Road off the Old Glenn Highway."

"What's the address?"

Malone shook his head. "I know how to get there, but don't know the address. It's one of those old log houses a mile or two around the loop on the butte side of the road. Been in her family for years. Her grandfather built it."

"Phone?"

He spilled that out easily, making it obvious that he actually knew the woman well enough to have memorized her number.

Except for the small sound of his pencil, the room was

quiet as Jensen added to the notes he had been taking in his pocket-sized casebook.

Becker broke the silence for the first time.

"You know Donny Thompson pretty well?"

"Well—yeah. We went to high school together, see, but he was a year ahead of me. My grandfather was a coal miner in the early days and my folks lived in Sutton until a few years ago when they moved to Wasilla. Out there we all knew each other, but Donny and I have always been friends."

"So you rode the school bus in to Palmer High School?"

"Yeah. There weren't enough of us in Sutton for a high school. Donny's brother Lee was a year older, so he rode it with us for a couple of years till he graduated. Their family was about the largest in town—seven of them, counting their mom and dad."

"Anyone you know who had problems with Donny— might be likely to shoot him?" Jensen asked, changing the subject.

"*Shit, no!* There were a couple of guys in high school who gave him a bad time for a while, but that was a long time ago and those guys gave almost everybody a bad time. You know—football jocks who thought they were hot stuff and got off on making things rough for other kids—nothing serious."

"How about the bikers he hung around with?"

Malone shook his head. "Naw, most of those guys aren't as tough as people seem to think. We hang with them off and on. Most of them're a pretty good bunch, actually. Nobody had a problem with Donny to my knowledge, and I think I'd know if they did."

Jensen gave him a long narrow-eyed look, knowing

from past experience that Malone's assessment was more positive than realistic for a few of the hard-core bikers with attitude, who maintained a well-earned rough reputation. He let it ride, however, and took a different tack on his next question.

"Donny into anything illegal? Drugs? Gambling?"

"Ah—well . . . oh, hell. We both tried a little pot for a while, but not for a long time. Nothing else. Any gambling we did was on pool games, or bets on the Super Bowl—maybe a poker game once in a while. You know, the usual small stuff."

"So you have no idea who might have wanted him dead—or why?"

"Not the slightest. It doesn't make any sense. He pretty much got along with everybody. Could it have been some kind of accident?"

"Could he have shot himself? Did he, to your knowledge, own or carry a gun?"

"I can't imagine that he'd do himself—had no reason that I know of." He hesitated slightly before saying, "But I guess you never really know everything about anyone, do you? He had a rifle for hunting in the fall, but no handguns. His dad won't have handguns around. Says they cause more trouble than they prevent."

There was another short silence before Becker asked thoughtfully, "Was there anyone in the Aces Wild or Oscar's on Friday that you would have avoided? Who might have caused Donny trouble, or who left about the same time he did? Bikers maybe, guys you don't know, or wished you didn't?"

Jeff frowned as he tried to remember.

"It *was* Friday night, so both places were pretty busy. We had to wait a couple of games after we got to Oscar's before we got a turn at the pool table. There was a woman there that Donny was interested in—a redhead. But I think she left just before he did. I don't remember her name, if I ever heard it, and I have no idea who she is, or where she lives. Oscar or Cole might know. But there wasn't anybody asking for trouble. Oscar won't put up with it—eighty-sixes anyone who starts anything."

Jensen leaned back in his chair, thinking.

"Did you happen to notice if Donny's motorcycle was gone when you left the bar?"

Malone frowned and shook his head. "You know, I didn't even look," he said. "Had no reason to. I just assumed he was riding it home. The lot was crowded, so we hadn't parked our bikes together. His was in a wide space between two cars, kind of in the middle of the lot. Mine was closer to the building, couple of spaces from the door. I just took it and headed for Robin's without looking for Donny's."

"What color is his bike?"

"Black and green."

"Yours?"

"Just black."

"Most of the Road Pirates' bikes black and green?"

"No, only a few. Most are just plain black, but a few put the logo on them somewhere."

There were a few other minor clarifying questions before Alex closed his notebook and tucked it into a jacket pocket, but nothing that gave the troopers any help, except to establish the times and places where Donny Thompson had been the first part of that night.

"Well," he said to Jeff Malone. "I have your address and phone, so I know where to find you if I need more information. If you learn anything I should know, get in touch, okay?"

"Absolutely. I'd like to know who killed Donny as

much as you would. I sure hope you catch whoever it was. Donny was good people. There's gonna be a big hole in my social life without him around."

He shook hands with both troopers and they stood together and watched as he went out the door.

"Not much help," Becker commented. "I don't know. There's something about him coming in so quick without our hunting him up. You think he's on the level about what he told us?"

Jensen nodded. "Yeah—pretty much I do. Still, until we get an answer to this one, he stays on my list. Sometimes you just can't tell, and there was a hesitation or two, as if he wasn't telling us quite all he knew—or wanted us to know. And he's evidently convinced that Donny didn't shoot himself."

Leaning back in his chair, he thought for a long moment, then gave Becker what seemed a combination of frown and reluctant grin.

"What I'd like to know is what made him come looking for me, instead of letting us find him with questions. What he told us was that he really had nothing significant to tell us, right? So why did he feel it necessary to hunt me down at home just to assure me he had nothing that would help? He didn't ask a lot of questions, so he wasn't looking for information. Who told him we wanted to talk to him? Something about it doesn't sit quite right with me. You?"

Becker agreed. "Won't hurt to keep him on the list. Maybe he's just an overzealous sort. Or maybe, as he said, he wants to know who killed his friend. Could get in trouble asking questions of the wrong people, if that's the case. Maybe we should have warned him."

"I think he's smarter than that—a lot smarter," Jensen said, then turned to the phone and dialed a number.

Becker raised a questioning eyebrow.

"No, not Malone. We'll keep an eye out for any med-
dling on his part, but right now I want to know if Donny's
motorcycle was still in the parking lot at Oscar's," Jensen
explained as he waited for an answer to his call. "It could
be, if he left there with someone else. When Cole locked
up and left he'd probably remember if it was. It'd be gone
if he really headed back to Palmer and from there to Sutton, or still there if, for some reason, he changed his mind.
If he did, he might have gone somewhere with someone
else. Not much chance, but worth checking."

Unsuccessful at reaching Cole Anders after several
rings, he hung up, then dialed another number.

"Hey, Jess," he said. "Would you do me a favor? I can't
reach anyone at Oscar's in Wasilla."

A pause while he listened.

"Yeah, I know it's closed this early, but I thought someone might be there restocking. So would you drive over
there, see if there's a green-and-black motorcycle still in
the lot, and call me back here at the office?"

Another pause.

"Yes—Donny Thompson's. He evidently rode his bike
Friday night and I just need to know if it's still there. If it is,
he may have left with someone else. Yes, please. Take
your cell phone and call me back when you know, okay?
Thanks, love."

Jessie hung up the phone, put on a jacket, took her cell
phone and car keys, and headed out the door.

She had washed, dried, and put away the breakfast
dishes on autopilot, her thoughts focused elsewhere. The
question of Donny's missing motorcycle was still bother-
ing her, and, with Jeff Malone's unexpected early arrival,
she had not had the time or inclination to broach the

subject to Alex before he left for the office. Now it seemed like mental telepathy that he should call and be looking for it.

If Donny had ridden it to town from Sutton on Friday and had not gone back there since, it had to be somewhere. Could it be somewhere he had parked and left it before hiking up the hill to where he died—somewhere close by? That he had ridden it up an unfamiliar trail in the dark now seemed highly unlikely. If he had parked it near the highway, wouldn't she have seen it on one of her training runs? So where was it? Maybe it *was* still, as Alex wanted to know, at Oscar's pub in Wasilla.

It was not. The place was closed up tight. There was nothing in the parking lot except for a ramshackle old Ford and the trailer Oscar sometimes used to haul things he needed for the bar, parked out of the way at the back of the building.

"It's not here, Alex," she told him on the phone. "No motorcycles at all."

"Damn. I was hoping to solve that problem. Well, thanks anyway, Jess. You saved me a trip from here and back to check and I appreciate it."

"Not a problem. I'll collect somehow later."

"You got it."

Pocketing her cell phone, Jessie drove out of the parking lot, headed for home and thought hard about where Donny's motorcycle might be.

There had to have been at least two people who went up the hill behind her house on Friday night—Donny and whoever shot him—maybe more. If there had been more, one of them might have driven the motorcycle away following the murder. But if there had only been one, with his own transportation—car, truck, or another motorcycle—then moving Donny's might not have been possible.

Could it be hidden somewhere near the road? It could have been moved from where he left it and run off into the nearby brush. If by some chance that were so, she might be able to find it.

Pulling back into her driveway, she thought about it.

It was as possible as finding it at Oscar's had been, she decided, and worth a try, though she might come up just as empty of results.

Climbing out of the pickup, she made up her mind.

She didn't feel like spending the day inside. As long as it wasn't raining, she would take Tank for a walk with a purpose. If she found nothing, nothing would need to be said to Alex about this bit of amateur sleuthing, which he would not necessarily have encouraged.

Inside the house, she put on a slicker and a wide-brimmed, waterproof hat in case it rained again. Pulling on a pair of knee-high rubber boots, she locked the door behind her and headed for the yard.

Several dogs, including Tank, were snoozing on top of their boxes, but raised their heads as she appeared, then jumped down to meet her and barked when she continued in their direction, obviously hoping that, snow or no snow, she had a training run in mind.

Ignoring them, she took Tank off his tether.

"Hey. Wanna go for a walk?"

The enthusiastic wagging of his tail and the doggy smile he gave her, tongue hanging out at the word "walk," answered that question.

Trotting close, he accompanied her down the driveway to the highway, where they took a right turn onto the path that ran beside it.

As they walked along it, Jessie carefully searched the

muddy ground for what might be tire marks from a motorcycle, but saw only the vague tracks of four-wheelers left by local mushers running their dogs before there was enough snow for sleds. They were not new, for the rain had washed the traces into vague patterns that were often filled with slowly disappearing puddles as the water soaked into the ground. Always they were the parallel tracks of four tires, double what a motorcycle would have made.

After ten minutes of slow walking from the house she stopped suddenly, halted by marks that had not been made by tires. In the damp shoulder of earth that rose up to the pavement of the highway were a few prints that had been made by human feet, in boots. Some of them came off the road on their way down the short incline to the path on which she stood and, very near them, some went back up.

The rain had blurred almost all of them. But as she followed where they led, across the path and into the trees, beneath the branches of a shrub that still clung to most of its leaves a few had been sheltered enough to be quite clear and distinct. The tracks disappeared where whoever made them had walked into the grove, onto the autumn birch leaves that heavily covered the ground, making a carpet that would preserve no marks of passage. But as she stood and looked carefully between the trees, she could see where some leaves had been disturbed, a track that could possibly be followed.

Even where the boot prints had been made vague by the rain and were less distinct, it seemed clear to Jessie that they had been made, perhaps, by more than one person, where they had left the highway in favor of the woods, and only one or two where they came out of the trees and regained the road. One of the most clear pairs of returning prints seemed to have been made by a person who had drug his feet at every other step or two.

Hunkering down to examine the prints more closely, Jessie saw that one of the boots had evidently been damaged, for a chunk of the sole was missing on the front outside of what was clearly the right foot. The prints had to have been left recently, because they overlaid the older four-wheeler tracks that had been left to dissolve on the trail.

Rising, she stared once again into the grove of trees, thinking hard.

It was very quiet in the woods. Most of the birds that filled the area with warbles and chirps throughout the summer had, as usual, fled south as the weather turned cold. A light breeze ruffled the few small leaves that stubbornly clung to the denuded birches, a sound much lighter than their whispered conversation with the wind a few weeks earlier. A squirrel chattered somewhere out of sight, probably in contention with another over the spruce cones they all collected and stored away in secret places for the winter period of hibernation. Then they would periodically rouse to nibble seeds from the pockets in the cones.

A bright beam of sunshine suddenly lit up a few of the pale birch trunks and the thick covering of gold that lay beneath. Glancing up, Jessie could see that the clouds had thinned a little and were drifting north with a few patches of blue between.

Taking a deep, appreciative breath of autumn, she turned back to her discovery of the footprints and the questions they had brought to mind.

Could the tracks really be linked to the death of Donny Thompson, or were they just the result of more than one someone walking home along the path and moving off the highway to avoid traffic? Would the track through the fallen leaves lead to where Donny Thompson's body had been found? If so, how many people had there been going up and coming down? Had one less person returned to the road because he was lying dead in the upper trail, where she had found him? Who had made the tracks?

Hesitant to try to follow the disturbed leaves into the woods and take a chance of ruining that indistinct track, she decided to leave it to Alex. What she should do was tell him what she had found—show him what she couldn't help assuming might be evidence.

Gathering several handfuls of the driest leaves, she spread them carefully and lightly over the clearest of the prints under the bush as some kind of protection in case it rained again before she could show him.

"Come on, buddy," she said to Tank, who was sitting where she had told him to stay, a few feet from what she had found.

Walking a short distance toward home, she took the cell phone from her pocket, called Jensen's number, and was glad when he answered.

"Alex, I think you should come home, soon if you can, before it rains again."

"Why? Something wrong, Jess?"

"No, but I've found some things I think you'll want to see—some things that *might* have to do with Donny Thompson's death."

CHAPTER TEN

Jessie had meant to go back to the house until Alex arrived, but the question of where the track makers had come from drew her and she decided to at least take a look on the other side of the highway. Climbing the short slope to the pavement, she waited for a truck to pass, lifted a hand to wave as she recognized the driver as a neighbor, then went across, Tank trotting by her side. There, she walked slowly along the shoulder looking for tracks to match those she had found on the other side.

A short way along, she found herself standing in front of what had been a dirt road sometime long before she had come to the area, built a cabin, collected her first few dogs, and began training them, and herself, to race. It ran at right angles to Knik Road and was half blocked with brush that had grown up along and out onto it, so that only the first forty feet or so could have been accessed by a vehicle. One had tried, however, probably a truck, for there were tire tracks sunk about an inch into the soil softened by years of weather and disuse, and turned muddy by the recent rain.

It seemed the truck had pulled in, then backed out again onto the highway, for there was a confusion of its tire tracks where the two roads joined and some of the mud had been carried out onto the pavement by the tires.

She walked slowly along the side of the old road, following where the tracks led her, careful to stay away from them.

What stopped Jessie and inspired her to clutch at Tank's collar to keep him close against her knee was identifying the singular track of a motorcycle's tires between the parallel truck tire marks.

As far from the highway as it was possible to go, halted by the obstruction of vegetation that had grown up in the way, she found the place where the driver had parked what she assumed must have been a pickup. There the tire marks where it had stopped were a little deeper than the incoming or outgoing ones.

The motorcycle track seemed to have stopped behind it and there were boot prints, indistinct from the rain, beside it, as if the rider had swung off, then someone had pushed it around the truck and the tracks disappeared into the brush on one side of the blocked and muddy road. There was no sign of its return to the highway, or of the motorcycle itself. But whoever had pushed it had walked back into the soggy disorder of prints behind the truck.

Even in the confusion of what she saw on the ground, she decided there must have been more than one person who crossed to the other side of the highway.

Alex, she knew, would be better at interpreting all she had found and she should leave it to him. It was time to go home and wait until he came, which from his reaction on the phone would be soon.

"She's got it all just about right," Becker said to Jensen as they followed the trail of disturbed leaves uphill through the grove to the west of Jessie's dog yard. "And she did a good job of preserving what evidence she could—those footprints and tire tracks on both sides of the highway and on that old side road."

Jensen agreed that she had, but frowned anyway.

"I just don't like her getting involved. And I *told her so, damn it.* I should never have asked her to check out Oscar's."

"I think you could give her a break on this one," Becker suggested. "Would we have found all she did before the weather took it, while there was enough left to work with? We've been sorting out people, not tracks. How long would it have been before we located Donny's bike? Now, at least we know, or think that it's out there in the brush where— *whoever it was*—moved it out of sight. And we know there were two of them who went at least partway up the hill, all the way to where we found Thompson, and that two came back down, so one of them must have killed him."

"Yes, but that's about all we know except for Thompson—obviously the one that didn't come back down. Only one of those boot prints has anything individual about it to prove whose foot was in it—that one with the damaged sole—if we can find it and whoever wears it."

About halfway back to Knik Road, the two men were still following what Jessie had thought might be the way the killers had come and gone up the hill, when Becker suddenly stopped and pointed at a birch they were about to pass.

"That branch isn't a dead one that broke from the weight of the snow. It would likely have broken clear off if it were dead dry. Going up or coming down, one of them probably grabbed at it to keep his balance."

Stepping close, the two examined it in silence for a few seconds.

"Yeah, you're right," Jensen agreed. "And here . . ."

He pointed a finger at some rough bark on the tree trunk. "What does that look like to you?"

"Like someone fell against it and tore his coat?"

"My thoughts exactly. But those few threads are the color of half the coats in the valley—Carhartt brown."

"Wait a minute. Look close. That's wool, not the usual waterproof stuff. See? And there's a green thread or two mixed with that brown."

"Right again," Alex agreed, looking carefully. He used his knife to ease away the bit of rough bark that held the threads and dropped it into an evidence bag he retrieved from a pocket. "Maybe the lab can give us something on it."

Though they had examined the hillside all the way to the spot Donny Thompson had died and back down, they found no other clue to the identity of those who had accompanied him to his resting place.

Back at the highway, they crossed to the old overgrown road on the other side. There they closely examined all the tracks, human and vehicular, and took photographs of them all, especially those made by the boot with the damaged sole. Following the tire tracks of the motorcycle into the brush, they soon found where someone had, as Jessie had suggested, shoved it down a slight incline to rest out of sight in bushes so thick they had a struggle to haul it back up. It was Donny's, green and black, and in one pocket of its saddlebags they found an insurance card and registration in his name.

"Might be fingerprints," Becker suggested at the end of the effort, when they, and the bike, once again stood on the old road, all three dirty and scratched.

"We'll get it back to the office, have the lab pick it up, and see what they can find," Jensen said. "But I doubt whoever it was would be that stupid. It was a cold rain and they probably wore gloves. Still, you never know."

In half an hour the two had loaded the motorcycle into the back of Jensen's pickup and were headed back to the office in Palmer, where it would be collected and delivered to the crime lab in Anchorage for a careful going-over for prints, or anything else that might be helpful.

Jensen wasn't hopeful, but every possibility had to be followed.

Monday afternoon was quiet and uneventful for Jessie. She spent an hour inspecting equipment she would need as soon as it snowed again and she could start serious training runs with her dogs. But all of it had been checked before, when she was unable to use it, so there was little to do.

It was frustrating to have had all the snow melt away so quickly, before she could take advantage of it. Still, patience was the name of the game at that time of the year. All she could do was hope it wouldn't, like some winters, start with a long, seemingly endless cold spell that continued deep into November with temperatures dropping toward zero and no snow at all.

At close to three o'clock that afternoon, with everything neatly in order, she closed and locked the storage shed and went indoors.

There she curled up on the sofa with a cup of tea and a book she had been meaning to get around to, but found herself reading the same page over more than once, gave up, tossed it aside, and, instead, decided to make a run into Wasilla for the items necessary to make a meat loaf.

Pushing a cart around the big Carrs store, she collected ingredients for the meat loaf, some baking potatoes, salad greens, tomatoes, and green onions. Heading for another aisle for tomato sauce, she hurriedly turned a corner and almost crashed into Hank Peterson, who was inconveniently parked crosswise in front of the spaghetti sauce, talking to a short redheaded woman, who was looking up at him and laughing at something he was saying.

"Hey," the woman called, spying Jessie.

"Hi, Stevie," Jessie returned, rolling her own cart up to add to the traffic jam in the aisle. "I haven't seen you in months. You been busy this summer building stuff with Vic Prentice?"

"Yeah, well . . . he had a job in Seward—a duplex that pretty much took the whole season. He took me on again this year, so I'm just back home for the winter. What're you up to? Gone to the dogs again? How's your knee?"

Stevie had been an energetic part of the construction crew responsible for building Jessie a new house after her old one was burned by the same arsonist who had torched Oscar's old place a year and a half earlier.

Shorter than either of her two friends, she looked as Jessie remembered her, an infectious grin on her face and a colorful bandana tied around her short hair. She had a way of being, or seeming to be, constantly in motion, even when she stood still.

Jessie had started to answer her questions when a woman with two small children, one in the cart, an older one following behind, came down the aisle, smiled, and waited patiently while the three carts blocking her access to the applesauce were moved to one side with apologies from their drivers.

"Thanks," she said. "Come along, Jill."

"Glad to hear you're okay," Stevie said, turning back to Jessie. "Are you gonna run the Idi—?"

"Hey," Hank broke in to ask a question. "Is what I hear

via local gossip true—that you found Donny Thompson's body in the trail above your house over the weekend?"

"Jeez!" Jessie answered, frowning and shaking her head. "Guess I should have known word would spread like wildfire in this community. Yes, unfortunately, it is true. Actually, it was pretty awful. I ran over him with the team and sled, but I didn't know who it was at the time. I was glad Alex was home to take care of it."

"Good Lord!" Stevie's eyes widened in reaction to this news. "Donny's dead?"

"You knew him?"

"Yeah. Well, I'd met him. What the hell happened?"

"He was shot, right?" Hank told her, glancing at Jessie for confirmation.

"Right."

"Any idea who might—?"

He dropped the question abruptly, as Jessie began to shake her head.

"I don't even want to know and I try to stay out of anything Alex is investigating. He didn't tell me much anyway, just asked a few questions."

"Like what?" Stevie asked, but gave it up at Jessie's frown. "You know . . . ," she said thoughtfully. "I saw Donny Friday night at Oscar's in town. He bought me a drink and asked if I was there with anybody. I told him I was, just to discourage him, then made sure I went out the door with Brody Kingston. I don't want anything to do with that wild crowd of bikers he's part of."

"Or was," Hank commented. "Well, back to the groceries. You be at the Other Place for pool Friday, Jess?"

"Maybe."

"See you then—*maybe*."

As he started to turn away, the floor suddenly began to vibrate under their feet.

As the vibration continued, Stevie's grin vanished, and she made a lunge for the handle of her grocery cart and clung to it desperately.

As they waited alertly, the shaking grew slightly and things began to rattle on the shelves around them and someone shrieked in the distance.

"I think maybe we'd better get out of here," Hank said, frowning. But just as he suggested retreat, the trembling faded and was gone.

Stevie took a deep breath and let go of her cart.

"Damn," she said nervously. "I just *hate* those things!"

CHAPTER ELEVEN

THE EARTHQUAKE ACTUALLY HADN'T BEEN THAT BIG, Jessie realized as she drove home. Aside from a number of people still standing outside their houses along Knik Road, it seemed quite normal. As she drove, she wondered how her dogs had taken it. Probably not much more than howling their dislike.

Turning off the road into her driveway, she caught sight of a familiar figure bending over a dog in the middle of the yard and recognized Billy Steward, the young man who often helped care for her kennel of dogs. He was learning to drive them, and was, to her way of thinking, developing into a very good musher. Already he had run a few junior races and done well.

"Hey, Billy. I didn't expect you today," she called, climbing out of the pickup and heading his way.

"Hi, Jessie," he greeted her with a smile. "I had nothing to do, so I came, thinking maybe you could put me to work. Too bad the snow we had all melted."

"Well, there'll be more sometime soon—I hope. Were you here when that last quake hit?"

"Yeah. It was interesting, huh? The whole kennel went a little crazy, as usual, but more so, since it lasted a little longer than most of 'em. The mutts are all fine, though. Where were you?"

She told him the tale of her marketing experience.

"Wow! A grocery store could be a bad place to be in a big one, couldn't it?"

"And I can think of places I'd rather be in anything bigger than that one—like out in the middle of an open field. Coming home it didn't seem like much, not much more than our usual, medium-sized ones, just went on a little bit longer. Everything here seems to be okay."

Before he could agree, several dogs stood up, moved nervously, and began to howl a protest as, a second or two later, a slight tremor briefly shook the ground under their feet, then stopped.

"Aftershock," Jessie said, as her dogs quieted. "The dogs feel it, or hear it, before we do."

"They do?"

"Yes. Most animals are more sensitive to it. Have you ever noticed how still it gets just before a quake?"

Billy shook his head. "Uh-uh."

"It's like all the birds are gone. You can always hear them in the trees here, like background noise you don't notice much. But you really notice when they stop chirping and aren't flying around. The ravens disappear just before a quake, like they know it's coming somehow."

"But the dogs didn't get quiet. They were howling and whining, and jumping around on their tethers like they wanted to run. Some of them crawled into their boxes and lay down. Then the ground started to shake."

"Yeah, it's odd. I guess different animals have different reactions. Some cats can disappear for days. I read somewhere that a woman's cat carried off and hid all her kittens—didn't bring them back home for several days. Fish have been seen swimming closer to the surface of the water. Bees may all fly out of their hive just before an earthquake and not come back for ten or fifteen minutes. Snakes have been known to crawl out of their hibernation dens and, being cold-blooded, freeze to death outside after a winter quake. Cows can be knocked off their feet and horses panic."

"Wow! Where did you learn all that?"

"Where do we learn a lot of things these days? Go online and Google 'predicting quakes from unusual animal behavior.' There's an interesting article by a guy named Brown."

"Cool. I'll do that. Now, what have you got for me to do?"

Jessie smiled and shook her head ruefully.

"I went through the shed earlier and there's really nothing much to do. You can help me water the guys, if you want. Then we could go in and use my computer to find that article. You could help me make an inroad on some cocoa. Then I've got to make a meat loaf for dinner tonight."

Billy readily agreed to this suggestion, reminding her that he was "remarkably skilled in predicting the merits of cocoa based on the number of marshmallows floating in it."

She assured him that she had marshmallows. "It's not the same without 'em."

They watered the dogs together and went indoors, taking Tank with them, and Bliss, a female soon to have a litter of his pups.

Inside, there was nothing to indicate there had been an earthquake any larger than the usual small tremors Jessie was used to and had learned to expect in living close to Alaska's maze of numerous fault lines. The potbellied stove was secure on its stone hearth, its tall stovepipe standing solid and straight up to the high ceiling. A drinking glass set too close to the edge had fallen into the kitchen sink and broken, but everything in the refrigerator was fine, if slightly rearranged. She was glad she had chosen hardware for the kitchen cupboards that held them closed and allowed nothing to fall out. A picture or two were crooked on the living room walls and a pile of books had spread itself out on the floor in front of the bookcase.

"Oh, good," she said, as she replaced all but one. "There's the new Margaret Maron mystery I was going to read and couldn't find after Alex removed them from the floor next to the sofa."

She was once again glad that she had elected to build another log house in place of the old one, as logs, which overlap and lock into place at the intersections, tend to flex and move in most earthquakes, rather than being pulled apart and tumbling down.

After putting the kettle on to heat water for cocoa, she glanced around in appreciation for the place in which she loved to live and noticed that her answering machine was blinking commandingly.

Alex! she thought, and hurried to call him back.

"Where have you been?" Alex asked when Jessie reached him on his cell phone. "I've called, but no answer."

"I saw it on the machine," she answered. "Until a few minutes ago I was in the yard with Billy. Before that, I ran into Hank and Stevie at the grocery. There was another earthquake. Did you feel it?"

"Yeah, one a little bigger than usual. Are you okay?"

"Sure. Where are you?"

"At Fred Meyer. We sent a forklift driver to the hospital with a broken arm and head injuries after the lift tipped over and the stack of crates he was moving up a ramp fell on him. But it wasn't quake-related. He was inexperienced and just drove it crooked—turned it over."

"Well, Billy's here and we're making cocoa."

"Tell him hi for me. I'll probably be late getting home, and just to be safe, you should check the propane connections to make sure they're tight."

"I'll do that. I picked up meat loaf ingredients at the grocery store. That okay for dinner?" Jessie asked, knowing it would be.

"You bet. I'll bring home some Killian's. We're about out. Now I gotta get going. There's an accident out near that gravel pit by the fairground. Couple of guys ran into each other and one's off the road. See you when I see you, I guess. Bake a couple of potatoes to go with the meat loaf?"

"I can do that."

An hour later Billy was leaving, clutching a copy of the article Jessie had mentioned about animal behavior before and during earthquakes. Tank walked him to the door.

"Hey, buddy," Billy said, tucking the pages under his arm and stopping to give the dog a pat or two before leaving. "Next time you start to howl before a quake, I'll pay attention, okay?"

"See you for sure as soon as it snows again," Jessie had called after him as the door was closing.

She picked up the mystery she wanted to read and sat for a moment on the sofa, but found herself feeling confined indoors and put it down unopened.

Probably a result of our grocery store experience, she thought, and decided to go outside instead.

"Let's take a walk," she said to Tank, then turned to

Bliss, who was sprawled on the rug by the stove. "You, however, are so fat you can barely waddle. We'll have puppies in a few days and I bet you'll be glad. I read somewhere that an earthquake could inspire an early delivery, so for now I'll put you in the puppy pen, just in case."

CHAPTER TWELVE

Dropping her cell phone in a pocket and taking the trail behind the house that eventually turned up the hill through the forest, Jessie went slowly, appreciating the scents and colors of fall.

Most of the birds had taken their music south to escape winter in the far north in favor of a warmer climate, so the forest was quiet. A slight breeze rustled curious fingers through the fallen leaves and whispered secrets to the dry grasses. When snow fell again to stay it would freeze into silence as well.

Scattered through the pale trunks and bare branches of the birch that surrounded them, the spruce appeared darker green and it was easier to see their shape. The snow had compacted the blanket of leaves on the ground, but their yellow and brown still made a colorful contrast to the white and green above them. Here and there a few blades of grass, still green, showed in bare spots, valiantly attempting to defy the change of season, but that wouldn't last long. By spring all the grass would be brown and dead, with early new blades coming up through them.

There was a distinctly different scent to the fall woods, a damp pungency of moist ground and rotting leaves.

From some neighbor's stove or fireplace a hint of wood smoke drifted in to add to the autumn potpourri, causing Jessie to wrinkle her nose and turn her head in search of the source.

Johnson, she decided. *Burning some of that wood he was cutting a few days ago.*

Tank, who had been wandering back and forth across the trail to investigate whatever caught his attention, stopped to look up at a squirrel he had caught on the ground and chased up a tree. Knowing itself safe on a high limb, it paused to chatter resentment down at him for interrupting its single-minded gathering of spruce cones to add to the winter larder. Tank, with dignity, turned away and ignored it.

In an open space between trees, Jessie spied the dried stalk of a sun-loving chocolate lily, its seed pod unopened. Though it was late in the season, with a folding trowel she had carried along in her fanny pack she carefully dug up the bulb with its ricelike kernels and put it away, with the seeds, in a plastic bag to add to others she had collected and planted near the front steps of her house. Tucking it into a pocket, she walked on and was soon climbing the hill.

Knowing that not much farther up the rising trail she would reach the spot where she and her team had run over the body of Donny Thompson, she hesitated, wondering for a long minute if she really wanted to go there.

Tank came to stand beside her and thrust his muzzle into her hand, as if to give her encouragement. Dropping to her knees, she put a hand on either side of his head and spoke seriously, face-to-face with him.

"You know, this is a trail we use often through the winter and can't abandon. There's no one but us here now and it'll be just the same as it always was—if we reclaim it. Don't you think we should do that?"

He licked her nose.

It made her giggle.

He did it seldom, seeming to view it as lacking in the dignity a leader should project.

"You old faker," Jessie told him, smiling as she stood up. "Come on then."

Turning, she started up the trail again, but Tank, attracted by another squirrel he couldn't resist, this one showing its umbrage from a lower branch, dashed off to stand looking up in hopes it would come down.

Stopping, Jessie grinned and called out sharply to bring him back. "Tank! Come back here, you. Leave that squirrel alone."

A second or two after her voice rang out there was the sudden sound of feet pounding the ground of the trail on the hill above. Someone moved swiftly up to the junction, then west on the upper trail.

For a moment Jessie hesitated, listening to the sound of running fading into the distance. Then, as Tank returned to her side, she sprang into motion, climbing the hill, hoping to catch at least a glimpse of whoever had been startled into flight by the sound of her voice.

It was a losing attempt at best, for she was slower going uphill than whomever it had been, and they had now disappeared on the more level ground of that upper trail as it traversed the hillside.

With Tank trotting behind, she went as swiftly as possible up the last few yards of the trail to the point where it curved and Thompson had lain hidden under the new snow until her sled brake turned him over. There she stopped in surprise.

Lying to one side of the trail, in clear sight on a pile of leaves that Jensen and Becker had searched from under the new snow before it melted, was a single bright spot of red.

For an instant Jessie thought it was blood left behind when Thompson's body had been removed. Then, stepping closer, she realized it was something else and completely foreign to anything that grew in the familiar woods. A long-stemmed red rose lay, fresh and perfect, atop and in contrast to the yellow and brown of the leaves that had fallen from the surrounding birch. Someone had evidently carried it up and left it, apparently in remembrance and tribute to the man who had died there, for it was inside a plastic bag that was tied closed around the stem with white ribbon—a thing florists did this time of year to protect their hothouse flowers from the cold.

Even more startling was the item that lay a few feet beyond it, in the trail. In stark incongruity to the glowing crimson of the single hothouse flower was a *revolver*, black as sin, as if it had been dropped by accident.

Like many mushers, Jessie was familiar with all kinds of guns—she usually carried a handgun of her own on training runs and in sled dog races, as defense against the many moose that freely wander the far north and can be extremely dangerous to dog teams and their drivers if confronted. In winter the huge ungulates are often reluctant to leave broken trails for deep snow. Stubbornly, they will sometimes turn aggressive and attack, kicking and stomping their way through a team of dogs that are held together by the harness that makes escape impossible. The driver may also be threatened in defending them and have no alternative but to use a gun, if he, or she, carries one, to put down the menacing animal.

Many, like Jessie, carry handguns that are easier to

retrieve from a bag that hangs on the back of the sled than from the sled bag itself, where a rifle is usually kept.

With a frown of confusion wrinkling her brow, she stood staring silently down at the handgun she had just discovered and could identify as a Smith & Wesson .38 Special—a black small-frame revolver of a size that could be carried in a pocket or sled bag and, hammerless, wouldn't snag or hang up on fabric when needed. Fully loaded, she knew it would carry five rounds.

But what was it doing there? In their careful search for a gun Thompson would have used if he had shot himself, Alex and Phil Becker would surely have found this one. So it had to have been dropped *after* their search. Who would have brought it there, and could that someone be somehow involved in the death of Donny Thompson?

There was no indication of the identity of the person who had hurriedly left upon hearing Jessie—no footprints, nothing. How could they have known exactly where to leave it and found this specific spot? She could think of only two possibilities: either someone who had been there when Thompson was shot had returned and left it, or someone else had been given exact directions to the location.

Whatever, she decided. It wasn't her business to figure it out and guessing did no good.

Retrieving her cell phone from her jacket pocket, she called Alex and was glad when he answered after two rings.

"Hey, lady! Need more groceries?" he questioned, a smile in his voice.

"No," she assured him. "But I could officially use a trooper here. I just found something else you'll want to see."

After telling him what she had found and its location,

at his suggestion, leaving everything else as she had found it, she extracted a Kleenex from her jacket pocket, used it to carefully pick up the revolver, wrap it, and put it away in the same pocket. She then went a short way back down the trail, to a place where, if she stood up, she could see the area in question above. There, facing downhill, she settled herself on a log to await Jensen's arrival, ears alert for any sign of the return of the person who had evidently left more than he intended in the place above. Tank followed, lay down at her feet, muzzle on paws, and fell asleep.

Except for the breeze that rustled the drying leaves that lay around the pair and the usual chattering of squirrels, it was peacefully quiet and, hearing nothing of anyone else around, Jessie was soon drowsy herself.

CHAPTER THIRTEEN

At the bar in the Other Place, Hank and Stevie sat sharing the tale of their escape from the grocery with Oscar that afternoon.

"Well," he said, giving Hank a new full bottle and removing his empty one. "Sounds to me like the possibility of an earthquake is a legitimate reason to do your grocery shopping as quick as possible. That's fine with me. I never liked doing it anyway."

"You're pretty well prepared here," Stevie commented, looking around and seeing little that would suffer in anything but a major quake.

Hank grinned.

"It sounded like you had a xylophone in the cooler when that one happened last Friday night—all those beer bottles clinking together."

"Yeah, but they stay put—no doors flopping open like the ones you describe at the grocery. Mine have secure fasteners. And you'll also notice that all my glassware and liquor bottles are held securely in place—planned it that way when we built this place. It would take a really big one to cause real damage in here. The whole building is bolted to the foundation with heavy brackets."

They nodded, still looking around, then turned back to the bar.

"Where were you Friday night, Stevie?" Oscar asked. "Didn't see you in here that night."

"No, but you'll be glad to know that I was spending my shekels at your place in town. We felt the quake there too. One of these days I'm going to give up on this country and move somewhere that doesn't shake, even a little bit. I do so *hate* those things."

"Good luck. Did you know that even if you don't feel it a big quake is a vibration that has an effect on the entire planet?"

"You're kidding!"

"Not a bit. Even though most people never felt it at all, our big one in sixty-four vibrated the whole world enough to alter the alignment of the North Pole by a measurable degree or two."

"Maybe you'd better apply to NASA for transport to some dead planet that doesn't move," Hank teased Stevie.

"Hm-m. There's a thought."

"They don't have grocery stores on Mars, though, or trees to make lumber for carpenters. You'd be out of a job—and food."

"And air—and beer." Stevie sighed. "Guess I'll have to stay here."

"Guess so. Have another beer and play some pool?"

"Naw," Stevie said and shook her head. "I gotta work tomorrow—an indoor job for Vic Prentice, finishing a house he's renovating out the other side of the butte off the Old Glenn Highway. Should keep food on the table for another month or so. I better get on home."

"Does he need anyone else? I'm free at the moment and could use an inside job."

"Maybe. You should ask him."

"I'll do that," Hank said and grinned.

Leaving a tip for Oscar, she climbed off the bar stool and started for the door. "See you guys when I see you."

"Make it soon," Oscar told her. "We missed you this summer, so you owe us."

"Right," she tossed back, reaching for the door handle. Before she could grasp it, it suddenly opened inward, giving her knuckles a painful rap.

"Oww!" Stevie yowled, stepping back and shaking her hand in an attempt to get rid of the hurt.

"Oh, Stevie. I'm sorry. Didn't know you were there."

"That's okay, Bill. Neither one of us can see through a solid door. I'll live. Nothing broken."

"You're the one who suffered. Can I buy you a beer?"

"Thanks, but I'm heading out. Got errands to run."

"Well, remind me next time then."

"I'll do that. You better watch out. Hank's cruising for a game."

"Good," he said. "I hoped I'd find him here. See you later."

"You bet!" she called back as the door shut behind her.

A few minutes later, Stevie was driving past the grocery, a frown on her face at the idea of the quake they had felt inside. Buying her groceries seemed like enough, as she didn't much like cooking, and she briefly considered the idea of eating out that night. Then, remembering the pile of clothes at home that needed washing, some of which she would need for work the next morning, she checked to be sure she had scratched laundry soap off the list written on the back of an envelope and resolutely drove on toward home.

Back on the hillside, Jessie had lifted her face to the slight warmth of a ray of sunshine that fell through the bare branches of a nearby birch and, eyes closed, was listening to the indignant chatter of another squirrel defending its territory somewhere nearby. Yawning, she opened her eyes when Tank suddenly sat up from where he had been napping at her feet and turned his head to stare up the hill behind them.

Standing up and turning to see what had attracted his attention, she saw nothing but the trees that lined the trail and cast their long shadows across the yellow leaves that covered the ground and heard nothing but their papery rustle in conversation with the slight breeze.

She sat down again and laid a restraining hand on Tank's collar.

"Lie down," she told him. "No more games of chase the squirrel. You know they always win, since you can't climb trees."

The condescending glance he gave her made her smile, for it seemed to express extreme tolerance with her assumption that he knew nothing about squirrels and would go chasing after them like a half-grown pup.

"Lie down," she said again.

But instead, he stood up, looking intently at something behind her off the trail, and growled low in his throat.

A raven suddenly came soaring over her head as if startled from a perch in some tree, a swift black silence that disappeared almost immediately among the naked birch and evergreen spruce below.

Beginning to turn to see what had attracted Tank's direct attention, thinking it might be a moose, she was startled when a voice not far behind her barked a sharp word of warning.

"Don't! I have a gun, so turn back and stay exactly where you are. Get hold of that dog and don't move."

The voice was low, gruff, and whispery. Jessie couldn't

tell if it was a man's or a woman's from the pitch, but something about it gave her a feeling she had heard it, or one very similar, somewhere else—would know and definitely recognize it again.

She reached her left hand to Tank's collar.

"Sit," she told him.

Obedient this time, he did as he was told, but remained alert and continued to closely watch the person behind her.

"Now," that person directed in that odd voice again. "Very slowly, take the gun from your pocket and toss it behind you. You turn and I'll shoot the dog first."

So, whoever this was, the object of this confrontation was to recover the revolver Jessie had carefully retrieved from where she found it. Did this mean this other person was bluffing and actually had no other weapon?

By herself, she might have tested that theory, but it was a chance she was not willing to take with Tank under threat.

"All right," she said. "I'm getting it now."

Very carefully and slowly she reached into the right-hand pocket and extracted the revolver, holding it by the barrel with the grip facing away, and tossed it as instructed over her shoulder—heard it land somewhere in the leaves behind her.

There were footsteps that crunched those leaves as the person, whoever it was, moved to pick up the gun.

"Get up—*slowly*!" the voice instructed, a bit closer this time. "Don't turn around. Just go back down the way you came up and don't look back. I'll be watching closely. *Do it!*"

Knowing that this person now had the revolver, and that it was loaded, Jessie did exactly as she was told: stood up, still holding tight to Tank's collar, and stepped away from the log on which she had been sitting. Without looking back, she moved carefully, slowly, as directed, to the trail and began to go steadily down it toward home.

Tank growled once, low in his throat, and resisted slightly.

"Hush," she told him, in a voice he would attend to. "Come along."

There was no further comment from him, or from whoever was behind her, but she felt watched and heard the scuff and rustle of feet through leaves, as if the person had moved to stand in the trail to keep an eye on her as she descended.

It wasn't far down to the first curve in the trail, one that swung to the right around a young spruce that would hide her from sight from above. Stopping with the tree between her and the upper hillside, without letting go of Tank, she risked peering through the branches back up the hill, hoping to see the owner of that odd voice, or, at the very least, catch a glimpse of its retreating figure. It made sense, she thought, that the person would go as quickly as possible back along the upper trail once she was no threat.

The trail closest to her was empty as far as she could see, though the place she had been sitting to wait for Alex was hidden by a rise in the ground and the thick brush and tall, drying grasses that covered it. Listening intently, she heard nothing at all like the sound of running feet that had caught her attention earlier. But vaguely she made out a rustling in the brush or dead leaves as someone passed on their way up. Then, through the spruce branches she caught a glimpse of a tall, slim figure in jeans, a brown jacket, and a denim hat with a brim, headed quickly into the trees that stood between Jessie and the upper trail. Almost immediately it vanished, cutting across through the woods from one trail to the other, and it was impossible to tell from such a brief and indistinct appearance whether it had been a man or a woman.

Should she try to follow? It was tempting, but she thought not. It would be a risk against someone with a gun. Better to go down and wait at home. There would be as much or as little to find now as there had been before, she decided. By the time she could reach the upper trail the person would be either far ahead or waiting for her. Better to let Alex examine it when he came.

"Come," she said, letting go of Tank, who had lost all suggestion of aggression and was sitting close beside her, waiting for whatever was next. "Let's go home."

As she went on down the trail and, finally, into the yard of her house and kennel, he trotted obediently beside her, even ignoring a challenge from a squirrel in a tree above.

Once there, she considered calling Alex to report what had occurred on the hill behind the house, but decided he could hear about it when he came home. So she made the meat loaf she had promised, and put it into the oven with two large Idaho russets to bake.

When Alex arrived later, he found her sitting halfway down the front steps, elbows on knees, chin cupped in the palms of her hands, a thoughtful expression on her face, and Tank occupying a step close below her.

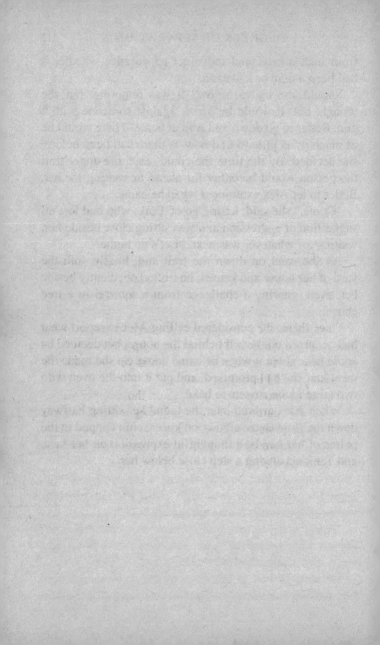

CHAPTER FOURTEEN

"Why did you go up there?" Alex asked again, frowning. "It's still a crime scene, you know."

"You took the yellow tape down. I'd have respected that, wouldn't have gone inside it, but there wasn't any."

"I *didn't* take it down. We left it where we put it up and neither Becker nor I have been back up there. Someone else removed it—maybe whoever it was you ran into."

"How could I have known th—?"

"I told you not to run your dogs on those upper trails."

"I *wasn't* running dogs. I was *taking a walk*!·Just me and Tank, like we often do."

"Not anymore. Not till I solve this case. Until then you *stay off the hill*! Got it?"

Jessie gave him an astonished, wide-eyed look that turned to doubt and resentment as he sat stiffly silent, waiting for her to promise agreement.

"Are you trying to *tell* me where I *can* and *cannot go*? On *my own property*?" she demanded in a thin, tight voice, her face flushed with annoyance.

He straightened in his chair at the table across from her, spilling a splash of coffee from his mug as he pushed it aside, leaned forward, and stretched his long-fingered hands out flat on the tabletop with a slap that made her flinch.

"Jessie—*Jessie!* I'm trying to keep you safe. But, okay—*yes*—if you must have it that way. *Officially I am telling you* to stay off the hill, until I tell you it's safe. Whoever it was, it could have been the same person who killed Donny Thompson. You could easily have been killed up there."

"I don't think so," she shot back.

They stared at each other for a long minute in an intractable silent standoff of sorts—she, knowing that his reaction and demand was fear and concern speaking, engendered by his caring for her—he, that he had pushed her too far in his apprehension for her protection, but meant it and wasn't about to take it back.

"I really don't think so," she said again.

"Why not?" he asked, eyebrows raised in puzzled surprise.

"The rose," she said, frowning thoughtfully. "I think it was a woman. She used a low voice and tried not to sound like one, but I got that feeling. I think she brought the rose and must have accidentally dropped the thirty-eight when she heard me coming and ran. Whoever she was, she wouldn't have killed him. She must have loved him to risk searching out the place where he died."

"Or she already knew. What about the gun then?"

"Maybe she was scared—brought it with her as protection."

"Hmm," Alex mused. "How could she have known where he died? If she wasn't involved somehow—was there when he was shot—how else could she—if it was a she—have known where to leave the rose—exactly? Only the killer could have told her where to look, so she'd have to know who that was, if it wasn't her."

"Maybe she had a general idea and went looking till she found the crime scene tape," Jessie suggested. "It would have been pretty hard to miss that spot with it in place. She might also have torn it down."

"You keep calling this person *she*. What was it, besides the rose, that makes you think it *was* a woman?"

"Like I said, her voice, the way she tried to disguise it in sort of a gruff whisper. Let me think for a minute."

"Okay. Then tell me what you remember."

She closed her eyes and tried to put herself mentally back on the hillside, on that log, and hear again the sound of the voice of the unseen person behind her who had directed her to throw the revolver—feel again what she had felt in response to it.

After a couple of minutes, she frowned and shook her head a little, opened her eyes, and spoke her thoughts.

"There was a thing that I can't quite get hold of. I never felt really frightened that she would shoot me if I didn't do what she said, though I didn't risk it. There was something almost desperate in her tone, but mostly something really sad. I think I'd recognize it if I heard it again."

"You should have come back down here to wait for me."

"Yeah, in retrospect I probably should have," she agreed. "Then I would have had the gun to give you."

"With your fingerprints on it."

"Alex—I'm not that stupid. I used a tissue to pick it up with and wrap it before I put it in my pocket."

"Did you touch it when you tossed it behind you?"

She thought for a moment, sighed, and admitted that she had held it by the barrel to throw it.

"Damn! Probably smeared any we could have got off of it."

"Well, you don't have it anyway, so that's not an option. Look, Alex, I'm sorry. I didn't hear her coming. She surprised me and I just didn't think."

"And you still think it was a woman."

She shrugged and nodded. "Yeah, I guess I do."

"That could make sense, considering that leaving a rose is something a woman would be more likely to do. And you *will* stay off the hill for now, please?"

"Yes." She smiled at his changing it to a request.

He grinned back at her.

"You are a very independent—possibly stubborn—woman at times, Jess."

"I know. But mostly when pushed."

"Agreed. I'll try not to do that. Okay?"

"Okay."

"Now," he said, getting up from the table, "I'd better call Becker, then go and see if there's anything at all that might help in figuring out who it was you ran into up there."

"Want help?" Jessie asked, with a mischievous twinkle.

"*No!* Thank you very much."

"Then why don't you ask Phil for supper, if you like? There's plenty of meat loaf and it'll be done by the time you come back."

"Good thinking. Would you also put that Killian's I brought home in the refrigerator," he said, waving a hand toward the six-pack that he had, more than a little distracted at the time, left at the door on his way in.

"Can do. Anything else, my lord and master?"

"You don't let go easy, do you?"

"Guess not. But we're about even now, I think."

* * *

Becker was not to be found at the office.

"He said he was heading your way," the dispatcher told Jensen on the phone. "You should try his cell phone."

As he was dialing that number, Jessie crossed to the window to assess the source of the sound of tires in the drive and turned to tell him not to bother.

"He just pulled in," she said, opening the front door for Phil. "Sometimes I think you two are psychic."

"Hey, Jessie," the younger trooper said to her with a grin as he waved a sheet of paper in Alex's direction. "Here's the coroner's report on Donny Thompson and you'll want to see it."

"Yeah?"

"Oh yeah. Besides alcohol, there were evidently drugs involved that night."

"Not just the marijuana Malone mentioned in the past tense."

"Nope."

"Well, bring it along and I'll take a look. We need to go back up the hill to where he died. I'll tell you why on the way."

They went out the door together, taking the conversation with them, leaving Jessie to look after them and shake her head with a smile. *It's almost like a couple of small boys with a map and a game plan on their way to a secret clubhouse in the woods,* she thought. But it was, after all, part of what made them successful at what they did—turning over the pieces of evidence like a puzzle to be solved—and they were pretty good at it, however humorous it sometimes seemed to an outsider.

She refilled her coffee cup and sat down at the table again, to think through what had happened earlier on the hill. There had been something about the person she still believed was a woman that nagged at her, but she couldn't quite identify just what it was. The single glimpse she had had of the figure slipping away out of sight into the woods would have been of more use if whoever it was had turned just once to look back, but that hadn't happened. From the back it could have been either a male or female, couldn't it?

Holding the coffee mug between her hands to warm her fingers, she stared out the window into the dog lot, seeing nothing of it as she worried the problem in her mind. Suddenly she noticed that small, icy flakes were drifting down and the dog boxes already had a thin, pale skift of snow that had begun to fall since she came indoors.

Setting the mug down, she hurried to the door and out onto the broad front porch to look up and see the sky full of clouds as white as the flakes that were silently, evenly falling through the quiet air. Perhaps this time they would continue, get larger, and stick, not simply disappear in a day or two. Maybe, just maybe, it was finally the start of winter and the sledding she loved. She could let Alex go on with his case. It would be easy to stay out of his way if she could get busy training her teams at last.

She went back inside, put on some upbeat music, and got busy with dinner and setting the table for three.

Up on the hillside, Jensen and Becker had searched the crime scene again, from where Jessie had sat on the log to the whole of the area around the spot where the body of Donny Thompson had been turned over in the trail by her sled. Aside from the missing yellow crime scene tape and one useless scuff mark near where he had lain, there was nothing but the rose someone had left on newly fallen leaves next to some that were still faintly stained with his blood.

The rose, however, protected in plastic and tied with white ribbon, was still unwilted by the cold and gave them a bit of evidence that might help identify the person who had left it. That person had evidently handled it bare-handed, for there were a couple of fingerprints on the plastic that could possibly be retrieved. Hopefully, they would not turn out to be simply those of the florist, when they found the one who had sold the flower to the mystery person who had left it.

Besides the reported blood alcohol level, the coroner's report confirmed a low amount of methamphetamine in his system. It also identified a number of bruises and contusions to his head and upper body that told them he had had a fight with someone.

Alex frowned. "It certainly appears that someone knocked him around a fair amount."

"But he gave whoever did it a hard time as well, from the condition of his hands." Becker handed over a photograph of the dead man's hands, which showed more lacerations and abrasions. Several of the knuckles on his right hand showed cuts that, from the coroner's assessment and comments, had bled prior to his death.

"So we should keep an eye out for some guy—or guys—who've obviously been in a fight. And who could have been at one or more of the two or three places we know he was seen that night."

"Might have another word with Cole Anders at Oscar's in Wasilla and Jeff Malone, who may know who Donny was at odds with."

"Right. He might also remember when both Donny and Jeff Malone left. I'd like to verify that Malone really spent the night with his girlfriend, as he says he did.

I've still got a feeling that guy knows more than he's telling us."

"You're probably right. Let's go into Wasilla and talk to Anders. He'll be there by now to take care of the after-work drinkers."

"Good idea."

But as they walked together down the hill Alex revised the plan. "Why don't I go see what Anders remembers about Friday night and you go see if you can track down Malone's girlfriend? We can compare notes tomorrow morning, unless you hear something I ought to know sooner."

Becker agreed it would be more efficient and was soon leaving in his pickup to see if he could find Robin Fenneli.

"He said to thank you for the dinner invite," Alex told Jessie, when he went into the house to change clothes and tell her where he was going.

"Why don't you come along? We can have a brew and you can probably work in a pool game while I talk to Cole Anders."

She agreed and turned the oven heat down so it would slowly finish cooking the meat loaf while they were gone.

"Did you notice that it's almost snowing?" she asked as she put on her coat and followed him onto the front porch.

"Not enough so you'd notice," he told her with a grin. "I think your imagination is working overtime in the direction of getting back on a sled. It's not snowing now."

Jessie sighed. "Well, it was—just a little. Maybe there'll be more tonight."

"Could be, but I wouldn't hold your breath over it. It's

gotta be like that old saying about how watching a pot never makes it boil, isn't it?"

She shook her head at that idea and shrugged before climbing into the passenger side of the truck.

"You may be right. But it has to snow sometime, and sooner than later, I hope."

CHAPTER FIFTEEN

ABOUT THE SAME TIME ALEX AND JESSIE WERE ON their way to Oscar's pub in Wasilla, for the first time since learning about the death of his brother Donny, Lee Thompson had bellied up to the bar at the Alpine Inn in Sutton and asked Pete the bartender to bring him a Budweiser.

"I was really sorry to hear about Donny," Pete said, setting the beer in front of him that, brought from the cooler into warmer air, immediately developed condensation that ran down the sides of the cold bottle.

"Yeah, well . . . thanks," Lee told him, frowning at it as he wiped a finger down the side closest to him, leaving a clear line on the glass before picking it up to take a long swallow.

"How're your folks doing?"

"About as you'd expect, I guess. Mom's taking it pretty hard. So's Sally. She and Donny were tight growing up together with the other three of us a little older. But you know Dad—he's stiff upper lip, as usual. They'll be okay in time."

"Well, if there's anything . . . just let me know."

Pete hesitated for a second or two before asking, "The cops have any idea yet who killed him?"

"Not that I know of," Lee growled, with a resentful glance at Pete's question. "But *I will*! You just wait. But I don't want to talk about it, okay?"

"Sure, Lee. Sorry. Just set back the bottle if you want another," he said as he moved away to answer a summons from farther up the bar.

It being a weekday, the Alpine Inn wasn't crowded. Only half a dozen people occupied the tall stools closest to the front door, two of them women casually dressed in jeans and flannel shirts, the other four men on their way home from work from the look of their clothing—one in Carhartt overalls over a faded green sweatshirt.

They had all looked around when Lee came in, nodded to him, and watched, most trying to seem not to, as he moved away from them to the other end of the long bar, clearly not wanting to hear their sympathy or answer their questions about his brother.

This behavior was not typical of Lee, who was usually a friendly sort, with a smile and a word for almost everyone.

One of the women gave the other a questioning look that got only a shrug in return as she turned back to her gin and tonic.

"How's Helen?" she asked in a quiet voice that wouldn't be overheard.

"Not good. But would you be if it were your youngest? Sally's the one who seems most upset by it. She and Donny pretty much grew up together as the last of the family and were pretty close. Still are—or *were*."

"Don't know what I'd do if it was either one of mine," the other woman said thoughtfully. "Wish there was something we could do. Helen's such a dear soul."

"I heard that Bill wanted Donny cremated, but Sally threw a fit when she heard, so there'll be a burial, I guess."

"I heard that too. There's the funeral Saturday, and you know that just about everybody'll be here afterward for potluck. That'll be the best time to let them know we're all here for them."

In murmured tones, the two went on to discuss what food they planned to bring to the potluck, their eyes drawn back to Lee as Pete took him a second beer when he set back the empty bottle. Noticing, he gave them a bitter glance and turned his shoulders so his back was toward them, clearly resenting the attention.

As they resumed their quiet conversation the door opened and another man came into the bar.

The women watched him walk across and take a bar stool next to Lee, laying a hand on his shoulder as he sat down.

Lee shrugged it off irritably, but the two men soon had their heads together in a clearly private conversation, pausing only when Pete set a pair of beers in front of them.

"Isn't that . . . ?"

"Yeah, Jeff Malone—an old friend of Donny's. Used to live out here, but he moved into Palmer when his folks left Alaska for Oregon over ten years ago. From what I hear, he spent most of the evening with Donny the night he was killed."

"Interesting. You suppose he knows something about it he's telling Lee?"

"Who knows?" She finished her drink and pushed her empty glass away, shaking her head to refuse another in answer to Pete's questioning look, and stood up. "I'd better get on. Charlie'll be home for dinner pretty soon and I left a chicken in the oven."

"Me too—going home soon, I mean. See you later—Saturday, if not before. If you need anything for that casserole, give me a call."

Watching her friend go out the door, she then gave the two men at the other end of the bar another quick look. It was impossible to hear what they were saying, but, from the look on his face, it seemed that Lee was aggravated over something Malone was telling him. Giving up her surveillance, she finished the last swallow of her drink, put a tip for the bartender beside the empty glass, and left the Alpine.

In Wasilla, at Oscar's, Alex had spent a few minutes talking with Cole Anders concerning who had been in the pub the previous Friday evening and their arrivals and departures. Most of their arrivals Anders could estimate, as he had been working behind the bar near the front door, but with the usual Friday-night crowd it was difficult, if not impossible, for him to recall when most of them had left.

Gena, the barmaid, filled in a few of the departures, but she had also been working hard serving drinks to those at the tables, and shook her head helplessly when she tried to remember.

"I honestly have no idea what time a lot of people came and went. I know Donny and Jeff Malone came in together and were both here for an hour or two in the middle of the evening and that Donny left first. Other than that, I'm not much help. Sorry. Friday's always slammed."

"Well," Alex told them, "that's okay. You've helped some. I didn't think there'd be much joy in finding out anything specific. You've both confirmed some things for me and that's good."

"Do you have any idea yet what happened to Donny—or who . . . ?"

He stopped Gena with a smile and shake of his head as he told her, "I can't talk about an ongoing case, you know."

"Yeah, I figured that. But it was worth a try. Good luck with it. Donny was usually pretty fun to have around and we're all going to miss him."

With a smile at the renewal of the Killian's he had emptied and handed back to Anders, Alex turned away to look for Jessie and picked her out of those present, not at a pool table but in the opposite corner of the room, in a dart game—with Lynn Ehlers.

Dismissing a mild pang of jealousy, he began to make his way between tables and chairs to reach the two. His feeling of suspicion, he knew, had no reasonable foundation, as Jessie had made adamantly clear more than once. But on his return to Alaska from Idaho a couple of years earlier, he and Ehlers had confronted each other unexpectedly and uneasily in Jessie's empty house, each wondering what the other was doing there with her not at home.

It had all worked out. But Jensen was aware that if he weren't around as a solid part of Jessie's life, Ehlers would be glad to take advantage of the opportunity to make himself available to her as more than just a friend. He also knew that as long as he and Jessie were a couple, Ehlers would keep his distance, romantically speaking.

It never hurts to walk your fences to be sure they don't need mending, Alex told himself with a grin as he moved in the direction of the dartboard on the rear wall, and the two people taking turns tossing darts at it.

"So who's winning?" he asked, settling into a nearby chair to observe the rest of the game.

"He is, damn it," Jessie told him. "I've obviously been spending much too much time at the pool table lately."

Alex watched and refused a round, appreciating the chance to sit and pretty much do nothing, though he had little to add to what he had already known about Donny's presence at Oscar's the night he was killed. *I'll have to talk to Malone again,* he told himself. *I think there's more there than he let on.*

Startled by a hand on his shoulder, he turned to find Gena standing next to him.

"You know," she said, "I don't know if it'd help you, but I just remembered that I noticed Donny was interested in a woman who was here that Friday—talked to her a lot, but she wasn't having any of it, finally left with another guy, though they hadn't come in together. I think it was her way of escaping Donny. Her name's Stevie Duncan and I think that, if you don't know her, Jessie does, because she helped build Jessie's new house after the old one burned a couple of years ago. About five four, red hair?"

He nodded, remembering being introduced to Stevie sometime in the past.

"Thanks," he told Gena. "That might be something useful. I'll check it out."

She gave him a smile and was gone to answer a call for drinks at a nearby table, so he turned back to watch Jessie put two darts in the center circle, but miss with the third, then lose another game to Ehlers as all three of his flew accurately.

"That's it, Lynn. I'm going to practice a lot before I play you again."

"Two out of three?" he asked, grinning.

"Not a chance, but I'll buy you the drink I owe you. You need another, Alex?"

"No," he said. "I'm good, thanks."

As she turned away to look for Gena, his cell phone rang in his pocket. Checking the identity of the caller, he found it was the dispatcher at the troopers' office.

"You better head for the hospital, Becker's been in an accident."

"What happened—and where?" he asked, leaving the last of his lager on the table as he abruptly stood up.

"Evidently someone ran him off the road this side of the Matanuska River Bridge on the Old Glenn Highway. His truck went into the ditch. He's pretty beat up, head injury and a broken arm. Wasn't wearing his seat belt, so he's lucky it's not worse."

"Who?"

"We don't know, and he can't tell us anything at this point, but Pritchard caught the call and said to tell you a bullet shattered the driver's-side window. He's waiting for you with a witness at the scene."

"I'm on my way—there first, *then* to the hospital."

"Check with me as soon as you know anything, please. The commander's gone to the hospital, but wants to hear."

"You got it. Tell him I'll be there as soon as I can."

Alex swung quickly toward the door.

As he reached the front of the room, pulling on his jacket as he moved through the people at the tables, Jessie turned from the bar, where she had been paying her game debt to Ehlers, and saw him and the concern written on his face.

"What's wrong?" she asked.

"Becker's been in an accident and I've got to go," he told her. He turned to Ehlers, who was standing beside her. "Lynn, would you take Jessie home? I've got an emergency to attend to."

"Sure. No problem."

There'd better not be, he thought, but only said, "Thanks."

"Call me when you know something and can," Jessie requested. "Anything else I should know? Is it really bad?"

"I don't know. Not good, but it doesn't sound life-threatening. I've got to go."

At her nod he took himself hurriedly out the door with a long-legged stride.

CHAPTER SIXTEEN

By THE TIME JENSEN REACHED THE PLACE WHERE Becker had gone off the road in his pickup, a large department tow truck was already winching it out of the ditch and onto the flatbed designed for transporting vehicles. He knew it would be taken to a lockup yard, where it would be examined in detail and he could see it later, so he turned to look for the officer in charge.

Round-faced with bushy eyebrows, Trooper Keith Pritchard was heavyset and shorter than Jensen. He raised a hand from the opposite side of the road, where he was questioning a young man who was holding up the bicycle he had evidently been riding toward the bridge when the accident happened.

The young man was taller and lean, with the well-muscled legs of a serious rider. His bicycle was, from the look of it, top of the line and well maintained.

"Becker?" Jensen questioned as he approached the two.

"At the hospital by now," Pritchard told him.

"How bad?"

"Concussion at least. Broken arm. He got thrown

around pretty good. Why's a cop not wearing his seat belt? Jeez!"

"I'll go and find out as soon as we're through here," Jensen said, and turned his attention to the young man with the bicycle. "Who's this?"

"This is Terry Larsen," Pritchard said. "He's Hardy's boy. You know Hardy Larsen?"

"Sure. Doesn't everybody? Did you see the wreck, Terry?"

The young man shook his head. "Got here just after it happened. I called 911 on my cell. But I saw the guy on the bike that must have run him off the road. There wasn't any other traffic coming toward me."

"Bike?"

"Motorcycle, one of those Harley hogs with ape-hanger handlebars and black leather saddlebags—headed for town."

"Who was driving? You recognize him?"

"No. He had on a helmet with a dark faceplate. Makes 'em all look alike."

"What was he wearing?"

"Leather, like the saddlebags—black, all black."

"Any chance you got a plate number—or a partial?"

"He went by really fast and he was on my side of the road. Swerved over just in time. I thought he was going to run *me* off, so I didn't have a chance to give the plate a look."

Pritchard, who was recording the conversation with a small handheld cassette recorder, spoke up when Alex hesitated.

"Do you think you could pick out the motorcycle if you saw it again?"

Terry frowned thoughtfully. "Well, maybe. But I might be able to pick out the guy's leather coat. There was a green skull and crossbones on the left shoulder and some white letters I didn't have time to read."

"You on your way home?" Jensen asked.

"Yeah. Just finished work at the photo counter at Fred Meyer."

"Feel okay to ride?"

"Yeah, I'm okay. It's just a little over a mile the other side of the bridge anyway."

"Trooper Pritchard's got your address and phone number?"

Pritchard nodded that he did.

Jensen thought for a moment before asking, "You live alone?"

"With my folks."

"Good. On your way then. Here's my card. If you think of anything else we should know, give us a call. If we need you, we'll be in touch."

The two troopers watched him pedal his bicycle away, then turned to each other.

"Good kid," Pritchard commented. "Hope he didn't see too much of that guy and his bike. Some of those guys could make trouble for him."

"You mean you hope the biker didn't see him seeing too much, right?"

"Right. Most of them are weekend riders who act tough, but some of those guys can be vindictive, and from what I've seen and heard so far, I'm convinced Terry's right. That guy ran Becker off the road on purpose. He won't want to be identified."

"Dispatch said you think a bullet shattered the driver's window?"

"Yeah. Becker wasn't hit as far as the paramedics could tell. I think there'll be a slug in the cab somewhere."

"Are you good to take care of everything here? I'd like to get to the hospital."

Pritchard agreed that he was.

At almost six thirty the sun had set and it was quickly growing dark when Jensen arrived at the Mat-Su Regional Medical Center. He found Ivan Swift, his detachment commander, already waiting for him with a frown of concern as he rose from a chair near the door.

"Becker's going to be okay," he told Jensen before he could ask. "There's a compound fracture of his right arm that will need surgery, but they're concerned about the concussion, so they'll wait a day or two, until they're sure it's okay to give him anesthesia. He's groggy, but awake. You can see him if you want, but keep it short."

"I will, but I don't want to make him go over what he's already told you. What did he say about the accident?"

"Not much. There was a motorcycle in his lane. He went into the ditch to avoid hitting it."

"I talked to Pritchard at the scene and a young man, Terry Larsen—Hardy Larsen's boy."

"Oh yeah." Swift grinned. "That Hardy, he's quite a talker."

"Well, Terry didn't see it happen, but he got a look at the motorcycle and rider heading toward town and thinks that's what caused it all. There wasn't anyone else on the road between him and the bridge."

"So nobody saw the actual wreck?"

"Not as far as we know. Did Phil say anything about who it might have been?"

"He was out cold when they got to him. Came to, but couldn't tell who it was—just a guy on a motorcycle."

As they spoke, they had been walking toward the room in which Phil Becker had been put to bed.

Pausing at the door, Swift stopped and waved a hand toward the door. "You go ahead. No need to crowd him with both of us in there. I'll wait for you."

Jensen nodded and went in.

Becker looked away from the nurse who was taking his blood pressure and gave Jensen a crooked half grin. His right eye was swollen shut from a cut and large bruise that ran cheek to hairline. He was lying propped with pillows in the hospital bed, and his right arm, supported on another pillow, was temporarily splinted and bandaged, broken between the elbow and shoulder.

"Hey," Alex said. "They tell me you're gonna live."

"Yeah," Becker responded woozily, moving nothing but his eyes. "They—ah—tell me that too. For a while there, wasn't sure I wanted to."

"I bet! Swift already filled me in on what you told him. All I want to know is do you think the guy ran you off the road on purpose?"

"*Know* he did!" The statement was quite clear and angry. "He fired a handgun at me as he swerved out of my lane and passed—hit the side window."

"You weren't wearing your seat belt. Why?"

"Wouldn't work. The receiving end was missing."

The nurse finished with the blood pressure cuff, removed it, and turned to Jensen.

"He really needs to rest," she told him. "Could it wait until tomorrow?"

It could—at least the rest of the details could.

He told Becker to take it easy and that he would be back the next morning.

Commander Swift was leaning against the wall outside the door.

"Anything?"

"He says it was definitely done on purpose. Also that

his seat belt wouldn't fasten. I'd like to have a look at that belt and see if I can locate the slug that he says came from the guy on the bike."

"We can do that now, if you want."

The pickup Becker had been driving, aside from front-end damage and an obvious need for total realignment, seemed in better condition than its driver.

"He's lucky it didn't roll," Swift commented, shaking his head.

"A bullet definitely shattered the driver's window," Jensen said, opening the passenger door and beginning a search through broken window glass for the projectile. In a few minutes he had it in hand from the floor beneath the seat. "We'll let the lab figure out what kind of weapon this was fired from."

Swift had been looking at the seat belt fastener.

"No wonder he wasn't wearing this. It looks like the end that the belt hooks into has been cut off."

Alex came around the truck to look and agreed. "Someone intended Becker not to be able to fasten it."

He frowned thoughtfully. "What I don't understand is how whoever it was could have known Becker would be driving out the road in that direction. We had only decided to split up maybe an hour earlier. I went to talk to the bartender at Oscar's in Wasilla and Becker was going looking for Jeff Malone's girlfriend, Robin Fenneli, who supposedly lives off the Old Glenn Highway on the Bodenburg loop. We decided who would go where just before we left and I had no reason to tell anyone, nor did he. So how the hell . . . ?"

"He could have been followed."

Jensen agreed. "But why, and who? It seems to me that this thing was planned. Was someone trying to keep

Becker away from the girl? Or just hinder our investigation?"

"Cuts your team in half, but that's not necessarily true
if I assign someone else to work with you on the case.
Could it have been Malone?"

"That's possible, I guess," Jensen answered slowly, still
frowning. "He rides a motorcycle, like Donny Thompson—
rode with Thompson, actually. And they both have—*had*,
in Thompson's case—associations with the bikers that
frequent Aces Wild."

"Interesting."

"Very. I think it's past time to have another little chat
with Jeff Malone."

Swift nodded agreement. "Keep me posted," he said as
the two men separated.

CHAPTER SEVENTEEN

DRIVING ACROSS THE RAILROAD TRACKS FROM THE troopers' office to the business district of Palmer, Jensen noticed several motorcycles parked in front of the Aces Wild on Colony Way. On impulse, he decided to go in and see which of the bikers who· habituated the place were hanging out on this particular night.

After parking and locking his pickup, he crossed the street and walked slowly along the line of motorcycles parked in front of the building, checking out each one. Two had the type of ape-hanger handlebars Terry Larsen had identified. Both were black with matching leather saddlebags, though the fenders of one of them were pin-striped with a green design.

Retrieving a notebook from his jacket pocket, Alex wrote down the license numbers and a quick description of the two. He went back to his truck, made a quick call on his cell phone, returned the notebook to his pocket, and went into the bar.

The place was more than half full; several tables and every stool at the horseshoe-shaped bar were occupied. Carl Thompson, as he had expected, was not working.

Instead, Mike, an older man, was mixing drinks and setting up beers, some for the barmaid on duty, a shapely
blonde wearing jeans and a yellow tight-fitting and low-
necked shirt, to deliver to the tables. Players were busy at
both the pool tables and the dartboard at the back of the
room. A group of bikers and their hangers-on were gathered across the room.

Hardy Larsen was sitting two stools from the corner
on the right-hand side of the bar, talking to a bearded
man who Jensen recognized as a dog musher.

He walked across to them and waited until Hardy finished the joke he was telling, which had something to do
with a couple of fishermen and a mermaid.

"Hey, Alex," Hardy greeted him as the chuckles of
those around him died. "Haven't seen you in a while."

"That's true," Jensen agreed, "but I saw your son, Terry,
an hour or so ago, headed for home on his bicycle."

"Yeah, he rides that thing everywhere, rain or shine,
even when there's snow on the ground. Wants to do the
Iditabike if they run it again. Crazy! You couldn't pay me
enough to ride a bicycle a couple hundred miles at down
to forty below. Buy you a beer?"

"I wouldn't object too strenuously."

"Here," said the bearded man next to Hardy, as he
drained and pushed back his bottle and stood up. "Sit
here. I've got to be on my own way home or Doris'll feed
my dinner to the dogs."

"Thanks, Bill," Jensen told him, and watched as he
went out the door before turning to Hardy.

"I was impressed with your boy," he told him. "He's a
sharp kid."

"He keeps his nose clean." Then, as Hardy cocked his
head slightly toward the group of bikers who had pushed

two tables together across the room and were noisily putting away drinks, he said, "That's more than you can say for some of them these days."

"Have to agree with you there." Alex nodded as the bartender set him up a Killian's. "Thanks, Hardy."

"No thanks necessary. Gotta take good care of the Mat-Su's finest."

"Seen Jeff Malone tonight?" Alex asked casually.

"Nope. He was in last night though. Donny Thompson's funeral is Saturday and he's bound to be there. Those two were tight. You going?"

"Hadn't thought about it. You?"

"Naw. Never did like funerals. Guess the next one I go to will be my own—when I won't give a damn." Hardy chuckled to himself, reminding Alex of something his father had once said about whistling past a graveyard.

A howl of laughter rose from the bikers across the room, turning heads at the bar. As it faded, the front door opened and Jeff Malone came in, stripping black leather driving gloves from his hands, and turned in the direction of the laughter. As he walked toward it, he took a look around the room. Seeing Alex watching him from the bar widened his eyes. He hesitated, then nodded slightly in recognition and moved toward the group of bikers without looking back again.

He wore black leather boots, jeans, and a black leather jacket, like many others. But, as he passed, Alex noticed a green patch on the left shoulder of the jacket—skull and crossbones with white letters under it: "Road Pirate."

He nursed his beer along slowly and kept a discreet eye on Malone until close to half an hour later, when the man chugged the last of his first beer. When he got up from the table and crossed the bar in the direction of the restrooms that were off a hallway in the rear of the place, the fact that he had taken his jacket with him did not escape Jensen's notice. With a quick good-bye to Hardy Larsen, he was immediately on his feet and following.

Malone did, indeed, visit the men's room. But when he came out, he didn't go back into the bar. Instead, he pulled on the jacket and headed straight for the back door, where he ran unexpectedly into Jensen, who was waiting for him just outside.

"Making an early night of it, Jeff?" he asked quietly, startling Malone, who hadn't noticed him leaning against the building in a shadow and whirled to face him. "Late to arrive and early to leave. My presence wouldn't have anything to do with that, would it? And where were you tonight before you came in here? Out the Old Glenn Highway this side of the Matanuska River Bridge, maybe?"

Malone stared at him as if he were crazy, opened his mouth, shut it again, and finally said, "Why would you think that?"

"Oh, an accident that was no accident, involving someone of your description who took a shot at my partner, Phil Becker, after forcing him off the road into the ditch and from there to the hospital. All of it was intentionally caused by a biker wearing a jacket with the same green patch on the shoulder as yours. You care to comment?"

"Yes," Malone said angrily, "I *would*. I'm not the only one who wears the Road Pirate logo. There are a number of us. And I haven't been anywhere near that bridge. I just came back from Sutton, where I went to see Donny Thompson's brother, Lee. You can ask anyone at the Alpine Inn, including the bartender."

"I *will* ask him. So tell me exactly what time you went to Sutton and how long you were there."

Malone told him and it was clear, if what he said was true, there was no way he could have been in both places at the same time. Obviously, he couldn't have bamboozled close to a dozen people in Sutton to lie about his whereabouts. The biker who caused Becker to wreck his pickup had to have been someone else.

"Okay for now, until I check it out—and I *will*. Who else wears that green logo on their jacket shoulders?"

"No way!" Malone returned sharply, shaking his head. "I'm no snitch to sic you on anyone else. Do your own investigating."

With that, he turned on his heel and walked back into the Aces, where, Jensen was certain, he would spread the word that *the law* was looking for one of the Road Pirates, or someone wearing one of their jackets. There was always that possibility. But somehow both Becker's accident and Donny Thompson's death were related—tangled in the same knot. Now it would be up to him to untangle it, and soon, before someone else got hurt—or dead.

There wasn't much he could do about it then and there. He would let the case turn over in his mind as he examined everything that he already knew about it. Maybe tomorrow morning Becker would have remembered something to add to the mix that would give him a better direction in which to aim his search than trying to track down and question every member of the Road Pirate brotherhood.

Besides, he hadn't had dinner yet and it was growing late.

Walking around the building, he noticed that the motorcycle with the green pinstriping was absent from the space where it had been parked earlier. Had someone else left the bar in a hurry? Did it belong to Malone? Or was it just coincidence?

Whatever! Circling a block to reach the road that led through Palmer and on toward Wasilla and Knik Road, he gave questions up for the time being and let his mind wander where it would.

The direction it took was toward the meat loaf Jessie had promised earlier in the day, that he knew was now waiting at home—as was she.

Time to be there!

The house was deliciously full of the scent of the meat loaf when Alex came through the door less than half an hour later.

Jessie stood up from where she had been watching television, Tank at her feet, and they both came to meet him.

"How's Phil?" she asked, taking his coat to hang next to the door. "How bad is it?"

"He'll be okay, I think, but it's going to take a while. Hit his head on something in the wreck and has a broken arm, but he'll mend. It'll just take time."

"Thanks be," she breathed. "I almost called the hospital, but decided I'd better wait for your report. You've been gone a long time."

"Yeah," he told her, bending to give Tank a pat. "I made a stop to check out a couple of things that might be important in finding out what happened. But right now I'm starving. I'll be strong enough to tell you a bit more after sustenance."

She grinned and headed for the kitchen, calling back over her shoulder, "You're just lucky it was my turn to cook. Wash up and I'll have food on the table when you come back. There's baked potatoes and salad to go with."

"Yes, ma'am!"

He headed up the stairs toward the bathroom to do as directed. Hopefully there would be enough leftover meat loaf for sandwiches tomorrow, as it was a favorite of his.

CHAPTER EIGHTEEN

AT THE HOSPITAL THE NEXT MORNING JENSEN FOUND Phil Becker awake but looking and feeling as bad or worse than the day before. The injured side of his face was a huge purple bruise that had swelled badly. An IV dripped pain medication into his unbroken left arm. His right lay as before on a pillow, still awaiting surgery to put the shattered bone back together.

"Thrown to the side. Caught the dash," he muttered, clenching his teeth to keep from moving his jaw as he saw Alex looking and attempted to explain. "Two teeth loose 'n' a som-bitchin' headache."

"Don't try to talk," Jensen told him. "I'm sorry, but I've got to ask you a couple of questions. Just raise a finger for yes, none for no. Okay?"

Becker lifted the index finger on his left hand.

"You have any idea who it could have been?"

No response from Becker.

"Terry Larsen, Hardy's son, was bicycling behind you on the road. You must have passed him on your way toward the bridge. Did you see him?"

Becker raised a finger.

"He told us the motorcycle rider was all in black, including his bike, and wore a full face-covering helmet?"

The finger came up again.

"And his motorcycle didn't touch your truck at all?"

No response.

"From what we can tell he was in your lane, riding directly at you, and swerved away just in time to miss and put you in the ditch. Right?"

Becker indicated that was correct.

"The receiving end of the seat belt was missing—had been cut off, as you said yesterday," Jensen told him. "Partly because of that, we think this was planned—done on purpose. Did you notice anyone following you on the way to and through Palmer on your way to the Fenneli woman's place?"

He shrugged his left shoulder to indicate that he didn't know—hadn't paid attention in that direction.

"Okay," Jensen told him. "You take it easy and don't worry about it. I'm going to find out who the hell was responsible, one way or another. I had a few words with Jeff Malone last night."

Becker nodded very slightly and once again spoke through clinched teeth. "Be careful. No chances."

"Right. I won't take any that aren't necessary. You just concentrate on getting well. I'll keep you posted, and if you want or need anything, we'll make sure you get it. Jessie wants to come and see you as soon as you feel better."

Hardly moving a muscle, Becker's concerned expression changed to a smile that involved only the corners of his mouth and a narrowing of the eye that wasn't swollen shut, so Jenson knew a visit from her would be welcome.

As he drove back into Palmer from the hospital he was thinking hard of the little that Jeff Malone had told him—and refused to tell him—the night before. Who were these Road Pirates? It was time to find out, especially as one of them, according to Terry Larsen, had been responsible for Becker's accident. Somehow all of what had transpired in the past couple of days since Jessie had run over Donny Thompson's body in the trail above her house and dog yard was related. But he could see no reasonable or obvious connection between someone causing Becker to crash miles from where the body was found.

Could the accident have been caused simply to keep him from locating and questioning Robin Fenneli? How could anyone have known that she was the objective of his drive in that direction? She was supposedly Malone's girlfriend. Could she have had something to do with Donny's death? Or did she know something that either Malone or the Road Pirates, whoever they were, did not want exposed? If so, what? That afternoon he would look her up, he told himself.

Commander Swift was probably right in suspecting that Becker had been followed. It was the only way Jensen could think of that explained how one lone biker could have known where he was headed, waited for him, and run him off the road. But there was also the seat belt that had been rendered unusable. When and where would anyone have had the opportunity to do that? And who had done it? The two things were clearly related and had been done with the intent to injure or kill.

Malone claimed that he had been in Sutton when the crash took place—that a number of people at the Alpine Inn had seen and could vouch for him. It was a thing that could and should be checked off his list of questions. After that, he decided, it would be time to both track down Robin Fenneli and to ascertain the identity of the Road

Pirates—one in particular. How hard could that be if they came and went from the Aces Wild, which seemed probable?

Straightening in his seat, he sighed and reached to roll down the window a little.

It felt strange not to have Becker to knock around the bits and pieces of information they usually gathered and shared until the facts of whatever crime they were investigating came together. Being on his own, with no response to his questions, made him feel a little out of balance, but no less determined in his quest for answers that would, hopefully, provide solutions.

Mind made up on at least the beginnings of a course of action, Jensen drove through the main intersection in Palmer and headed on out the Glenn Highway toward the pub in Sutton. Time to have another talk with Pete the bartender—who supposedly knew everybody there. And best to do it in person. One could learn a lot from the expressions on a person's face.

Remembering Jessie's description of degrees of separation, he smiled. ". . . around here it's definitely less than the proverbial *six* degrees of separation. Everybody knows somebody. If you ask one or two people, you can usually find a connection to number three."

Perhaps it was as simple as asking the right questions of the right people in the right order, so one would lead him to the next. In time, with focus and determination, he should be able to get answers that would provide clues enough to solve the conundrum that confronted him and had put his partner in the hospital.

At that thought the smile vanished and he pounded a fist on the steering wheel in anger at Becker's accident and current condition. It must be something someone thought pretty important to risk getting away with possibly killing a state trooper.

Only two vehicles were parked in front of the Alpine Inn when Jensen reached it and pulled in next to a battered orange pickup that was at least twenty years old and showed hard use. Next to it sat a motorcycle—black, with green pinstriping—the same bike he had seen the night before in front of the Aces Wild and believed to be Malone's. Was he here again? If so, why?

Trying the door, he found it locked, but peering in through its small window he saw a light at the far end of the long bar and the silhouette of someone moving in front of it. Probably it was Pete the bartender. His hard knock was rewarded by the man himself coming to open the door when he saw who was waiting outside.

"Hey," he said with a smile. "Johnson, isn't it?"

"Jensen."

"Oh, sorry. But I was close at least. Come on in."

Alex stepped inside and watched as Pete relocked the door, talking as he did so. "As you can see, the place isn't open yet. Not for another half hour. I'm just restocking the coolers."

Turning with the keys in his hand, he led the way across to the bar and quickly stepped behind it to stand facing Jensen. "Sit down," he said. "Make yourself comfortable. Can I get you some coffee? There's a fresh pot. Maybe a Killian's?"

"No, thanks," Alex told him, wondering if the man was always so gregariously talkative. "I just have a few questions."

"Sure—sure. How can I help?"

As he started to ask Pete about Jeff Malone's claim to

have been at the Alpine Inn the evening before, from somewhere out of sight beyond the bar in what he judged to be a storage area came the sudden sounds of hurried footsteps and the sharp clap of a door closing.

Frowning, Pete glanced over his shoulder toward the open doorway between the two rooms.

"Who *was* that?" Jensen asked, remembering the motorcycle he had seen parked in front of the building and beginning to suspect that the bartender's flow of words had been a nervous attempt at cover for whoever he had just heard leaving.

Pete shrugged, but before he could answer, they both heard the engine of the motorcycle growl to life in the front parking lot. Knowing Pete had relocked the front door, Jensen sprinted to look out a window as the bike roared onto the highway, headed fast in the direction of Palmer, giving him just a glimpse of its black-leather-clad rider, unrecognizable in a correspondingly black helmet.

He turned and walked back to the bar, where the two men stared at each other in silence for a long moment before Jensen asked the obvious question: "Malone? Here to make sure you covered him for last night?"

Alex Jensen wasn't the only person that Tuesday morning who was interested in soliciting information from people who might know something that, whether they realized it or not, could relate to Donny Thompson's death. From past time spent in the Aces Wild, Hank Peterson knew several bikers who wore black leather jackets with the green Road Pirate patch. He also knew that others who frequented the bar would be familiar with the identity of those he didn't know.

When he arrived there at shortly before eleven there

were only four other customers at the bar, none at the tables.

Swinging himself onto a bar stool next to Hardy Larsen, he was prepared to ask a few questions, hopefully without being nosy enough to elicit notice from members of the Pirate gang, though, as he had hoped, none were present at that time of the day.

"Hey, Hardy. How's it going?"

"'Bout as usual, I guess," Larsen answered with a grin. "You're in early."

"Yeah, well, I gotta see a man about a job, so I thought I'd see what was happening first. A beer, please, Mike," he requested of the substitute bartender, who was quick to set it up.

"Hear your boy, Terry, almost tangled with that accident out by the bridge that put Jensen's trooper partner, Becker, into the hospital. He know who the guy on the bike was?"

"Naw. But the guy, whoever it was, passed him headed into town. He called 911 and waited for the law and paramedics to arrive."

"Smart kid."

"He'll do. Jensen was in here for a few minutes and said he'd seen Terry, but he kept mum about the accident. Just asked about Jeff Malone, then went out the back door after him when he showed up. Could it have been Malone, do you think?"

"No idea, but I doubt it. Doesn't seem like his kind of thing. That's not to say it couldn't have been one of those hard-core types he runs with sometimes—those Road Pirates."

"Well, he wears one of their green patches."

"Yeah, but I'd say it's more bravado than commitment. He and Donny both liked to seem tough."

"Never saw Donny with one of those patches."

"I have. But he never wore it in here where Carl would see it and carry that bad news home to his dad. Bill Thompson would never put up with that kind of gang thing."

Hardy frowned. "Good for Bill," he said. "Neither would I. Thank God Terry's never been inclined in the direction of anything on two wheels but bicycles. Got him his first one when he was just a little tyke—had training wheels and he went from—"

He broke off what he was saying as there was a sudden rumble, like a passing truck. It grew louder and the room started to shake with another earthquake. At first it was minor, but it didn't stop, as they usually did, in just a few seconds. It grew and things began to rattle, then fall. Two unoccupied stools tipped over after a rattling walk away from their places at the bar.

The barmaid, with no one to serve at the tables, was sitting on another of the tall stools with a cup of coffee in front of her and a cigarette in her hand. She shrieked and dropped it into the coffee cup as she scrambled down and stood clinging to the padded edge of the bar.

Mike, the bartender, tried at first to catch the glasses and liquor bottles that were dancing off the shelves and crashing into shards on the floor. But, as the shaking continued and grew stronger, he gave it up and got out of the confined space into the open area. As he passed the glass-fronted cooler door it opened and dumped out a shelf or two of unopened beer bottles, which exploded into fragments as they hit the tile below.

"Best get out of here," he suggested, grabbing a bar towel to wrap around a bleeding cut on one hand from the flying glass, and headed for the front door, setting an example for his customers. The warning wasn't necessary.

They were all close behind him in exiting the Aces as quickly as possible.

Hank grabbed the girl, who was still shrieking and clinging to the bar, and pulled her with him to the door, where they were the last to make it to the sidewalk outside. Once there, she clung tenaciously to him, hysterically crying for someone to "make it stop. Please, make it stop."

Instead the shaking grew worse. With a whine of stressed metal and a crash, the sign from La Fiesta, the Mexican restaurant on the corner, fell onto the sidewalk. Luckily it hit no one on its way down to splinter on the concrete, for along the street people were pouring out of other businesses, many yelling or screaming as they staggered, alone or together, across the street to get away from the buildings into open space next to the railroad tracks, where there was nothing to fall. Some lost their balance and went down, then struggled to regain their feet, or stayed where they were on hands and knees. Others helped one another, or crawled.

As the street rolled, a car and a pickup collided in the intersection of Evergreen and Alaska streets, piling up traffic in both directions. Another car ran off the pavement that crossed the railroad tracks and now sat astride them, empty, both doors flapping back and forth in rhythm with the heaving of the ground. Some people simply left their vehicles in the street to bounce erratically on their tires like bumper cars at a carnival, crushing fenders and side panels against one another as the quake continued. Some drivers evidently felt safer inside and remained seat belted as they were agitated in place. The pavement cracked, making a jigsaw of the road, and pieces of blacktop were shoved onto one another.

It was chaos as people screamed and shouted. Bricks

began to fall from the cornices of an older building on the corner across the street, scattering people still trying to get out and sending some back inside. An older woman clung to the door frame, too terrified to move or even attempt to escape. Farther along that block, Hank saw two clerks from the Fireside Bookstore carrying out the limp form of the owner, blood running down the side of his face, probably from something falling, a shelf tipping over, or some heavy book.

In the distance he could hear the sirens of police cars or ambulances, their drivers already trying to make it to wherever, whoever needed them.

With a couple of hard jolts for emphasis, the rocking and rolling continued for perhaps another minute before the trembling slowly died away, leaving what seemed like a dead silence.

"Is it over?" the barmaid sobbed, finally letting go of Hank's arms.

"I hope so," he told her. "There'll be aftershocks, but they won't be anywhere near as bad."

"Well!" Hardy Larsen, who Hank noticed was still holding the beer he had carried out with him, heaved a great sigh of relief, then grinned before draining the bottle. "Didn't equal the one in sixty-four," he assessed what they had just been through. "I'd estimate it was about a six-point-five. You think?"

CHAPTER NINETEEN

THE MATANUSKA RIVER WINDS NORTHWEST IN A DEEP, beautiful valley between the soaring slopes of the Talkeetna and Chugach mountains. The highway from Sutton to Palmer runs high above the river like the coils of a snake along the Talkeetna side, following the curvatures of its ridges.

Alex, having radioed in a request for a trooper on duty to stop the motorcycle rider he knew could be between himself and Palmer, was headed west on its loops and turns in a hurry when the earthquake began. At first, concentrating on apprehending the suspect, he didn't notice the shaking, simply wondering in a distracted way at the unevenness of the highway. Soon, however, he could actually see that the road ahead of him was moving in waves and cracking. Small dirt and rock falls were beginning to litter the highway. Dodging a few boulders, he pulled over onto a wide spot off the pavement on the inside of a curve, could then feel the ground shaking the truck, and sat watching the road move for a long moment.

Suddenly, ahead of him a large crack appeared in the pavement between the centerline and the far side of the road, where the hill fell away toward the valley. The fissure widened, separated from the rest of the road, and he could see that the ground had opened to a depth of perhaps eight or ten feet. Climbing out of the cab, he watched it slowly grow wider.

There was a sharp jolt, then another, and with a roar that side of the road split completely open and the outer section collapsed, sliding down out of sight, leaving a cloud of dust in its wake. What had been a perfectly good two-lane highway abruptly became adequate for one-lane travel only.

Thank God there was no one on it, Alex thought, and, as he had that thought, around the curve came a green station wagon. Traveling at normal speed, it was heading straight for the section of the highway that was no longer where the driver would expect it to be.

Anxiously, Alex stepped forward, yelling and waving his arms, trying to warn the traveler of the danger into which he was heading.

The vehicle slowed slightly; then, at the last minute the driver applied the brakes hard, swung to his left, and came to a screeching halt on the remaining side of the road.

The two men stared at each other through the windshield of the car for a few long seconds as the shaking of the earthquake slowly subsided.

Then the driver opened the door, got out, stepped to the side of the road that had fallen away and looked down at the distance it had fallen, bent over with his hands on his knees, and threw up as he realized just how close he had come to disaster.

Two hours later Alex finally made it back to his office in Palmer.

The man he had kept from driving off the road, one

Harold Spenser, had wiped his mouth with the back of his hand and come across to give pale-faced thanks to his benefactor.

"You saved my life," he said.

"No, you saved it with quick thinking and reactions," Alex told him. "We'd better do something about this to warn other drivers before someone does go over the edge though."

Together they had used sticks broken from the brush on the uphill side of the road and thrust into the earth to support the yellow tape that was part of the kit Jensen carried in a lockable metal box in the bed of his pickup for use at crime scenes and emergencies. Hanging the tape on the sticks along the edge of the cave-in, they then took cans of yellow spray paint from the same kit and walked in opposite directions from the slide to paint warnings on the surface of the road: SLOW! SLOW! SLOW! ONE-LANE ROAD! APPROACH WITH CAUTION!

That much accomplished, he left Spenser giving him more thanks for his rescue and drove on toward Palmer, watching the road carefully for more cracks and slides, seeing several.

Three curves later, on an inward curve of the road, he found a group of people standing near three cars and a truck, looking down over the edge of the road. Pulling up behind a black Subaru wagon, he joined them and identified himself.

"Some car go off the road?" he asked.

"Not a car," a woman told him. "A motorcycle."

"It's down there in the brush," said a tall man. "I had pulled over to wait until the shaking stopped and saw it leave the road during the last of the quake. Seemed to just lose his sense of direction with everything moving like it was. Instead of following the curve around, he drove straight off, flew through the air, hit a tree, and dropped like a stone. I saw him go."

"How long ago?"

"Just a few minutes."

Well, Alex thought, *unless he stopped somewhere to wait for me to go by, it can't be Malone. He left Sutton half an hour ago.*

When he and the tall man had climbed carefully down to reach the site where the motorcycle had come to rest, his prediction proved accurate.

The rider was, as expected, not Jeff Malone, though the motorcycle was painted like his and the rider, now clearly deceased from the face-first impact with the tree, wore the patch of a Road Pirate on the left shoulder of a similar black leather coat. But when Alex removed what was left of the battered helmet, a cascade of blond hair that had been tucked up under it fell down over the shoulders of a *woman.*

Nowhere on her body or the motorcycle did he find any kind of identification, but he knew the license plate number would lead him to its owner as soon as he could get back to town and look it up. He didn't even try to call his office for backup, knowing the switchboard would, as usual, after even a minor earthquake, be jammed with incoming calls, and this one had not been small. Also, there would be little help available for assessing the scene at which the woman had died, for every officer, trooper or policeman, would be occupied indefinitely in assisting victims of the quake.

With the help of the tall man, it took the better part of an hour to implement the retrieval of the woman's body, wrap it in a blanket from someone's car, and drag up the damaged motorcycle using the winch mounted on the front bumper of Jensen's truck. Both secured in the bed of the pickup, he continued his drive into Palmer, where he would take them to the state troopers office for transport to the morgue and, possibly, the crime lab in Anchorage.

The description of the motorcycle going off the road at enough speed to launch it into the air made him wonder why the driver had seemingly made no effort to slow or stop. Most riders were quick in handling their bikes, which were more responsive than automobiles, and he would have expected at least an attempt to avoid the deadly flight. The woman had evidently made none. Could something have been wrong with the brakes, the steering? Or was the cause simply the earthquake? It would be worth examining.

Reaching the top of the long hill toward Palmer's most heavily trafficked intersection, where the Glenn Highway crossed the road out of Palmer all the way to Wasilla, Jensen could see chaos ahead and traffic backed up in all four directions with fender benders, the result of several cars and trucks having collided there. Making a quick left turn, he made his way down Arctic Avenue, weaving his way through a lesser but similar confusion of traffic, and turned right on Alaska Street, which ran parallel to the railroad tracks. Reaching Evergreen, which crossed the tracks to South Valley Way and the state troopers office, he was forced to swing wide around a wreck in the intersection, where a police officer was now directing traffic.

"Hey, Jensen," he yelled, recognizing fellow law enforcement, and holding back a line of slow-moving cars to create a space for a left turn. "Pull through here."

As he made the turn, Alex saw Hank Peterson trotting

toward him and waving a hand to attract his attention. He hesitated just long enough for Hank to open the passenger door and hop in, and was already in motion as Hank closed it.

"Hey," Hank said. "What a pain this—"

"Hold that thought," Jensen requested. "Let me get through this turmoil first, okay?"

With that, he continued on over the tracks, watching carefully for erratic drivers and negotiating a route between several other vehicles before making the turn onto South Valley Way, pulling up in front of the office and turning off the engine of the pickup. Leaning back in the seat, he took off the Western hat he was wearing and fanned himself with it.

"What a mess. Was anyone badly hurt?"

"Couple of people that I know of were sent off to the hospital," Hank told him. "One broke an arm when she fell off a curb into the street, and the owner of the bookstore has a nasty head injury. Otherwise just scrapes and bruises—at least in or near this intersection. I haven't been anywhere else, but I hear the Fred Meyer store is a real mess and some people got hit with stuff falling off the shelves up there. Where you coming from?"

"In from Sutton. There's a place or two where the road caved in between here and there. I'm carrying the body of a female biker who sailed off the road six or seven miles out. She hit a tree on the way down and it killed her."

"Who?"

"No identification on her."

Hank nodded slowly, frowning. "Well, if she rides a bike I might know who she is. There aren't that many women who do."

Jensen stared at him for a long minute in silence, then

shook his head and said, "Two degrees. Jessie's right, I think."

"Degrees?"

"Of separation. She says that if you ask one or two people around here you'll find someone who knows the person you're interested in. You are one degree in answering my question. If you can identify the woman, that makes two."

"Oh, that old *six degrees of separation* thing. Yeah, Jessie's got it figured. Around here it wouldn't take six. Two or three is about right." He hesitated thoughtfully for a moment or two.

"You have something I need to know?" Jensen asked finally.

"Yeah, I guess," he said slowly. "I think maybe you should know that I was talking with Jeff Malone at the Other Place last night. He'd come out from town looking for his girlfriend, Robin. Seems no one's seen her the last couple of days. He said she isn't at her place out on the loop near the butte, she doesn't answer her cell phone, and wasn't at work yesterday."

Jensen frowned, his mind racing back to the wreck of the woman on the motorcycle.

"She a blonde?" he asked.

"No," Hank answered, shaking his head. "Brunette."

"Well, this one's blond—but dyed, I think."

"Then it's not her. But before he started dating Robin, he was tight with Sharon Parker, and she's a bottle blonde."

"Does she ride a bike like Malone's, black with green pinstriping?"

Hank nodded.

"Wear black leather with a Road Pirate patch?"

"Yes, but—"

Jensen interrupted with another question. "Where will I find Malone this morning?"

Hank shook his head and waved a hand toward the confusion across the railroad tracks caused by the earthquake.

"In this? I have no idea. You might try his place here in town. He might be home. I haven't seen him this morning and he wasn't at the Aces."

"Well, until we know for sure who this woman is, I'd appreciate it if you'd keep this to yourself. No sense making mistakes in identification if it isn't who you think it might be. Okay?"

"Okay." He opened the door to climb out of Jensen's truck. "For now, there's a lot of upset people in town. So I'm going back over to see if there's anything I can do to help."

"Good idea. Be careful."

"You bet."

Hank climbed out of the truck and headed back across the railroad tracks toward the historic station that stood alongside them, raising a hand in a farewell salute.

In the yard on Knik Road over an hour earlier, Jessie had known another earthquake was probably on the way when the dogs began to howl, whine, and move about uneasily, as they usually did just before one occurred.

She went down the porch stairs and walked across to Tank, who was howling with the rest, but stopped when she reached him, gave him a pat, and unclipped the line that restrained him.

"Too bad Billy isn't here to hear you guys sing," she told him as the shaking began.

Expecting another minor event, she waited, then

frowned as it grew worse and with a rumble under her feet began to move in waves across the ground. All around her both the dogs and their boxes rose and fell as the earth rolled and rocked them. Most of the howling stopped and the sound of earth moving and grinding was all that could be heard, except for a whimper or two. Several vanished into their boxes, but most remained outside staggering and bracing themselves to keep their footing, as did Jessie, who moved to hold on to the roof of Tank's, which was nearest.

Looking across at the trees that formed the woods beyond the yard, she watched them whip back and forth, coming close to sweeping the ground with their top branches. With sharp cracks, two or three broke off or had their trunks split vertically.

A car on the road screeched to a halt. The driver leaped out and ran away from it into her driveway, apparently leaving the engine running, though she could hear nothing but the roaring, breaking, tearing sounds that were coming from the woods and yard around her—up from the ground itself as it moved violently under her feet. As she watched, he tripped and sprawled full length on the rough ground.

As the quake continued she dropped to her knees and, hugging Tank close, turned to look at her house. Four or five feet off the ground on its basement foundation, it was moving. She could see that the supporting concrete had developed more than one crack, though it seemed to be holding together due to the required earthquake reinforcement the builder had used. She could imagine that the jars of fruit, jelly, and jam she had canned during the summer and stored in the basement were probably falling from their shelves to shatter on the cement floor. It would be a sticky, glass-filled mess to clean up later.

Glad she was not inside, she wondered what was happening in her house, knowing there would be similar clutter to clean up in the kitchen as well when a quake this size finally stopped. She hoped the gas lines wouldn't break and was relieved that the fire in the potbellied stove had burned itself out earlier and she had neglected to start another. Glad also that she had quakeproofed the kitchen cupboards with latches so they wouldn't fly open and dump out the dishes, pots and pans, and canned goods, she hung on and waited as the shaking continued. The refrigerator, she thought, was another thing, and most of what it held would without a doubt be emptied onto the kitchen floor—milk, juice, yogurt, cottage cheese, fresh rhubarb jam, and other things—to make a colorful coating on the tile.

Where was Alex? she wondered. He had gone early to visit Becker in the hospital and see what he could do about finding the biker who had run his partner off the road.

She had left her cell phone in the house and was not about to go back in after it until things calmed down. Probably wouldn't be able to get through anyway, she decided, and best just to take care of what she could where she was.

He would be in contact soon enough.

Finally everything stopped shaking and it was very still, except for the engine of the car left on the road, which had bounced almost onto the shoulder. Not a bird flew or made a sound for a few moments. Then a raven came soaring out of the woods with a squawk of protest at the treatment it had suffered as it clung to some branch, making her smile.

"You okay?" the man who had abandoned his car

called to her, then went back to it and drove away when she assured him she was.

Taking Tank with her, she went to check the gas lines, see what the inside of the house had to offer in damage, and find out if she could get any information on the radio, or get through to Alex on the cell phone.

CHAPTER TWENTY

It was almost five o'clock before Jensen found time to consider what Hank Peterson had told him concerning Malone's search for his missing girlfriend. He now knew, from a check of the license plate on the motorcycle on which she had crashed off the highway, that the dead women was indeed Sharon Parker. Her body rested at the troopers' office until transport to the crime lab in Anchorage could be made available, along with her damaged motorcycle. Jensen went off to see where he could be of help in Palmer.

Midway through an afternoon of helping to rescue people stuck or injured in the quake, clearing traffic-snarling vehicles from the roads and intersections, contacting the military to establish guards at banks and other businesses to halt looters, checking to make sure schoolchildren got home safely, and generally making himself useful wherever he was needed, after several tries he finally got a call through to Jessie's cell phone and they spoke briefly.

"You okay?"

"Yes, you?"

"Yeah. Damage report?"

"Not much, actually. Gas lines held. Kitchen and pantry are a mess, but I'm working on it. The dogs are fine. I am fine. Would have called, but couldn't get through and knew you'd be incredibly busy anyway."

"That and more. Have no idea when I'll be able to get home tonight, so don't expect me till you see me. Don't light fires or use the gas. If you've got power—"

"Amazingly, I do."

"Then use a couple of space heaters."

"Already got 'em running. We'll be okay for the time being."

"Good. I'll be home when I can."

"Becker?"

"Okay. I called. They were flooded with people hurt in the quake so they couldn't do surgery on his arm today, but will try tomorrow. He said to tell you hi and be safe."

"You take care."

"You too, love. Gotta go. Bye."

And he was gone.

It was full dark when he could finally take a few minutes to turn his attention from quake-related business to that of tracking down Jeff Malone to tell him of his prior girlfriend's death and obtain any information he might be able to provide.

Rather than try to find where he lived, on a hunch he went to the Aces Wild and was successful on that first try. Several members of the Road Pirates, including Malone, were helping Mike, the substitute bartender, finish cleaning the place.

Taking him outside, away from the listening ears of those in the bar, Alex first demanded to know where he had been for the last couple of days.

"Around," Malone told him with a shrug and a frown. "What's the problem?"

"I understand you've been looking for Robin Fenneli all over town and not finding her—that she hasn't been home for a day or two, or anywhere else you've looked. What's that all about?"

"What business is it of *yours*?" The question carried a decided tone of resentment.

"I'm making it my business in the investigation of Donny Thompson's death, among other things, that's what. And I suggest you give me answers and get a better attitude while you do."

"What the hell could Robin's whereabouts have to do with Donny's death? I told you she went home from the bar that night and I know because she was home when I got there not too long after seeing her at Oscar's in Wasilla."

"Anyone else know that?"

"I don't know. I may have mentioned it to someone. Maybe she did."

"Not too long, you say. But you didn't go out to her place that night until almost midnight."

"So? It was less than two hours."

"You been out to Sutton today?"

"Why?"

The stress of the last two days, Becker's accident, the problems in Sutton and Palmer, the results of the earthquake, the death on the road—everything mixed together and finally caught up with Jensen as he had all he was willing to take of Malone's evasion.

"Look," he said sharply. "If necessary, I can provide you with a night in lockup for obstruction if it helps remind you how to cooperate with law enforcement. You *will* answer my questions, one way or another, but I

don't have any responsibility or reason to answer yours. Got it?

"Now, get in my truck. We'll finish this interview at the office. On the record."

"All right," Alex said, when they were seated across from each other at a table in an interview room, with Commander Swift sitting in at one end to listen in and with a recorder running. "First I want to know if you were out at Sutton today."

"No, I was not," Malone snapped back. "But I was there last night at the bar with Lee."

"And what was that about?"

"He called and asked me to come out, so I went. He wanted to know where we were on Friday night and when Donny left Oscar's place, which I told him, just like I told you—between nine thirty and ten, headed for home."

"You say you spent that night with Robin Fenneli. Have you seen her in the last two days? Do you know where she is?"

Malone sank back in his chair, resentment fading from his face to be replaced by an expression of concern.

"No," he said slowly. "I left her place Saturday morning and talked to her on the phone that afternoon. Asked her to meet me for dinner, but she said she was busy. Haven't seen or talked to her since and can't find anybody else who has."

Frowning, he shook his head and leaned forward to put both elbows on the table and address Jensen seriously. "Okay. Here's the thing. I went out there yesterday—mid-afternoon, about three thirty—when I tried to reach her at work and they said she hadn't been in all day. But she wasn't home either. The house was locked. Her car was there, but not her bike, and there were a couple of things in the mailbox, so I assumed she hadn't been there all day."

"Bike?" Jensen questioned. "She rides a motorcycle? With the Road Pirates? Black jacket, green patch?"

"Yeah, sometimes, with me and the guys. There are several women who ride with us. She drives her car to work, but at times, if the weather's good, she rides the bike by herself. I thought she'd put it away for the winter when it snowed the other day. But I looked in her shed and it was gone. So she evidently took it somewhere. And what worries me is that nobody's seen her since Saturday, possibly Sunday—two whole days."

"What time did you come back to town and on which road?"

Malone sat up straight with a jerk and narrowed his eyes, catching the sharper tone in Jensen's voice. "Why?" he asked cautiously.

"Oh, don't start that again," Jensen told him impatiently. "Just answer the question."

"I went on out to where the Old Glenn Highway meets the new and rode on to Peter's Creek, where Robin's brother lives. I thought she might have gone there. I came back on the new road."

"But she hadn't been to her brother's?"

"No. He said he hadn't seen or heard from her in days."

The two men glared at each other without speaking for a space so long that Commander Swift leaned forward with a question of his own.

"So this Fenneli woman has a black jacket with the green Road Pirates patch? And she wears it when she rides?"

Malone nodded. "Usually. But I have no way of knowing if she wore it whenever she left her house."

"Does she own a handgun?" Jensen asked.

"Not to my knowledge. Why?"

"One of your biker buddies took a shot at my partner, Phil Becker, and ran him off the road this side of the Matanuska River Bridge on Monday," Jensen told him angrily. "That's why. A witness gave us a description of a black motorcycle and a rider in black leather with the green shoulder patch. Becker's in the hospital with a concussion and a badly broken arm. You know anything about that? It couldn't have been you. I've already verified that you were in Sutton at the time it happened, so don't climb back on your high horse. But, from what you tell me, it could just possibly have been Robin Fenneli."

"Or one of a bunch of other bikers," Malone shot back. "It *wasn't* me. And I know it wasn't Robin either. Couldn't have been. She hates guns."

"Well," Jensen said thoughtfully. "The thing to do is find her. Tell us where you've already looked for her and anywhere else you can think of that she might go. We'll get our people looking for her too."

He hesitated, thinking. "I also want as complete a list as possible of all the Road Pirates—every name you can come up with, and where they're from, here to Anchorage and beyond—if there are any who come from beyond there."

"There are a few, but most are pretty local."

"Is the Aces Wild the only local pub they hang out in?"

"There are a couple of others, including the Alpine in Sutton and the Knik Bar sometimes, but usually they collect at the Aces."

They made the list and Malone cooperated in its creation, though Jensen thought that there was a name or two he had reluctantly added to it and wondered about repercussions from some of the members of the Road Pirates, should they learn who had supplied the information. Several of the names listed he recognized from prior arrests, and two from Anchorage were known to be involved with drug dealing. There were five women's names on the list, including Robin Fenneli and Sharon Parker.

As they finished it, a mechanic for the troopers, who had been taking a look at the motorcycle Parker had ridden off the road to her death, interrupted to call Jensen out of the interview room with some new information.

"Parker's wreck was no accident, Alex. Someone messed with the steering and the brakes, though I'm not sure how yet—haven't taken it apart. I'll let the lab do that. But whoever it was, they intended her to lose control. The brakes failed, she couldn't stop, and went straight off that corner."

Returning to the interview room, Alex changed his mind about informing Malone of Sharon Parker's death and decided to wait until he received an autopsy report from the crime lab after the coroner's examination of her body.

CHAPTER TWENTY-ONE

JESSIE AND ALEX WERE UP EARLY WEDNESDAY MORN-
ing, both focused on what needed to be done after the
large earthquake of the day before. There were all kinds
of things that would require the assistance of law enforcement, as people reported everything from a gas leak to a
robbery in progress. Alex needed to check in at the office
and prioritize what would call for his attention, so he was
leaving earlier than usual. Becker's surgery was scheduled
for later that morning and the surgeon had promised to
call as soon as it was over with his report, so Alex intended
to keep his cell phone handy.

It was still dark enough to activate the motion sensors
on the tall pole between the house and the dog yard when
he drove his pickup down the drive and turned left on
Knik Road, headed for Palmer. Jessie, warmly dressed
against the temperature, which hovered just below freezing and had deposited a thin layer of frost on the top of
each dog box, stood on the porch to wave him off, hoping
it would soon warm up enough to melt the frost.

She stepped down the stairs and went to prepare breakfast for her dogs. Not long after she started filling bowls
throughout the kennel with food and water, the sun's first

rays crested the eastern hill and reached narrow fingers through the birch woods east of the log house and into the yard. Many of the bowls had held a thin skift of ice from the previous day's water, which broke and began to melt as she poured fresh water, warmer from the faucet, over it. The dogs ate hungrily and were not bothered by the chill in the air, for they were bred with thick coats to withstand cold weather. To them it was normal for at least half the year.

Too bad mushers aren't covered with such protective coats, Jessie thought and grinned at the idea, picturing some she knew who wore heavy beards all winter for just such protection from the icy winds of the far north when they were out on the trail.

Finished with her immediate dog yard chores, she walked to the mailbox to collect the morning's paper. Then she headed back inside to plan the day ahead, which she knew would be filled with finishing the cleanup from the earthquake. Though the upstairs was clean and the unbreakable items were back where they belonged, she knew that during the quake some of the canned goods in their jars had rattled to the edge of the storage shelves in the basement and fallen to shatter on the cement floor, mixing her homemade spaghetti sauce with raspberry jelly and gooseberry jam.

Inside the door, she kicked off her boots, hung up her warm coat and scarf, gloves and hat, and crossed sock-footed to add coffee to her cup. As she stirred a little sugar and cream into it, she glanced around the kitchen, now cleaner than it had been before the quake.

"Ought to be one more often," she told Tank over her shoulder, for he was already relaxed on the brightly colored rag rug in front of the cast-iron stove. "Or, since I could do without the shaking, maybe I should just clean the floor more often. It didn't seem dirty, but it sure looks cleaner now."

Alex had checked the connections to the propane that provided fuel for the new furnace in the basement and declared them tight and safe to use. The metal chimney that reached to the ceiling high above had suffered no damage, but it needed a little straightening, which he had taken care of with the assistance of a tall ladder. As a result a cheerful fire now crackled in the potbellied stove, warming the room, and the space heaters had been put away.

Sitting down at the table, she opened the paper and found the whole front page dedicated to news of the earthquake and its results. Pictures of the chaos created in the aisles of the grocery store where she had met Hank Peterson and Stevie Duncan two days before caught her attention and made her glad she had been elsewhere, for it was littered with items that had fallen from shelves and coolers. The accompanying article mentioned that a dozen people had been injured before they could escape, one with a serious head wound from a falling display rack.

A colored photo showed a clerk with a broom in one hand standing in the doorway to the back of the store near the produce section, which now resembled a giant salad. The carefully piled pyramids of apples, oranges, lemons, peaches, even pineapples had evidently rolled and fallen in cascades from their countertop displays and crowded the floor below. Across the space, next to the wall, some of the stacks of vegetables had followed similarly—tomatoes, potatoes, red, yellow, and green peppers, lettuce, cabbage, and onions. A few carrots, celery, cucumbers, and others less likely to roll because of their shape had fallen anyway and added diversity to the mix.

Good thing Stevie wasn't there, she thought. *She'd have hated it worse than the one we felt two days ago.*

Jessie had decided years before that living in earthquake country was just a thing you either got used to and took for granted or you didn't. You made preparations where possible and got on with living normally. Most people who couldn't take the shaking as it came and were terrified of it eventually left Alaska for places where they felt safer and were not regularly reminded by small, minor tremblers that a big one would arrive sooner or later.

As she flipped pages to another section of the paper, Jessie wondered just how much of New York City, for instance, was actually built to withstand an earthquake, if and when one came. This, she recalled from something she had read, was not an impossibility. It was much less likely than in Anchorage, Seattle, Portland, San Francisco, Los Angeles, or any city that lay around the Pacific on the Ring of Fire, where volcano eruptions and earthquakes happened frequently, but nonetheless. . . .

The colorful section of ads for the local grocery store fell out onto the floor, and as she picked it up, a special on a London broil caught her attention. Along with asparagus and a salad, it sounded tempting. There were also items that had been expelled from the refrigerator, broken or spilled, and needed to be replaced—milk, mayonnaise, the rest of the stew in a glass bowl. Though she knew a trip was necessary, the idea of braving the chaos of the local store was not appealing.

"I could run into Anchorage," she said, causing Tank to lift his head from his nap, yawn widely, and lay it back down again.

"Yes, I know. I could replenish the supply of food for you too—and the rest of the guys outside. We're running low. How about it? You want to go along?"

He raised his head and sat up at the word "go."

The roads will be clear by now, Jessie thought. *The basement will wait till—*

The phone rang, interrupting that thought.

"Arnold Kennels," she said.

"Jessie? Oh, good. It's Maxie in Homer. Are you okay up there? Of course we've all heard about the quake you had yesterday—epicenter was somewhere on the Denali Fault, from what the paper says. We felt it slightly and I've been trying to reach you, but the phones have been jammed. Are you and Alex both all right?"

"You dear woman," Jessie responded, pleased. "Yes, we're both fine, just a few minor problems—half my jelly and jam, for instance, is mixed with spaghetti and glass on the basement floor, so it won't be used for topping toast this winter. But nothing critical is broken. All the utilities are back to normal—light, heat, phone—obviously.

"But how good of you to call. What are you doing in Homer? I expected you'd be long gone down the road to the Lower Forty-eight for the winter and I'd hear from you eventually from somewhere in southern or middle America."

There was chuckle from the older woman, an Alaskan resident, who, after her second husband died, had bought a motor home and for several years had spent the winters "Outside" in the contiguous states, mostly the southwest—a snowbird, following the warmth and sun with her mini-dachshund, Stretch, for company. Jessie had met her on a spring trip up the Alaska Highway and they had been friends ever since, talking often and seeing each other when they could.

"Well," Maxie confessed, "I did mean to go down the road, maybe see a bit of Texas or even Mexico. But somehow I just couldn't get myself geared up for it this year.

Would you believe me if I told you I've a hankering for snow and northern lights?"

"You're asking the pot to call the kettle black with that one," Jessie told her. "You've no idea how much I've been yearning for snow, now that my knee is well enough to get back on a sled."

"We haven't had any yet, though, have we? It's going to be a beautiful sunny day and, with that in mind, I have a question for you. Could you put up with a houseguest for a day or two starting this afternoon? I've decided to store my house on wheels in Anchorage for the winter this year. It needs some minor repairs and one big one—something hokey going on with the cooling system. So I thought before it decides seriously to be winter I'd drive it up and fly back. But I'd love to see you. If you would give us—Stretch and me—shelter for a couple of nights, I'll rent a car and drive out."

"What a great idea! We'd love it," Jessie told her with a grin that evidently carried over the line along with the enthusiasm in her voice, for Maxie laughed again before she spoke and Jessie could picture her expression clearly.

"Well, then—"

"Wait a minute," Jessie told her. "I've got a better idea than your renting a car. I had just decided to drive into Anchorage on a supply run. Our store, as you can imagine, is total chaos—impossible for the moment. So I'll be headed that direction and can pick you up wherever you leave the Winnebago. When you're ready to go home— hopefully more than two short days—I'll drive you back to Anchorage. There's always some excuse to go to the big city, even if I don't want to live there with over three dozen dogs. How would that be?"

"Just dandy, as you know. But you're sure you were already planning to drive in?"

"Definitely. Gotta have supplies for the mutts and sustenance for the lawman. We're low on Jameson as well, and you can't ever be too prepped for the winter with a case or two of Killian's. Can't be caught out of the necessities of life now, can we? And your company will make it perfect."

Another two minutes of phone time and they had arranged for Maxie to call Jessie's cell phone when she was ready to be picked up at the address she provided on the Old Seward Highway in Anchorage.

"Good. About three, you think? I'll go in about noon, get the shopping done, and be ready to find you there. Oh, Alex *will* be pleased. Me too, of course. See you then."

Jessie immediately called Alex, who was delighted to hear that Maxie was coming to visit and added a few things to her grocery list before he gave her the news on Becker's successful surgery.

"It evidently went just fine. They found setting the arm was easier than anticipated and he's resting comfortably, sleeping off the anesthetic. Even the concussion was less serious than they thought at first. It's a relief."

"I thought I'd take some flowers to the hospital," Jessie told him. "That okay with you? Something bright and cheerful."

"Works for me. By the time you get back from Anchorage he'll be out of recovery and you could probably stop by the hospital and say hello. You and Maxie would be a double ray of sunshine and could bring the flowers with you. He'll probably be groggy, but you know Phil—he's tough, and besides, he likes you a lot and has met Maxie before."

"Great idea. Then I'll be able to pick up a humorous card as well. I'll do that and put your name on it too. Okay?"

"You bet. Get chips and some of that spinach dip at the grocery, will you? And filling in the Killian's supply isn't a bad idea."

"Anything else?"

"You'll have your cell phone. If I think of anything I'll call you."

After giving the dogs in the kennel extra water, cleaning the floor of the basement after all to have it out of the way, and changing the linen on the bed in the second upstairs bedroom, Jessie was ready to leave for Anchorage just before noon, as planned.

She closed and locked the front door, walked with Tank to her truck, and headed down the driveway to Knik Road, pleased to be heading for Anchorage and seeing her friend.

Waiting for a blue van to pass before turning left, she didn't notice a car more than half hidden in the old overgrown road where she had found the evidence of a truck and motorcycle on Monday. Focused on the idea of welcome company, she also missed seeing a person in a green jacket who stepped quickly behind a spruce and peered out cautiously to watch her leave before walking to the drive and up to the house. Passing along the north side of it, the figure went on into the trees and started up the hill.

When it had vanished from sight, the dogs stopped barking at the trespasser. Some went into their boxes, others jumped atop them, but some simply stood staring in the direction it had gone and might return.

CHAPTER TWENTY-TWO

"IT WAS PRETTY EASY ON DRY ROADS UNTIL I GOT through Cooper Landing to the Seward Highway junction," Maxie told Jessie in answer to her question about the two-hundred-plus-mile drive from Homer on the Kenai Peninsula to Anchorage. "Then it was icy in spots, mostly over Turnagain Pass, where it snowed several inches a couple of days ago and caught a little more last night from the look of it. It's beautiful up there this time of year, but it can be treacherously slick, so I took it slow and easy, and made it the rest of the way with no problem. From Girdwood to Anchorage the road was dry. Have to admit, though, that I'm glad I don't have to drive the rig back down till spring."

"I'll bet you are," Jessie agreed. "I hadn't thought about there not being winter tires on your motor home. But then you wouldn't need them if you were going someplace warm, would you?"

"No. Lots of Alaskans do have them, of course. Those who take their rigs out during hunting season, for instance, and mushers like you, who drive with dogs and also have helpers to drive them from checkpoint to checkpoint during races."

"That's right. I have all-weather tires on this truck

now, but will trade them off for studs when it finally snows enough to need them, especially if I run the Iditarod or the Yukon Quest."

Arriving in Anchorage just afternoon, Jessie first stopped at Alaska Mill and Feed to pick up a number of large bags of dry dog food she had ordered by phone and which were waiting for her to load with the help of two young employees and a low rolling cart. It would be part of what she fed her forty hungry sled dogs and had to replenish often. The bags filled much of the bed of her truck and the rest was taken up with people food in boxes from the grocery store, where she spent well over an hour and filled three carts, adding significantly to her list in terms of unbreakable canned and frozen food to have on hand in case of future earthquakes. Knowing she and Alex had not paid enough attention to the things they should have on hand in quake country, she had also replenished their supply of bottled water, flashlight and radio batteries, and a few items for the first aid kit.

Along with Maxie's small suitcase, all this now filled the truck bed under a canvas tarp she had tied down to keep anything from flying out and as protection against the small icy snowflakes that had begun to fall just enough to cause Jessie to turn on the windshield wipers.

At three thirty in the afternoon, the two women were almost to Eagle River with a ways to go to the Mat-Su Valley, with Tank and mini-dachshund, Stretch, good buddies from prior time spent together, in the backseat of Jessie's truck. Stretch had curled up for a nap and Tank was watching the world go by out a side window.

Jessie was quiet for a long moment, then burst out suddenly with an expression of her unexpected relief in seeing her friend.

"Oh, Maxie, it's so good to see you! Alex said to tell you you're welcome to stay all winter if you like—and I totally agree with him. Your company is just what I needed right now."

"You sound like you need a good talk," Maxie commented, hearing the frustration in Jessie's voice. "That all can't be due to the earthquake. From what you said on the phone, it didn't do too much damage."

"No, you're right. It could have been much worse—didn't come anywhere close to the sixty-four quake. Considering how badly some parts of the community were hit, we got off lucky, nothing major. But the last few days have been more than just frustrating, they've been downright frightening."

"What do you mean?"

"Well, it all started when it snowed just enough to take out a team with a sled on a training run. Then on the way back we ran over a dead man on the upper trail behind the house."

"*A dead man?* Did I hear you correctly?"

"Yeah, you did. It turned out to be a young man from Sutton named Donny Thompson who someone shot and left there. Alex is working on the case. So was Becker, until one of the bikers Donny rode with ran him off the road and put him in the hospital."

She proceeded to tell Maxie everything she knew that had transpired since the previous Sunday, ending with the incident with the rose she had found and the gun she had found and lost to a stranger in the woods.

"Good grief, Jessie. You *do* need at least some comic relief, and if I can provide it along with a listening ear, I'll be more than glad to."

So for the next half hour the conversation centered around the events Jessie had just described, and Maxie encouraged her to talk and get some of the disquiet out of her system. The older woman was quietly and thoughtfully glad she had decided to come up from Homer. If nothing else, she could listen and be moral support, and the timing couldn't have been better from the sound of it. She knew it took a lot to rattle Jessie's personal cage, for past history had tangled her in more than one death, and she was pretty good at keeping a clear head. Still and all . . . sometimes enough was enough. And this clearly seemed to be enough, so she listened carefully, asking only a few clarifying questions.

Half an hour later, by the time they reached the hospital, which stood high on a hill over the intersection where the Parks Highway branched off the Glenn to run the few miles to Wasilla and on to Fairbanks past Denali Park, the snow had strengthened enough to deposit a light coat over the parking lot and the cars and trucks crowding it.

"Probably people either taking care of injuries from yesterday's quake or visiting people who were hurt badly enough to be hospitalized," Jessie guessed as they crossed the lot to the building after pulling into one of the remaining empty spaces.

They found Phil Becker in his room with an IV running into his good arm, bandages on the other that lay on a pillow. A sleepy-looking smile spread over his face at the sight of Jessie's armful of the brightly colored flowers she had found and purchased at the grocery store along with a vase to hold them.

"Pretty colorful for this late in the year," he said. "You didn't need to bring flowers, Jessie. A visit from you is plenty. Alex was here a while ago and said you'd be stopping by on your way back from town."

"Thought I'd better check on you. Make sure you were behaving yourself and not chasing the nurses," she teased and turned toward the bathroom. "Say hello to Maxie while I get some water for these. I know you've already met her."

"Sure have. Hi, Maxie. Where'd you spring from? Feel left out when the quake didn't reach Homer?"

"Hardly. We get enough of our own not to be jealous of yours. If they're any bigger than a vibration you can have 'em all. How're you feeling?"

"Not bad, considering. I'll be here another day or two. Then it'll be a while until I do anything but desk work. But the doc said the surgery went better than he thought it would and I'll be fine as soon as it heals, but there'll probably be some physical therapy in my future."

"That's good to hear."

"Yeah, it could have been worse—a lot worse."

By the time the two women had driven to Wasilla, out Knik Road, and were turning into the drive at Jessie's place, it had stopped snowing for the moment, though it had come down a little more heavily there and left a couple of inches on the ground, house, and kennel.

Jessie noticed footprints and tire tracks in the drive, and Alex's truck was parked near the house and bare of snow.

"Hey," she said. "Alex is home and must have just come in. He'll be a help in unloading groceries. The dog food can wait until later, but I want to get the vegetables in so they don't freeze."

Expecting him to appear upon hearing the sound of her truck in the drive, she climbed out and was surprised not to see him in the doorway.

Maxie had come around to lift Stretch from within the truck and clip a leash to his collar before he escaped into the kennel full of excited sled dogs.

Tank had, of course, jumped down on his own and stood waiting to escort them inside.

Though the dogs in the yard had met Stretch before, they had, of course, put up a rumpus at the appearance of the small, short-legged canine, and their barks of greeting should have been enough to attract Alex's attention if, for some odd reason, he had not heard the truck, but the door of the house remained closed.

Quieting them in a firm voice, Jessie went up the steps and opened the door, which she found to be unlocked, so Alex had definitely arrived home, but the house felt empty and he did not respond to her calling his name.

Maxie had followed her into the house with Tank and Stretch and closed the door.

"Not here?" she asked.

"He's around somewhere," Jessie told her. "Sometimes he rides with one of the other troopers in a squad car. But he wouldn't have left the door unlocked if he was going somewhere else. He'll show up soon."

Meanwhile, she ferried in the boxes of groceries, leaving the heavier ones of Killian's and all the dog food for his help later, when he came back from wherever he was, and insisting that Maxie make a start on unpacking the boxes rather than carrying them.

"If you want to help, you can put the veggies that need to stay cool in the refrigerator. But leave out the Jameson and what you think we'll need to make a salad. I thought we could have the London broil for dinner with some of those small red potatoes. Does that sound good to you?"

"Certainly does," Maxie agreed.

"Great. I think we might start," she suggested, "by

checking the Jameson to make sure it didn't go bad on the way back from Anchorage. If that suits you as well, the glasses are in the upper cupboard to your left."

"That suits me just fine," Maxie assured her with a grin, reaching for the glasses. "I'm an expert at testing the quality of Irish whisky, as you well know. Jameson very seldom goes bad, especially so quickly. But we should definitely test it to be sure."

Groceries stashed away, except for what Jessie would need to make dinner, they settled comfortably on the large sofa, toasted each other, and began to catch up on what, besides finding Donny Thompson, had transpired since their last meeting.

"After your trip to Hawaii, I'm sure you spent the first few weeks at home working in your garden," Jessie said.

"You're right. By midsummer I had some of the tallest and best deep blue delphiniums ever. Mixed with my deep orange tiger lilies they put on quite a show. I took some pictures, but they're only a hint of what those blossoms were really like."

"One of these summers I'm going to—"

Jessie stopped and got up and started toward the window as the dogs in the kennel began their vocalizing again, but Alex Jensen stopped her in her tracks by coming in the front door, bringing a young woman in with him.

Tall as his shoulder, dressed warmly in outdoor clothing that did nothing to conceal her slimness, she stopped just inside and stared across the room at the two women, who were looking at her in surprise. The lids of her brown eyes were red and her face was streaked with tears—she had clearly been crying. She snuffled and blinked, but said not a word.

"Hey there, Maxie," Alex said with a smile. "Good to see you and that you can spend a few days with us before the winter sets in for good. Have a good trip up, did you?"

She agreed that she had, glancing at Jessie, who was staring with pleasant but questioning looks at both him and the strange girl he had brought into the house.

"You can take off your coat, Sally," Alex suggested gently, reaching to take her green jacket and hang it beside his own when she complied, stuffing her knit hat and mittens into the pockets and, before handing it over, retrieving a soggy tissue, obviously already used. After blowing her nose, she wadded the tissue in the palm of one hand.

"Boots too," Alex told her. "It's warm, so they'll dry on the mat. We all go sock-footed around here."

Turning toward the two older women, he put an arm around the shoulders of the girl he had brought into that warmth and guided her forward a step or two.

"This is Jessie Arnold," he told her. "And Maxie Mc-Nabb on the sofa there. Jessie, this is Sally Thompson, Donny's sister. I followed her tracks up the hill and discovered her where she'd come to leave another rose at the place where we found him—where you found the first one on Monday.

"Some of that Jameson would do fine for me, but could you make some hot cocoa? Sally's been up there quite a while and could use some warming up."

CHAPTER TWENTY-THREE

THE FOUR OF THEM SAT AROUND THE TABLE NEXT TO the kitchen, Sally Thompson hugging her hot chocolate mug between her two hands to warm them and the other three sipping Jameson.

Alex explained to Jessie and Maxie how he had followed her tracks in the snow and found Sally on the hill, sitting on the trunk of a fallen birch and grieving the loss of her brother Donny, another rose clutched tight in one hand.

"So it must have been you who left the rose I found last Monday. How did you find out where he died?" Jessie asked.

"Pete, the bartender at the Alpine Inn, told me," Sally said. "I went in and asked if he knew and he did—Jeff Malone had described the place. The first time I came I went up through the trees over there." She waved a hand toward the woods beyond the dog yard. "When I found a trail I followed it along until the one that comes down to here branched off and went down it till I found the place with all that crime scene tape and knew it was the right place."

She glanced at Alex nervously. "I took it down," she said to him. "It was so awful to look at."

"That's okay, Sally," he told her. "I can understand, so don't worry about it."

The mention of Malone's knowledge of the place Donny had been killed narrowed Alex's eyes and brought a hint of suspicion to his frown, but he had said nothing, filing the information away for later, when he intended to make good use of it.

"Why did you go up there?" Jessie asked, knowing the answer, but asking anyway to see how the girl would answer.

"I just wanted to know. It was the only place I could think of to say good-bye the way I wanted to—without my father telling me to stay at home and my mother crying all the time, or everybody in town watching me at the funeral. It's been just awful at home in Sutton the last few days. I wanted something bright and happy-looking to remember him. He was a great brother." Her eyes filled with tears again and she swiped at them with the back of a hand.

Jessie got up and retrieved a box of Kleenex, which she handed her.

"That's a long ways. How did you get here?" Maxie questioned. She had been listening closely, knowing Jessie and Alex would explain the details of this odd situation to her later. "Sorry, Alex. I should let you ask the questions."

"Don't be sorry," he told her with a smile. "It's a good question. Sally?"

"I drive my own car to work at Fred Meyer in Palmer, so I told Mom that's where I was going. She didn't ask any more questions and Dad wasn't home to stop me."

"Where is it?" Alex wanted to know.

"The car?"

"Yes."

"Across on the other side of the highway. There's an old road that used to lead somewhere down the hill. It's pretty overgrown, but there's room to park on the top part of it. I could see that other people had. So I pulled in there—both times."

"Did you bring a handgun with you, take it up the hill?"

"A *handgun*? No way! Where would I get one and what would I do with a gun? Besides, my father would have a fit. He hates handguns."

"Thought you might have wanted some protection."

"From who? Whoever killed Donny wouldn't come back, would they?"

"Possibly. Did you see anyone else either time you came?"

Sally shook her head. "No, but there had been someone else there. I saw tracks in a muddy place in the trail this time that weren't the same as the ones the police—you—made. These had heavy soles and a piece was missing from the right foot."

Jessie, who had been staring into her glass as she listened, looked up sharply enough to distract Alex's attention.

"What?" he asked.

"That same print was near the highway the day I called you and Becker about the truck and motorcycle tracks and the footprints in the mud that came and went into the woods. Before you came and found the bike in the brush."

He nodded. "We took a cast of it. I'd probably better make another as soon as we finish here, which we almost are. Do you know anything about the guys Donny and

Jeff Malone ride motorcycles with? They call themselves Road Pirates."

Again Sally shook her head. "Nothing, really. Donny was afraid my father would find out he was hanging with them. I knew he was doing some kind of wild things and overheard that name when he was talking to Jeff on the phone a couple of weeks ago. He made me promise not to tell my parents and to forget it. Which, of course, made me remember it. I've seen a couple of them at the Alpine and their bikes are there once in a while, but I don't know any of them or what they do except ride together."

"Did Donny have a girlfriend?" Jessie asked.

"Not that I know of, though there was someone he was interested in. He wouldn't tell me who when I teased him and tried to find out."

"How about Jeff Malone?"

"Yeah, he does. He's been dating someone named Robin who lives somewhere the other side of Palmer. I've seen them together a couple of times, but I don't know her. Listen," she told them, getting up from the table nervously. "I need to get home before my father somehow finds out I'm not at work."

The conversation ended with Alex walking Sally to her car, then going up the hill to make another cast of the footprint she had mentioned. He came back to find Jessie filling Maxie in with the details she had left out on their ride from Anchorage, including the loss of the handgun she had found near the first rose Sally had left in remembrance of her brother.

"I think maybe I picked a bad time to invite myself to be your houseguest," Maxie said thoughtfully.

"Not at all," they both reassured her.

"You know you're always welcome," Alex reminded

her. "And I have to admit that I feel better having you here with Jessie. If Sally isn't the person who brought the handgun Jessie found up there—and it's pretty clear she isn't—then there's someone else who did and who took it back. That makes me uneasy, so I'm glad you're here for more than just company."

"And I can certainly use the company," Jessie added. "Maybe you can think of something we haven't about all that's been going on. And there're lots of other things to catch up on."

As long as it's just talk, Alex thought. If nothing else, he decided, but kept to himself, *it would be a distraction for* Jessie—better than an earthquake. Though that had certainly kept her busy. He found himself hoping Maxie would stay for more than a couple of days. *At least until I figure out who's responsible for Donny Thompson's murder.*

Later, when he thought back about it, it was to remember the old saying "Be careful what you wish for."

By then, however, when he recalled that the two women had helped solve a case before, on their way up the Alaska Highway, it would be much too late.

"Let's take Maxie over to the Other Place," Jessie suggested after they had eaten dinner and made short work of the dishes—Jessie washing, Maxie drying, Alex putting them away. "Let her meet some of the people we know around here."

"Good idea," Alex agreed. "I could use a break from the pieces of this puzzle that I can't quite fit together somehow. The earthquake didn't help—just turned my focus elsewhere for most of two days."

"I assume the Other Place has to be that local pub you

talk about," Maxie said, joining them at the door to put on her coat and boots. "Sounds interesting, and there must be a story behind the name."

As they drove the short distance to the Other Place, they took turns telling her the tale of how the bar's name had come to be through the reluctance of its patrons to call it anything else.

"You'll like it," Jessie told her. "It's a gathering place for half the mushers here in the valley and their fans and friends. There's always something going on at the Other Place."

It was half full of people when they walked in the door a few minutes later, many of them mushers enthusing over the snow that had finally fallen and had a good chance of sticking if the temperature gave it a chance.

"Another foot and we'll be in business for the winter," Lynn Ehlers was saying to another kennel owner who was seated next to him at the bar. "Hey, Jessie. Ready for the season to start?"

"You bet. I'm tired of four-wheeling behind my guys. Time to get them back in front of a sled. Think snow!"

She introduced him to Maxie, who smiled as she took the hand he offered. "I recognize the name. You ran the Yukon Quest with Jessie a year or two back, right?"

"Ran with?" Jessie corrected. "He practically saved my life on that one."

"Hi, Lynn," Alex said, and nodded in his direction, his hands too full of three drinks, Jameson for Maxie and bottles of Killian's for Jessie and himself, to shake hands.

They found a table in the middle of the room and settled comfortably.

"Where's Tank?" Oscar questioned, coming out from behind the bar with a piece of jerky in his hand.

"Sorry, Oscar. We left him home this time. Only room for three in Alex's pickup."

"Well, take this home for him so he won't have hurt feelings."

Introduced to Maxie, he also found a reason to connect her to Jessie.

"You came up the highway with her the year they were building her a new house, didn't you?"

Alex grinned and threw up his hands in a gesture of defeat.

"It's true," he said, chuckling. "It's all true. And it's not just here in the valley. I think the whole state's full of people with less than six degrees of separation. All you have to do is ask the right question about someone and the person you're asking either knows them or they know someone who does."

"Here comes another illustration of that theory," Jessie agreed, as Hank Peterson came across the room from the pool table, where he had just won a game.

"Hey, Jessie," he said. "I bet this is your friend Ms. McNabb from Homer, right?"

"Just Maxie, please," she told him, as the laughter rose and fell once again. "I'm beginning to feel right at home at this Other Place, so I'd best be on a first-degree-name basis."

Hank had soon enticed Jessie to the pool table, where she proceeded to thrash him two games in a row and was about to continue the streak with a third.

"She's very good," Maxie commented.

"She says it's more luck than talent," Alex said and grinned, setting a fresh drink for her and a Killian's for himself on the table before sitting down across from her.

"What you're seeing is an ongoing, never-ending battle. They don't really care who wins. They just like to play and are about equally good at it. You should have been here to see the night there was a small earthquake. It rolled the ball she needed to sink for the win right into the pocket without her help."

He was quiet for a minute; then he leaned forward with a serious expression.

"I'd like to ask you a favor, Maxie," he said quietly.

"Ask away," she told him. "I think I've an idea what you're aiming at already."

"You may at that," he said, nodding. "You're pretty insightful."

"You'd like me to stay around for a few more than two days," she said. "Till you catch whoever killed that young man on the hill behind your house, right?"

"Exactly right. There are a couple of reasons why. One is that I think whoever killed Thompson is pretty ruthless and will be more so and running scared at this point. Scared enough to run my partner, Becker, off the road and shoot a hole in the window of his truck. And enough to compromise the steering and brakes of a motorcycle that sent a woman off the road and into a tree that killed her between here and Sutton. If the same person is the one who took back the handgun from Jessie on the hill two days ago, then I'm justifiably concerned.

"The second reason is Jessie herself. You know how stubbornly curious and independent she is. I can't protect her all the time . . ."

"You wouldn't want to," Maxie interjected. "Neither would I."

"No, you're right. I wouldn't, and wouldn't want you to. But, nonetheless, it concerns me that she might get herself into a dangerous situation unintentionally. With you around she wouldn't be as tempted—at least less so."

They sat looking at each other thoughtfully for a moment.

Then Maxie spoke seriously.

"Yes. The answer is yes, I will stay as long as you both feel it necessary and as it relieves your mind. But I mean *both*. I want her to know what you've asked me—also the terms under which I've agreed. I'm not comfortable otherwise. It's got to be open and aboveboard or not at all. Okay?"

He frowned at her while he took in her terms, then he nodded.

"I can accept that if she does. Thanks, Maxie. We'll talk about it later, at home."

"Good. Now—I see an empty dartboard holding up the wall over there. You up for a game where you could get beat by a senior citizen?"

CHAPTER TWENTY-FOUR

Alex went out early again on Thursday morning, leaving Maxie at the table, taking her time over a second cup of coffee after breakfast, which he had cooked.

Jessie, who had gone out to take care of feeding the dogs and to bring Tank into the house to keep Stretch company, came back inside smiling and rosy-cheeked from the cold as she kissed him good-bye at the door.

"Have a good day, Trooper. We'll keep the home fires burning, but if we're not here, you might try the Other Place."

"You going to take a team out today?"

"Maybe. It snowed another two inches last night and that's probably not enough to keep from wearing out runners on rocks and rough spots on the big trails. But it might be fun to take Maxie for a ride on the local ones. Another four inches and there'll be no keeping me off the sled runners—along with everyone else who runs dogs."

"Well, stay warm then. Bye, Maxie. Have a good day."

After refilling her own cup with coffee and topping off Maxie's, Jessie returned to her chair and leaned forward, both elbows on the table, cup between both hands, settling in to enjoy the company of the older woman she liked so much.

Tank and Stretch were already snoozing peacefully on the rag rug in front of the sofa.

"As if they hadn't just had a full night's sleep," Maxie said and smiled. "Stretch usually keeps my feet warm at the foot of the bed, but here he prefers that spot on the rug when Tank's inside."

"We can take them out for a walk later," Jessie suggested. "Before they get fat and lazy?"

"Not bloody likely, that," Maxie said, a comment that held a bit of the accent and words she had picked up from Daniel, her second husband, an Australian expatriate.

Jessie's expression grew serious, and she abruptly changed the subject. "What do you think of all this about Donny Thompson?"

"Now there's a curly question," came the response, once again tinged with a suggestion of Aussie. "Give me a bit to mull it over. I do think, though, that Alex is right and you must leave it to him and the law to answer the questions and solve it, which I'm sure he's doing capably, yes?"

"Absolutely. Still, it happening here on home ground haunts me."

"I'm sure it does. Remember how uneasy I was thinking that someone had been in my house while I was in Hawaii? Then it turned out to be completely explainable, didn't it? When you have an explanation for this situation it will seem much different, I assure you."

"Well, I hope so. Still . . . oh, hell! Let's talk about something else. How's your son, Joe, and his lady, Sharon? I really liked her—and him too, of course."

"They're both fine and decided to come up for Christmas this year when they found out I meant to spend a northern winter and would be here. You and Alex should come to Homer and make it five. That would be a treat!"

"We'd love to. But if I can find someone to take care of my mutts for ten days or so, we may go to Idaho and spend the holidays with Alex's mother. She's alone now that his father has passed on."

"Where does she live?"

"In Salmon, right where the panhandle widens into the lower part of the state, very close to the border with Montana. If you go north over Lost Trail Pass, you come down into the south end of the Bitterroot Valley."

"Interesting. I came through that way on my way north last June, but had no idea that Salmon was where Alex is from. Had I known, I could have stopped and visited with his mother. It's beautiful country. You should go and see it."

They proceeded to catch up on what had been part of their separate lives since last they met, enjoying every minute of it.

In downtown Palmer, at the troopers' office, Alex first called the hospital to see how Becker was doing and found him ready to, as he put it, "get sprung from here."

"It's a little soon, isn't it? How soon does the doctor say you'll be ready to leave?" Alex asked, not surprised at his partner's frustration. Becker, an active sort, had always disliked enforced idleness.

"Maybe tomorrow, he says, but probably the next day. I feel pretty good though. Think I could go now, except for the cast they're going to put on later, when the swelling goes down some. I wanna go *home*!"

Alex couldn't help laughing.

"You sound like an old bear who wants to get back into his own cave for the winter," he teased Becker. "You know you're not going to be ready to come back to work for a while yet, so why not take it easy? There won't be any pretty nurses at your place to bring you food and baby you—and fewer visitors with flowers."

"That's a point," Becker agreed. "Still . . ."

The call ended with Alex agreeing to bring him something to read.

"If you could stop at Annabel's in Wasilla and pick up Lee Child's latest thriller that Carol's holding for me, I'd owe you big-time. Plus, I'd promise to stop whining for at least another day or two, if necessary."

"I'll do that later this morning," Alex promised.

He then focused his attention on making a list of anyone he could think of who could possibly know anything at all to do with Donny Thompson's death—or who might know someone who did.

He missed his partner. Discussing their cases together was often helpful to both in providing different perspectives. Maybe, he decided thoughtfully, this *degree of separation* thing could be made to work to his advantage. There was something—and probably more than one something—that he was simply not seeing, or had yet to learn about the situation. The details he had gathered didn't seem to fit together in building a reasonable pattern, so he spent part of an hour making a chart of exactly what he knew and did not know, and trying to organize it into some kind of order on paper.

First he listed all the people he could think of who might have something to do, directly or peripherally, with the case, or know someone who did. Then he thought about each of them individually and added what he knew or suspected about each.

There was Bill Thompson, of course, and his family.

Bill, it seemed, was a traditional, head-of-household sort of person who was fairly strict with his children, disliked handguns, and evidently disapproved of bikers like the Road Pirates.

His wife, Helen, would probably back him up on those things and was unlikely to know much that would be of help. But if she did, she might be inclined to keep it to herself.

Their children presented other questions.

If Sally knew that Donny was riding with the bikers, then all or some of her brothers might know it too, and other things their parents did not.

What little Alex knew of Carl, the oldest, seemed to indicate that he pretty much followed his father's example of likes and dislikes, disapproving of the Road Pirates and his brother Donny's connection with them. As bartender at the Aces Wild, in a position to observe and learn about the bikers, he probably knew more than Donny, or his buddy, Jeff Malone, thought he did. Putting a question mark next to Carl's name to remind himself to have a chat with him as soon as possible, perhaps after the funeral Saturday afternoon, Alex moved on to the next in order of age.

He knew even less about Garth, except what he had seen of him at their house when he and Becker had gone with the news of Donny's death. From that observation he thought that Garth must pretty much follow his father's lead as well. He was the one, after all, who worked the most with Bill Thompson and had been at the Alpine Inn with him.

As Alex looked at his list of the family names it occurred to him that the Thompson children seemed to be divided into two groups according to age. Carl and Garth were the eldest, Garth a full two years older than the next in age, Leonard, or Lee, as he was called. The three youngest, Lee, Sally, and Donny, were nearer in age, only a year or a bit more between them. There seemed to be a separation in attitude as well, as Carl and Garth formed a trio with their father in values, while Lee, Sally, and Donny formed another, less strict group.

Lee was another uncertainty in Alex's mind and received another question mark. He was the pivotal sibling, probably feeling a certain amount of desire to please his father and to fit in with his older brothers, but conforming more to the position and way of thinking of the younger two. He had, according to Pete the bartender, been at the Alpine with Malone on Monday night, talking seriously about something, which had provided Malone with an alibi when Becker was run off the road near the Matanuska River Bridge. As one of the three younger Thompson children, he had probably known about his brother's ties with the Road Pirates, as did his sister, Sally.

Sally had evidently grown up closest to her brother Donny, and was willing to overlook his deviations from his father's values, as she herself had done in choosing to bring the roses on her own to mourn her sibling in her own way. Still, it seemed she was not apparently willing to incur her father's disapproval in letting him know that she had done so—twice.

Donny Thompson, it seemed, had been the wild child of the family, the one most likely to bend or break the rules his father laid down and go his own way. Being the youngest, he had probably been babied by the rest of the family, who would have found his antics amusing and assumed he would outgrow them. Later, "rebellious" would probably be a good word to describe his attitudes and behavior.

Looking at the others on his list of names, he shook his head in dissatisfaction.

Jeff Malone had left as many questions as he provided answers concerning his relationship with Donny and the events of the weekend he was killed. What had he been talking to Donny's brother Lee about at the Alpine Inn on Monday night? Could he have been there again on Tuesday before the earthquake to meddle with the steering and brakes on the motorcycle Sharon Parker had driven off the road? Pete had not been forthcoming with that information.

This question raised another in his mind that stopped him cold, remembering something he had meant to pursue but that in the aftermath of the quake and its demands on his time and efforts had completely forgotten.

Now he suddenly remembered the sound of the door closing at the Alpine Inn, the rumble of a motorcycle starting up outside and taking off on the road to Palmer. There had been something about it that bothered him at the time, but he had later assumed that it had been Sharon Parker, who he had found not long afterward where she had died in her flight off the road and into the tree.

But there had been a motorcycle he had noticed on arrival that had been parked in front of the building, not on the side, where it would have been out of sight. Had there been two of them? If so, whose had been parked in front, whose had been out of sight, and which had he heard leave? According to the mechanic who examined Parker's machine, someone had tampered with the brakes and steering. Was that second person the one who had disabled it to a lethal extent? If it had been Malone . . . why?

Sharon Parker! *Sharon!* Hadn't that been the name of

the woman who took over behind the bar for Pete on the day he and Becker had stopped after apprising the Thompsons of Donny's death? He knew it was. But was it the same woman who had died in the motorcycle wreck on Tuesday? He thought it must be. If the bike parked in front of the bar was Malone's—or anyone else who rode with the Road Pirates—why would Sharon have been a target?

He drew a circle around her name to make finding out a priority.

Robin Fenneli was next on the list, and her name received its own circle before he even started writing down the reasons for it. Where was she? Why was she making herself so elusive that even her boyfriend, Malone, hadn't been able to find her? Or had he?

Alex was frowning at the implications of that thought and what it might mean as he picked up the phone to make a call to one person he knew who might be of assistance in getting information on both these women and whether there was any connection between them—and a few others, including Malone.

It was definitely past time for answers that made sense, and Hank Peterson, a gregarious sort who lived alone, and spent a lot of time in the valley pubs, could be an extremely good source of information.

CHAPTER TWENTY-FIVE

Aʟᴇx's ᴄᴀʟʟ ɢᴏᴛ ʜɪᴍ ɴᴏᴛʜɪɴɢ ʙᴜᴛ ᴀɴ ᴀɴsᴡᴇʀɪɴɢ machine that promised its owner would "get back to you as soon as I can," so he shrugged on his coat, took the list he had been making, and headed out the door. It was too early to try the pubs Hank usually frequented, but ten minutes took him halfway to Wasilla on the highway that connected it most directly to Palmer. Turning west on a side road, he soon arrived at the small house he knew Peterson rented. If he wasn't answering his phone there was a very small chance he might be there anyway, but it was worth a try.

As half expected, Hank was not at his house, but he had left a note taped to the door for Stevie Duncan, which Alex took the liberty of reading. Evidently he had gone to work at the same job she was working and she had been expected to give him a ride, but he had decided to take his own wheels and left the note to tell her so. The last sentence asked her to "tell Vic I'm coming, but will be late—have something that has to be done in town."

Vic, Alex knew, had to be Vic Prentice, the contractor who had built Jessie's new log house and who lived in Palmer and often had projects in the Mat-Su Valley, as well as other locations around south central Alaska. Jessie had mentioned that Stevie was working for him on an older house he was renovating somewhere off the Old Glenn Highway near what locals called the butte. A quick phone call reached Prentice on his cell phone and gave Alex the location.

I'll kill two birds with one stone, he thought as he drove back through Palmer, headed in that direction, remembering that Malone had said Robin Fenneli lived on Bodenburg Loop Road, which was also off the Old Glenn Highway, in "one of those old log houses a mile or two around the loop on the butte side of the road." It shouldn't be hard to find her place after he talked with Hank. Hank might know where it was, for that matter. It always surprised Alex just how much Hank *did* know about just about everybody. He was a prime source of one-degree-separation information.

When he reached the construction site, a two-story house just over half a mile on a side road off the Old Glenn Highway, the yard was busy with workers. As expected, Vic Prentice knew how to get a job done fast and well, so the number of people engaged in the project wasn't a surprise to Alex.

The outside of the building had been stripped and a lumber company truck was preparing to unload a pile of new siding from its tilting bed onto several old four-by-fours that would keep it from resting on ground that was wet and muddy from the skift of new snow that had fallen in the night.

High overhead, four men were stripping old shingles from the roof. Directly behind them, four more were efficiently attaching new ones to the roof. A worker with a forklift was raising more bundles of roofing from pallets on the ground. Evidently Vic intended that they should have it weatherproof by the end of the day and didn't hesitate to hire enough labor to get it done.

There was a smell of fresh paint in the air, and through an open door and two windows Alex caught glimpses of painters at work in what appeared to be a living room.

He saw Prentice, in coveralls and a warm work jacket, talking with Stevie Duncan, who was similarly dressed and holding a clipboard. Behind them, from a panel truck with the logo of a Palmer hardware store, a man unloaded a stainless steel sink and took it into the kitchen through a side door. Another followed with a roll of vinyl destined for new countertops.

"Hey, Jensen," Prentice called out, noticing the trooper approaching. "Looking for work?"

"Nope. Sorry, Vic, but I've got enough on my plate for the time being—though at the rate it's progressing I might be better off taking you up on that offer."

As the two shook hands, Stevie grinned as she teased Prentice, knowing him well. "Good save, Alex. He's a real slave driver."

"Yeah, but I make it worth your while, don't I?" the contractor questioned with a mock scowl. "Be gone, Stevie Wonderful, and take care of ordering that water heater and a new window for the bathroom, once you get the measurements."

"Yes, sir! Right away, sir!" She gave him a saucy salute and was gone.

No wonder Prentice never lacks for workers, Alex thought as Vic turned to him with a smile, *he treats people well.*

"That Stevie. Nobody works harder, or does a better job," Vic said. "What can I do you for, Alex?"

"Well, actually I'm looking for Hank Peterson," he

answered. "He around somewhere? I need a few minutes of his time for answers to some questions on a case I'm working."

Prentice shook his head. "Sorry. He's not here. Asked Stevie to tell me he had something important to do in town and would be late. He'll be along, but probably not until afternoon, from what she said. I just put him on the crew yesterday so I'm not surprised that there was a thing or two he had to take care of before starting."

"Any idea what?"

"Nope. Stevie didn't know either, but it's okay with me. Everybody has personal priorities and lives to live. He'll be along as soon as he takes care of whatever it is. Good worker. I'll hire Hank when I can get him. He knows that and doesn't abuse it."

"When he gets here," Alex said, "will you tell him I need to see him after work? If he'll stop at the Aces, I can arrange to meet him there."

"Sure. We'll knock off here around five thirty. That okay?"

Alex agreed it was and was turning to go when a call to Prentice from one of the roofers made him pause and look up at two faces that were looking down from the already shingled edge.

"Hey, Vic. I'm out of nails for the gun. You got some more down there?"

"Hold on, Sean. I'll send some up on the lift. Eric, you out too?"

"Totally."

"Sorry, Alex," Prentice said, already in motion. "Can't have these guys sitting on their hands. I'll tell Hank to meet you."

"Thanks, Vic."

* * *

Driving west a mile or two, Alex soon came to the turnoff to Bodenburg Loop Road and took a right onto it. For several miles he drove along it, looking carefully for an older house that could belong to Robin Fenneli and checking the rural mailboxes for her name. Halfway along the northern part of the loop road he finally came to one with FENNELI printed in block letters on the side.

South, down a long gravel drive, half hidden in a small grove of tall cottonwoods, he could see a log structure, its single story low to the ground and weathered gray with age. Most of the snow that had fallen in the night was melted, but there were no tracks of a vehicle in the drive, so no one had come from or gone to the residence since the day before at the latest.

Getting out of his truck, he opened the mailbox and retrieved what appeared to be a couple of days' mail from inside, mostly flyers and advertisements of a kind that most people toss away in annoyance without reading. There were two envelopes with windows revealing Robin's name and address, probably bills or bank statements, he decided, nothing personal. He replaced them in the box and closed its door.

Turning onto the drive, he drove the length of it into a yard, where it made a left into an open space in front of another log structure that was obviously meant as a garage, with a double door that would open outward and a small four-paned window on the side toward the house.

He got out of his truck and stood, looking around. It was very still except for a pair of ravens holding a raucous conversation from their perch high on a limb of one of the trees. Instinctively, he felt there was no one at home, but hesitated long enough to examine the place in some detail.

He could see no recent footprints anywhere in the

muddy parking area or mud tracks on the path that was formed of cement pavers and ended at a step in front of the cabin door.

A heavy lock secured the double doors of the garage.

He walked across to its window and peered into the dark interior. The glass was coated with accumulated grime, but after rubbing at it with a gloved hand he could see enough to tell there was a car inside, dark blue or black, and that a narrow workbench attached to the wall beneath the window was littered with old paint cans, a few tools, and oily-looking rags. A scattering of faded plastic flowers lay incongruously among the tools, and at one end a red helmet like those worn by motorcycle riders sat abandoned and covered with dust.

Red. Interesting. Maybe she thought red would not go well with the black worn by the Road Pirates. Probably she had another, a black one, like the one worn by Sharon Parker.

Her motorcycle was not inside the garage. This was worthy of note, as she certainly couldn't have taken both if she was alone when she left the place, whenever that had been. Wherever she had gone, she had gone on the motorcycle Malone had told him she owned.

Leaving the garage, he walked up the path to the house and knocked loudly on the front door.

As expected, no one answered.

There is a silence that occupies an empty house and Jensen recognized it, had expected it and that no one would come to the door in answer to his knock. It was clear Fenneli had been absent, as Malone had said, for at least a couple of days.

He tried the door. It was, as anticipated, locked securely.

Stepping to one side, he cupped his hand around his face and peered through a front window that showed him the interior through half-drawn curtains. The inside was clean and tidy, but totally and surprisingly empty of personality. Most houses reflect the people who live in them, and you can tell a lot about them by examining their place of residence, of safety, where they feel most at ease and themselves.

This house, though aged and small, told more about the person who had built it years before than it did about the woman who now owned and lived in it. It clearly had just four rooms: the living room into which Jensen looked, a kitchen he could see part of through a doorway opposite the front door, a bedroom through another to the left, and probably a bathroom out of sight in the rear.

The living room furniture was average in design and color, mostly brown and not new. The carpet was brown with worn areas in the obvious places most trafficked. That was also the color of the sofa and a couple of chairs, with a pillow or two in blue. The walls were plain white and held no decorative pictures or photographs of family. There were no houseplants, no knickknacks, no books or magazines, no sound system, no television, nothing personal at all that he could tell, except a pair of leather gloves on an end table by the front door, as if Fenneli had dropped them there on her way in or out, perhaps meaning to put them away somewhere later.

Through a window in the rear of the kitchen he could see that the trees were thick and fairly close behind it. He walked around the side of the house to that window and was surprised to find it unlocked. Raising the lower half, he leaned in to take a look at the part of the kitchen he had not been able to see from the front window. It was clean and empty, the cupboard doors all shut and the countertop bare of clutter. Not so much as a cookbook lay in sight.

The only thing he noticed, with his face inside the house, was a faint and interesting hint of something herbal in the air—rosemary, or lavender perhaps—pleasant, but unexpected in this impersonal residence.

Taken aback at the blandness of the house, Jensen stepped away, closed the window, walked around to the front, and stood thinking as he looked back up the drive he had come down from Bodenburg Loop Road, but saw little of it. The fact that the house revealed almost nothing of its resident made him feel somehow sad and a little incredulous. What kind of person was this Robin Fenneli anyway? Her name, Robin, had caused him to assume a cheerful, attractive idea of her that was now in contradiction to what her living space had told him.

Maybe he was evaluating it incorrectly, he thought suddenly. Maybe it revealed much more than he was assuming. Could the lack of personality in her living space really reflect the same sort of deficit in her as a person? It certainly was not his idea of the kind of woman in whom Malone would be interested. What a pair of opposites they must make, if this proved true.

Or did it simply mirror a woman whose character was distinctly at odds with the name she had been given?

What a cold thought!

He shuddered, suddenly wanting very much to be away from this place and its blankness.

Walking swiftly to his truck, he climbed in, turned it around, and drove quickly back to the road at the end of the drive without looking back.

CHAPTER TWENTY-SIX

THERE WAS NO NEED TO GO WEST TO PETER'S CREEK and look up Robin Fenneli's brother, Alex determined on his way back into Palmer. Malone said he had already checked that possibility and come up empty—she hadn't been there. A phone call to the insurance office where she worked had told him she was not there either, and had not been since the previous Friday.

So where the hell was she, he grumbled to himself, and did it matter?

Evidently it did to Malone, who had been looking for her for days. Was his concern what was making it an issue for Alex as well, or was it simply because he'd still like to dot the i's and cross the t's in confirming Malone's whereabouts on the Friday night Donny Thompson died and Fenneli was the person who could verify it?

It seemed that he might be giving himself a bad case of tunnel vision. There were other things and people besides Fenneli that he should be paying attention to and it was time to do so.

Who had tampered with Sharon Parker's motorcycle, for instance? Who was the person who must have been at the Alpine Inn before the earthquake on Tuesday? And why had Pete refused to tell him who it was? Keep his own counsel, indeed! There were times when that attitude was out of line, and this was one of them. Perhaps it was time to confront Pete again and . . .

Crossing the Matanuska River Bridge, he dropped that idea as he thought of Becker and suddenly realized he was ignoring a superior source of assistance.

If he couldn't talk to Hank, who knew everybody, or knew someone who did, until late that afternoon, rather than make the drive to Sutton, which might or might not be worth it, he could at least talk to Becker, who was bored and restless in the hospital and would welcome the chance to speculate on the things his partner had learned, or needed to learn. He would probably, as usual, have ideas Alex hadn't come up with. It was part of why they worked well together, and he missed it.

Encouraged and relieved with this idea, he drove through Palmer and on to Wasilla, where he stopped at Annabel's bookstore, Carol and Richard Kenney's terrific source of hundreds of new and used books. He picked up the one Becker had requested, and one he knew Jessie had been looking for. Then, though he was tempted to do a little of his own shelf reading, he gave it up and, in much better spirits, headed for home, where he intended to have lunch before going to the hospital.

A couple of hours earlier, Jessie and Maxie, noticing it was not snowing and the sun was making an attempt to peek through spaces in the clouds that covered most of the sky, decided to dress warmly and take their dogs for a walk.

"Where shall we go?" Jessie asked when they were standing on the porch.

"Well . . . ah . . . ," said Maxie, with a hesitant and

concerned expression. "If you wouldn't mind, I'd like to see the place where that poor young man was killed."

"You *would*?"

"Yes, I would. I know it sounds rather morbid. But his death sort of haunts me and I'd like to have a real place in mind instead of my imagination. I'm sure it's much less disturbing for real."

"It is," Jessie agreed. "That's really a lovely part of the woods."

So up the trail, on which Alex and Sally had left their footprints the day before, they went, past the house and storage sheds where Jessie kept her sleds, harnesses, and other gear, and on into the woods.

The birch, now bare of their leaves except for a few that still clung, displayed lacy patterns of branches and twigs against the sky. Dark green spruce were interspersed here and there between the pale trunks of their deciduous neighbors. The small amount of snow that had fallen between them also made a pleasing contrast.

"How nice it is," Maxie said, "to be able to walk from your house right into the trees."

Jessie nodded and started to answer, but a scolding from overhead reminded her that there were still a few squirrels about, and the small birds, chickadees, siskins, and sparrows, many of which did not migrate south for the winter, were making cheerful sounds. Several larger birds also remained—the omnipresent ravens, a few magpies, jays, and, though seldom seen, snowy owls that did most of their hunting at night or late in the day. Jessie recalled a story for Maxie about a cross-country skier who had his fur hat snatched from his head one evening by a hunting owl that left talon wounds on his head and flew away with his headgear, thinking it had captured dinner.

They climbed on a little farther.

"Here's the log I was sitting on when whoever it was demanded that I return the handgun I had found," Jessie said, stopping in front of it. "I still think it might have been a woman."

"Looks like it might have been where Sally was also sitting when Alex found her."

It was, for the larger prints of his boots stopped there, where he had turned around to accompany the young woman down the hill to the house.

Around a curve in the trail, they came finally to the place where Donny Thompson's body had been rudely disturbed by the passing of Jessie's team in training.

She pointed out where it had lain in the snow, turned over by the sled's brake, exposing the carpet of yellow leaves beneath.

There was really nothing left to indicate what had transpired at that location. The thin new snow had covered any blood that remained on the leaves or ground, along with any other reminder that a man had died there not quite a week earlier.

The only tracks around the spot were those that obviously belonged to Sally Thompson, coming up to and going back down from where her brother had died.

It was very still, except for a slight breeze that whispered through the denuded birch, rattling a branch against another somewhere close at hand. The sun shone briefly through a space in the slow-moving clouds to light up the place temporarily.

A raven swooped its blackness through it, casting a swiftly moving shadow on the ground, coasting downhill as it rode the air currents, but making almost no sound in passing.

The two women stood in silence for a minute or two.

Then Maxie turned completely around in an unhurried circle where she stood, looking carefully at the forest that surrounded them, the hill beyond the upper trail that paralleled the highway that lay out of sight far below in front of Jessie's house.

"You know," she said thoughtfully, "this seems such a strange place to kill a man. Why here? There are two trails close by, including this one that joins the one that runs above it, which a significant number of mushers use on a pretty regular basis, right? It's as if whoever did it wanted him to be found and I find that surprising."

"It's more like the wild country we cross in races, but safer, away from a road or highway with the traffic that's getting busier with all the new people who are moving into this area. When we run beside Knik Road, going up and down as we cross streets that run away from it, they forget to watch out for us sometimes.

"A team was hit last year by a car turning off Knik Road onto the access that led to the house the driver was still building back in the trees. The team was dragged, three dogs died, and the musher was badly injured."

"Then would it be reasonable to make the assumption that either the killer didn't know there would be mushers using these trails, or that maybe he—or she, for that matter; it could be a *she*, I suppose—wanted him to be found, or didn't care if he was?"

The question startled Jessie. It was not a conclusion she would have come to on her own and not one that she had heard from Alex.

"I think it's reasonable," she answered slowly. "You should ask Alex about it. Is there anything else you've noticed?"

Maxie looked again at the slope above them.

"Well," she said, "not exactly noticed, more like questioned. What, for instance, is on the other side of that hill?"

"I feel like a total idiot," Alex said when Maxie had presented her questions to him at Jessie's urging when he stopped in for lunch just before noon. "How'd you like a job, Maxie?"

She smiled from where she sat across the table and shook her head.

"I think not. The Winnebago is enough for me, thank you. I'm a little over the hill to be chasing around in anything with flashing lights and a siren. Though it might be fun to come up behind people and startle them, and it'd be useful to be able to clear out slow-moving traffic ahead of me at times.

"But I would like to know what's on the other side of that hill."

"So would I," he said, as he got to his feet, a frown drawing lines on his forehead. "Let's go find out."

"You really want us to go with you?" Jessie asked, coming back from the kitchen, where she had put the lunch dishes in the sink.

"Why not?" he said, heading for the door and reaching for his coat. "If Maxie wants to know what's on the other side of the hill, she'd better come along. Maybe she'll see something else I haven't noticed."

Taking Knik Road toward Wasilla, he soon turned his truck off on a road that he knew led to a local builder's new housing development in progress. Before what was now a street was put in and paved, however, there had been an older, narrower gravel road that provided access to a small log cabin in the center of a kennel that had belonged to an older musher. Though it was still there, the musher and his dogs were gone and the cabin, Alex supposed, would probably be torn down in favor of more like the first two brand-new houses they had passed, which were finished and occupied, though the yards around them would have to wait till spring for grass and shrubbery.

"Damn," said Jessie. "Chuck's sold his place and they'll tear the cabin down, won't they? I wonder where he's gone with his dogs. Pretty soon we'll all be crowded out if this keeps up, and it will."

"Not for a while," he told her, pulling to a stop in front of the seemingly abandoned cabin. "You own enough of the land surrounding your place so they can't get close. We'll be okay, I think, as long as you want to stay there."

"The Johnsons aren't about to sell their place either," she told him, thinking of her nearest neighbors. "So if we hang together they can't build too close."

"Right. Let's get out and take a look," he said, turning off the engine. "Isn't there a trail out back that Chuck cleared to go up the hill from here?"

"Yes. It hooks up with the upper trail just on the other side, like mine does."

As the three walked up the drive to the cabin, Alex noticed that there were tracks in the new snow, single tire tracks that had to have been made by a two-wheeled vehicle, and footprints that led to the door. *Maybe Chuck came back for something,* he thought. *But he wouldn't have been able to move much on a motorcycle, would he?*

"Jessie," he asked, "does Chuck ride a motorcycle?"

"Not to my knowledge," she told him. "Most mushers drive trucks, so they can transport their dogs. I've never seen him show up anywhere in anything but his battered old orange pickup with its permanent dog hotel box on the back."

"Well," he said, hesitating to turn and examine the tracks more closely. "Someone has been here on a bike and left again since it snowed. Interesting.

"Hold on a minute," he told them, stepping toward the cabin to try the door.

Unlocked, it opened easily with a small complaint from the cold hinges.

Alex stepped in.

Jessie and Maxie followed close behind and the three of them stood together, silently looking around.

As expected, the place was empty of anything that had belonged to the musher who had built it many years earlier. It was cold and slightly damp inside, but not as cold as it was outside, and there was a trace of wood smoke in the air.

Alex pulled off a glove and moved across to lay a hand on the old cast-iron stove that sat on the far side of the single large room in which Chuck had clearly lived, cooked, and slept. It was very slightly warm under his palm, or at least not as cold as the air surrounding it.

And as he had moved across that space something else had caught his attention. There was, once again, under that trace of wood smoke, a subtle reminder of rosemary or lavender, something herbal—the same scent he had noticed in Robin Fenneli's impersonal and empty house.

CHAPTER TWENTY-SEVEN

Back outside, the three walked around to the back of the cabin, where, as expected, they found a snow-covered trail that led past an outhouse and disappeared into the trees as the hill took it up into the woods that, like Jessie's, were a mix of spruce and birch, the latter now bare of yellow leaves.

"Let's follow it up," Alex suggested and led the way around the outhouse and into the first of the trees.

Single file, Maxie in the middle, they tromped in their boots through the undisturbed light snow that covered the trail as it wound gently around several large spruce that Chuck had evidently been unwilling to sacrifice in creating it. Soon the hillside grew steeper and, like the one on Jessie's side of the hill, the trail went up in curves laid out to teach dogs to swing themselves and a following sled successfully around trees and shrubbery. Halfway to the top there were two switchbacks, and Jessie paused briefly to examine the second of them.

"See how well this is supported?" she asked the other two. "He really knew how to build a track. His dogs were always ready for almost anything and this is obviously where he started teaching the new ones. Only another musher would appreciate just how carefully he laid out and built this trail. It will come out on top at the main trail, just west of the one that runs down to my yard."

She started on up with a shake of her head. "Oh, I *am* going to miss him. He taught me a lot in the early days. Gotta find out where he's gone from here."

"Have you ever met Robin Fenneli?" Alex, who had looked carefully, but said nothing as they climbed, asked Jessie a moment or two later.

"Don't think so," she answered. "Have you?"

"No, but the more I find out about her, the more I want to," came the answer, as he momentarily disappeared around a last spruce and came out on the upper trail, where she had said they would.

The three of them stopped there and looked around carefully.

Some musher—*probably a rookie,* Jessie thought—had been too impatient to wait for more snow, for there were parallel sled runner tracks in the snow of the trail, with dozens of dog prints between them. They disappeared not far beyond where she could see that her home trail turned down the hill.

"Well," said Alex, turning to Maxie. "What do you think?"

She frowned and bit her lower lip for a second or two as she examined the area more closely before answering.

"I'm thinking just about what I expect you're thinking," she told him finally. "That it was just as possible that whoever killed this Donny Thompson came up here from *either* side of the hill. And just as possible that they went down the way they came, or that they went on over the hill and down the opposite side.

"It's, of course, impossible now to tell which, but knowing that much might have told you something about whether the shooting was planned, or happened spontaneously. And, if you knew that, it might explain something about *why* he was killed and *who* killed him."

He stared at her, eyes narrowed in thought for a long moment after she stopped speaking, then reached up to run a thumb under the band and resettle the Western hat he favored wearing. Then he smoothed both sides of his handlebar mustache around the grin that spread itself across his face before he spoke.

"Your mama raised no dummies, did she, Maxie? I'm getting more serious by the minute about that job I mentioned."

"Fenneli's been in that old abandoned cabin, Phil," Alex told Becker at the hospital later. "I know she has. I can smell it."

"Get serious, Alex. You can't tell the difference between a guilty and an innocent suspect by smell. Guilt doesn't have a specific smell. They don't *smell different.* Well—maybe if they're scared or nervous, or have spent a long time hiding out without a bath."

"I *am* serious. There was an herbal scent of some kind of lotion or perfume inside her house—the one out on Bodenburg Loop Road that you were heading for when you went off the road. I caught a whiff of it again in Chuck Landers's old cabin. So I know she's been there, and not long ago. The stove had been used. It wasn't completely cold. There were motorcycle tracks in the drive and I know she's riding hers because her car was locked in the garage at her house. She was at that cabin earlier today, probably this morning after staying the night. It makes a great hiding place. Who would know? Chuck's gone and everyone thinks it's empty."

"Okay! *Okay!* I believe you. So where's she now? How are you going to find her?"

"I don't know. But I do know who *will know* how to find Jeff Malone, and I think that eventually Malone will be the key to finding Fenneli, if he hasn't already. Hank Peterson knows half the valley's population and somebody he knows will know somebody else who knows something. So I'm meeting Hank at the Aces at five thirty to find out what he knows, or who he knows who may know that something."

Becker nodded. "Sounds like a plan to me. Wish I could help, but . . . Hey, I didn't tell you that the doc says I can go home tomorrow and I'll need a lift. So can I count on you for it after he checks me out in the morning—sometime after ten o'clock?"

"Sure. And if for some reason I get hung up on this case, I'm certain that Jessie and her friend Maxie will be glad to transport and mother you."

"No mothering will be necessary. My sister's flying in from Spokane tomorrow afternoon. She'll do just fine in that department."

"You want one of us to pick her up at the airport in Anchorage?"

"Again, not necessary. She's going to rent a car and collect some groceries and stuff on her way out here—has already made a list of what she thinks'll be good for me. You haven't met Alvina, but I've always been her baby brother. Need I say more?"

"Got it! Good luck with that. Just don't expect similar treatment when you come back to work. I'm more Grendel than Mother Goose, if you remember."

"Ah, yes. That does ring vague bells. Go on and talk to Hank. If he doesn't have an answer, he will know someone who knows something."

"I will, but first I'm going to see Cole Anders at Oscar's in Wasilla. I want to know as much as he can remember about who was there the night Donny was killed and when they arrived and left. I've a hunch the timing could be important on this."

Becker agreed. "I think you're right. We already know that at least two people went up the hill from the Knik Road side and that one of them was Donny, because we found his motorcycle there in the brush on the other side of the road. So he didn't go home to Sutton as he told Malone he was going to. Malone supposedly stayed at Oscar's playing pool until almost midnight—at least that's what he *claimed*. Could be you'd better find out who he played, if Cole or anyone else can remember. He could have slipped out and come back, I guess. The restrooms are next to the back door and it's unlocked when the place is open so people can come and go to the parking lot in back."

It was an idea Alex hadn't considered.

"I'll do that now," he agreed. "I have time before meeting Hank." He left the hospital reflecting on several new possibilities.

Just prior to four o'clock in the afternoon, the bar held only a few people when Alex walked into Oscar's and looked around.

Cole Anders was, as expected, working behind the bar, and the same waitress he remembered talking to the night of Becker's accident was across the room, delivering drinks from a tray to a table by the dartboard, where a game was in progress between two couples. Two men in shirts and ties that said they probably worked in offices somewhere in Wasilla sat across from each other at a table in the middle of the room, their sports jackets hung from the backs of their chairs. A young blond woman in jeans and a blue sweater was practicing shots at the pool table. The stools at the bar were all empty.

"Hey, Alex," Cole greeted him as he took the stool farthest from the door. "How you be?"

"Pretty good. You?"

"Same ole, same ole. What can I get you?"

"Just coffee, please. I'm still on the clock. But I have a couple of questions for you if you've got a minute."

"Sure. Give me five," Cole told him, setting the requested caffeine-filled mug on the bar in front of him. "Cream? Sugar?"

"No, thanks."

In less than five minutes, he was back to stand leaning toward Alex across the bar, bracing both hands on the edge of it.

"You sound serious. What can I help with?"

"I know it's been almost a week, but think back to last Friday night and tell me what you remember about Jeff Malone—when he came in with Donny Thompson and when he left. Robin Fenneli supposedly stopped by as well. Do you remember her?"

Cole frowned, thinking.

"Yeah. Can't say I *know* her, but I'd recognize her in a crowd. As I remember it, Jeff and Donny came in just after eight, maybe eight thirty. They waited for the table so they could play a game of pool, which I assume Donny lost, because the next time I noticed, Jeff was playing someone else who had put a quarter up. I kept an eye on Donny because he was trying to make a date with Stevie

Duncan, who wasn't having any of it. He bought her a drink, but she left not long after that with Brody Kingston, just to get away, I think. It amused me. Stevie's pretty good at getting rid of guys she isn't interested in, and she clearly wasn't interested in Donny."

"What time was that?"

"Oh, must have been about nine thirty, but by that time the place was packed. You know, Friday night and all. We're always busy on Fridays, so after eight or nine I'm pretty slammed behind the bar."

"But you saw Malone's girlfriend, Robin, come in?"

"Yeah, I did. Robin's one of those women you tend to notice—tall, not pretty, but striking, all that dark hair and those eyes. Pretty well stacked. I don't know what she sees in Malone, but . . . ah well." He grinned.

"I understand she wasn't here long."

"She only stayed for one drink. I heard her say she'd worked late and wanted to go home. Jeff told her he'd be along soon, but I didn't see him go out the front door until after eleven."

"And when did Donny leave?"

"Honestly, I didn't notice, but it must have been shortly after Robin. I noticed later that he was gone but Jeff was still here playing pool. Like I said, it was really busy that night. He played several games, but sat out some when he lost and someone else took over."

"Could you say that he was here all the time between eight thirty and when he left, after eleven?"

Cole looked at him thoughtfully.

"Officially, you mean?"

"Well—yeah, if it has to be, I guess. Could you testify to that if necessary?"

He shook his head slowly. "No. I think he was, but I couldn't say for certain. There's no way I kept any kind of close track—had no reason to. He could have been sitting down somewhere close to the pool table with a quarter up, waiting for his next game, and I wouldn't have seen him through the crowd that was sitting, standing, or moving around between here and there. Or he could have gone out and come back. A lot of people were coming and going from nine to midnight, and both the front and back doors are unlocked. To make it more complicated, the restrooms are just inside the back door. I was busy as a one-armed paperhanger and more concerned with making sure I got the orders right than who was here. You could ask Gena, she was serving tables that night and might have noticed."

"I'll do that. Thanks, Cole. Keep it to yourself, will you?"

"No problem."

Alex left a few minutes later, none the wiser for having spoken to Gena, who, like Cole, was unable to swear that Jeff Malone had been in the bar the whole time between when he said he arrived and when he left.

"There was too much going on," she told him. "I have to agree with Cole that he could have been here for the whole time if he says he was, but there's no way I can be sure. I practically run my legs off going back and forth to the bar on Fridays with the usual crowd. It was raining that night, so it was even more crowded. But the tips are good."

Alex hoped they were. He decided he'd rather have his job than hers, but wished Malone had picked a less busy weeknight to play pool—if that was what he'd been doing for those three hours.

Whatever it was, he still didn't know how Donny Thompson had wound up on the hill behind Jessie's house.

It seemed that there was no way to ascertain for sure the whereabouts of Malone, Fenneli, or Donny during the time between nine thirty and sometime after eleven that Friday night.

CHAPTER TWENTY-EIGHT

HANK PETERSON WAS LATE AND DIDN'T ARRIVE AT THE Aces until almost six o'clock that evening, and when he came he had Stevie Duncan with him.

"Sorry," he said, taking a seat on the bar stool Alex had saved for him on the far side of the bar, where several were empty and he had figured they could talk without being overheard. "We stayed to help Vic get the site under wraps in case it snows tonight. Hope you don't mind I let Stevie tag along."

"Let me tag along?" Stevie protested with a grin. "I drove myself here and will drive myself home. Nobody has a right to a particular bar stool, but"—she turned to Alex—"I'll be glad to move across the bar if you want to talk to Hank about trooper stuff."

"Not a problem," Alex told her. "It's kind of trooper stuff, I admit, but I think maybe you can help. Buy you both a beer?"

"Sure. Don't want to go dry in a land of plenty. Thanks."

"So you've gone to work for Vic Prentice again," Alex said to Hank, while waiting for the drinks to arrive.

"Yeah, it's nice to have a job close to home."

The bartender set up the beer, and as Hank raised the bottle to his mouth, a small earthquake suddenly trembled the place, making him set it back down untasted and wait for the shaking to stop, which it did almost immediately.

"Damn! Don't those things ever stop?" Stevie said, clutching at her beer with both hands.

"Nope," Alex said with a grin. "It's just the fault settling after the bigger one we had Tuesday. We've had several in the last couple of days. One woke me up in the middle of the night last night."

"I'm beginning to hate them almost as much as Stevie does," Hank said. "And she hates them a lot. Still, quakes and all, I'd rather live here than any place I can think of Outside."

Alex agreed, though he thought of Idaho as he did so, and reminded himself to talk to Jessie again about going to his mother's in Salmon for Christmas. They would have to make up their minds soon and take care of making flight reservations for the trip.

"So, what's up?" Hank asked.

"I'm looking for Jeff Malone and his girlfriend, Robin Fenneli," Alex told him. "Have you seen either of them anywhere in the last couple of days?"

"You know, I haven't. For a couple of days the first of the week, it seemed like I saw him everywhere. He was looking for Robin, but she had sort of made herself scarce and he couldn't find her. Maybe he did and they're together somewhere. But it's not anywhere I've been. You might try her place out on Boden—"

"Bodenburg Loop Road," Alex said, shaking his head. "Already been there earlier today and they're not—neither of them. The place seemed like it'd been empty for a couple of days, but her car is locked in the garage."

"I saw her late the day before yesterday," Stevie said and leaned forward to look past Hank to tell Alex. "She went past our work site headed for town on the Old Glenn."

"That would be Tuesday afternoon?"

"Right."

"You were at Oscar's in Wasilla last Friday night, weren't you, Stevie?" Alex asked.

"Yeah, for a while. I left when . . . Oh, that was the night Donny was killed, wasn't it? He was there for a while."

"I talked to Cole earlier," he told her and gently teased. "I understand he was giving you a bad time."

"Not really. Donny is—was—just Donny. He asked me to go riding with him and I don't want anything to do with those Pirates and their motorcycles. So I told him I was there with another guy and left with him so Donny would leave me alone."

"Brody Kingston," Alex said, surprising her.

"How'd you know that? Oh, yeah—Cole, of course. Not much gets past him, but he was really busy that night, so I didn't think he'd noticed."

"Well, he evidently did. Good save, Stevie," Hank told her. "Nothing much gets past you either."

"Have either of you got any idea where I might find Malone or Fenneli? Any ideas at all? I've already checked his house and hers, and where she works."

Hank frowned, thinking, then shook his head.

"I think she's got a brother in—" Stevie started, but Alex interrupted.

"Peter's Creek—another dead end."

"Seems like you've covered all the bases I can think of, unless you catch up with him floating around some-place," Hank said slowly. "Maybe Bill Monroe would know something. He plays pool at both of Oscar's places pretty regularly and must have played Malone at one or the other, or both, for that matter."

"He was at the Other Place Friday night."

"Yeah, he was. I was playing him when you guys got there."

There was little else to learn from Stevie. Hank, however, did know old Chuck Landers and where he had moved with his dogs to another old cabin at the far end of Knik Road near the historic town of Knik.

"He's got a friend out there who sold it to him when that housing development started to go in and they made him an offer for his land. They'll probably tear down the cabin on it though. Wouldn't fit well with those uptown houses and condos they're building."

"I'll tell Jessie. She was wondering where he'd gone," Alex said, putting on his coat. "Thanks, guys. If you see either Malone or his girl, let me know, will you?"

Five minutes later he was on his way to Wasilla and on out Knik Road, hoping that something hot and filling would be waiting with two cooks in the kitchen at home.

There was. Maxie had volunteered to make a kettle of what she said her son Joe called her infamous firehouse chili. And Jessie had a pan of corn bread keeping warm in the oven.

"Could you just move in and spend the winter, Maxie?" Alex asked after scraping the last spoonful of chili from his second bowlful.

"You'd regret that invitation when you began to realize the limitations of my culinary repertoire," she told him. "I'm not even second cousin to a natural-born cook. If I don't have a recipe for things they can turn out to be very strange and, at times, inedible. Nobody starved at my house, but both my husbands were much better cooks than I am, and so is my son Joe.

"I once got creative and tried a batch of lemon cookies with my own improvements on the recipe. Joe called them incredulies. You could have used them for hockey pucks."

"Well, anytime you want to do more of this chili, I'm up for it."

"Me too," Jessie chimed in. "Will you at least write it down for me, please?"

"Sure."

"Becker asked if one of us could give him a ride home from the hospital in the morning just after ten," Alex remembered to tell Jessie. "The doctor is springing him as soon as he's checked him once more. His sister, Alvina, is flying in tomorrow afternoon to take care of—and I quote—'her baby brother.' So he won't need mothering."

"We can do that," Jessie assured him. "I thought Maxie might like to go for a drive around the valley anyway, if the weather's decent. The viewing up the Knik River road is nice and there's one place where you can see the glacier from just off the road. We could do that after taking Phil home and getting him settled."

"I'd love that," Maxie agreed. "I've always driven right through Palmer, aiming to make it at least to Tok Junction on my way Outside. It'd be nice to take a look. Could we go out to the end of Knik Road and see old Knik and the part of the Iditarod Trail that passes through out there?"

"Good idea. We'll do that too."

Dishes done, kitchen cleaned, they had settled back at the table with coffee and a plate of cookies.

"Store-bought," Jessie informed them. "Sorry."

Then she said, "No, I'm not. These are pretty good, and I don't make great cookies either, Maxie. But Alex does a pretty fancy job on double chocolate brownies."

"As long as somebody does," Maxie said, smiling. "How'd the rest of your day go, Alex? Find out anything helpful? Or can you tell us if you did?"

He took a bite of the oatmeal cookie he was holding and chewed it thoughtfully, deliberating, while the two women waited patiently.

It would be unusual, Alex knew, to open the door to information concerning an ongoing case to anyone not law enforcement and directly involved with the investigation, especially of a murder case. Part of his willingness to do so now, he was sure, had to do with Becker's absence and the need to talk it out with someone. Jessie and Maxie, already involved, could be trusted to keep anything he told them to themselves and would, he hoped, not take it upon themselves to seek answers to subsequent questions on their own if he was not around to provide them.

Finally he nodded.

"Considering that you both know a fair amount about this case anyway, I don't see any reason why I shouldn't tell you most of it. Maybe you'll come up with something useful that I haven't got a handle on yet. You certainly did that about the other side of the hill, Maxie. I bet you've been thinking about it some, haven't you?"

She had to admit that she had. "Yes. I know it's really not my business, but I can't stop wondering about it all. And I keep running up against a lack of information on how the people who seem to be involved relate to each other," she said. "It's how people relate to each other that really counts when they hurt each other, doesn't it? There doesn't seem to be a reason for someone to kill Donny, so there's something, probably several somethings, about his relationship with whoever did that we don't know."

"I know what you mean," Alex agreed. "I'm still having some of the same trouble. But let me start at the beginning and set the scene and what I've learned for you. That may help you some and it may help me to put it in order.

"As you both know, this all started for us last weekend, when Jessie ran her team and sled over Donny Thompson's body in the trail above the house."

Jessie and Maxie both listened carefully as Alex went on to tell them pretty much in chronological order what he had discovered that might or might not have to do with Thompson's death. He talked for close to half an hour with few interruptions, and when he had finished they all three sat quietly for a minute or two, thinking it all over.

"There are several things I don't understand," Jessie said finally. "Like how does the woman from Sutton who ran her motorcycle off the road and hit the tree fit into all this? Or does she? Also, why would someone try so hard to hurt Becker, disabling his seat belt, shooting at him, running him off the road, and how did they know he'd be going out that way at all?"

"I don't know the answer to either of those things yet," Alex told her. "But I do think that whoever sabotaged the brakes and steering on Sharon Parker's bike meant for her to have an accident, and that that person was the one who went out the back door of the Alpine Inn that the bartender refused to identify. He said he didn't know, and though I didn't believe him, I couldn't pry an identification out of him.

"As for Becker, it was no accident. Someone tried hard to kill him and I have no idea who or why. It could have been one of the Road Pirates, or at least someone wearing one of their coats. Whoever did that may have thought he knew something they didn't want known. But if he did, or does, he isn't aware of it. It may be as totally unrelated as it seems. We've talked about every possibility we could think of—in this and other cases—and couldn't come up with anything he thought would lead anywhere in terms of a reason."

As Jessie leaned back in her chair, thinking so hard she was frowning, Alex turned to Maxie, who had been sitting quietly, taking sips of her coffee and listening intently.

"You've got a look on your face that tells me you've got a thing or two on your mind that I haven't touched on," he said. "What? I'm more than interested in a new point of view."

"You're right," she told him, reaching for another cookie. "Bear with me while I talk around this idea a bit, okay?"

"Better than okay."

"Well, to begin with, I think that with Becker unavailable to share responsibility for this case you've taken on a huge task by yourself. So much that there simply hasn't been time to put it into perspective as you would if there were two of you working, both adding facts, ideas, and, particularly, balance to keep your analysis on track.

"Second, I think there are too many details—too many people and places and things that have been happening. It feels as if you are walking around and around something, trying to see it from every possible angle. Perhaps you only need one or two—the important one or two, of course.

"You've told us a lot in chronological order. Some of it's relevant, but I think some of it's not and has inadvertently been included along the way as you tried to gather everything that could lead you to a conclusion. Becker's accident may not signify at all, for instance. But to figure out what does and what doesn't, you might consider going back to the basics of a week ago and take it one thing at a time, just the things you know for sure are true and pertinent to Donny's death, yes? Follow each thing or idea one at a time until it runs out, then ask yourself what else you need to finish it. Does that make sense?"

He stared at her, thinking hard, then nodded.

"You're right, Maxie," he told her. "It reminds me of that old thing about trying to fit rocks, pebbles, and sand into the same jar. If you don't do it in the correct order they won't all fit in. But if you put the rocks—the essential stuff—in first, then the pebbles—important and related stuff, but not so essential—in second, they'll all fall down among the rocks. Then, last, you pour in the sand—the related but not really important stuff. And it will all fit nicely into the jar."

"Exactly!" she said, and told him what she considered were the three rocks he should consider essential enough to put in first.

CHAPTER TWENTY-NINE

Two hours later the three of them sat in Alex's truck next to a half-built condominium across the street from Chuck Landers's old cabin—headlights off, engine silent.

All three were warmly dressed against the late October temperature, which hovered just above freezing. In addition, Alex wore insulated ski pants and Maxie shared a wool blanket with Jessie.

The streetlights for the new housing development had yet to be installed, so it was very dark. Heavy clouds, which Jessie hoped promised snow, had swept in earlier, canceling any light from an almost full moon.

They had been there just over half an hour, but the cabin they had visited earlier that day had remained dark and there was no hint of anyone inside or out.

"Maybe she won't come back," Jessie suggested. "And if she does, won't she notice the tire tracks and footprints we left this afternoon?"

"Probably," Alex agreed. "But she'll have no way of knowing who it was, will she? Could have been Chuck coming back for something he forgot."

"He wouldn't have left the tracks of three people—or gone up the hill."

"Give it a little," Maxie advised. "It's pretty dark to count tracks. If she thinks she's found a good hiding place, she won't want to search out another one this late in the day. I bet that even if she notices someone's been there she'll choose to stay the night and consider moving tomorrow."

"I agree," Alex said. "Besides, when you think about it, there can't be too many places that would be empty and so convenient to hole up in."

They waited another half hour, and even Maxie was beginning to think it was a hopeless idea when Alex sat up suddenly to peer through the frame that would eventually be condo walls at a single headlight coming slowly, quietly down the street in their direction.

"Want to make bets?" he asked. "Anyone else you can think of would be riding a motorcycle on this street? It's gotta be Fenneli."

As they watched, a motorcycle hesitated in front of the cabin across the street, seemed to be looking the place over carefully, then, evidently seeing nothing suspicious, pulled into the drive and up close to the front of it.

Alex had rolled down the window an inch so their breathing inside the closed cab wouldn't fog up the glass, and they heard the low mutter of the engine across the street die as the rider shut it down. Cautiously, still alert, the person, who was almost a shadow without the motorcycle's headlight on, climbed off, took a duffel bag off the back of the machine where it had been secured, something else from a saddlebag, walked quickly to the front door, opened it, hesitated again looking in, turned on a flashlight, shone the light around the interior, then disappeared into the cabin and shut the door.

Inside, the soft glow of light moved as if the person were looking around carefully, then it became stationary, as if it had been laid down. In a minute or two another smaller light appeared below the level of a front window, grew larger, then disappeared.

"I think she's lighting a fire in the stove," Alex said softly.

He was correct, for shortly a thin wisp of smoke, pale against the dark hillside behind it, floated up from the stovepipe that extended above the shingled roof.

"Stay here," he told the women quietly. "I'm going over there."

"But . . . ," Jessie started to protest.

"No," he said, opening the driver's-side door carefully to avoid making noise and stepping out to stand on the icy ground. "If she has a gun—and she may—I don't want to have you over there dividing my attention."

"Okay—for now. But close the door. We're about to freeze in here."

Through the windshield they watched him walk slowly and as quietly as possible away from the truck, across the street, and halfway up the drive toward the cabin.

He had almost reached the spot where the motorcycle was parked when the cabin door suddenly opened. The person inside, still dressed in warm clothing, stepped out and turned the flashlight beam toward a pile of wood that was stacked next to the front step.

Alex attempted to freeze in place. But, unfortunately, he had taken his last step onto a puddle that had frozen solid, flat, and slick in the cold. The interruption of his forward motion threw him off balance, his feet went out from under his tall frame, and he fell backward to sit down hard on the very ice that had caused his fall.

At the sound of this, the person in the doorway swung all attention in his direction, saw him struggling to get up, whirled and, leaving the door wide open, moved swiftly to the opposite corner of the cabin and vanished around it into the dark, turning off the flashlight on the way.

Alex regained his feet and took off in pursuit, careless now of any sound he was making in the effort.

"That's it," Jessie said. "Now I *am* going over there." Without further delay, she slid across the seat of the truck under the wheel, threw open the door on the driver's side, and hopped down onto the ground, clearly intending to follow.

"Not without me, you aren't," Maxie told her, opening the door on her side to exit the truck. "Hold on. I'm coming."

Together they trotted across the road and up the drive, carefully avoiding the slick spot where Alex had fallen, and around to the back of the cabin. There they stopped to listen.

There were sounds from the lower part of the hillside of two people in motion, Alex and whomever he was chasing. Then they heard a thrashing of brush and curses as he stumbled off the trail, probably at one of Chuck's carefully built switchbacks. It was clear he was all but blind in the dark in his attempt to follow the figure, who was climbing steadily ahead of him and gaining ground with the aid of the flashlight that had been turned back on.

"It's too dark and the ground's almost bare. If there was more snow he could see better against it," Jessie said, stepping forward. "Let's go up and see if we can help. I know this trail better than he does."

"Wait."

Maxie clutched at her arm to retain her.

"Whoever that is up there for sure won't come back this way. With the help of that light they'll be over the top and gone down the other side before Alex reaches it. Once out of sight, if they turn the light off they could hide anywhere in the woods and wait unseen for a chance to make a break. Or they could go straight down the trail to your place and be at the road long before Alex could make it there."

"So?" Jessie asked. "We can't just let them get away."

"So, Alex left the keys in the truck, didn't he? Let's go back and drive around to the other side. It's not that far and I'll bet we can make it before either of them."

"Then what?"

"Then we can at least see who it is, yes?"

"You're right. Let's do it."

Trotting back to the truck, they clambered hastily inside and in minutes were back on Knik Road, heading swiftly for Jessie's place. As Jessie drove, Maxie continued to assess the situation.

"You realize," she said, "that person left their only transportation—the motorcycle—back in the cabin driveway. On this side of the hill they'll have none."

"Interesting you should mention that," Jessie replied. "I was just wondering what they would do if they made it to the road ahead of Alex—and they probably will. If they try to catch a ride, we could offer them one as if we were just passing by. But I don't think that would be too smart, considering that he—she—might have a gun and we'd be instant hostages."

"Agreed," Maxie said. "What occurs to me is that we're driving Alex's truck. Yours is still in your driveway. Is it locked? Does it have the keys in it?"

"It's locked and the keys are in my pocket," Jessie assured her. "I never locked it when everybody out here knew everybody else, but with all the new people who I don't know moving into the area, I'm not so trusting anymore."

"Good girl! Then there's no way they can make a getaway in your truck."

"Nope! But I hope I remembered to lock the shed. There's a couple of four-wheelers in there and the keys to them are hanging inside the door."

"I very much doubt they'd take the time to go looking," Maxie reassured her. "It'd be a case of try your truck, then go to ground or try to get away before Alex catches up."

Jessie slowed as they neared the driveway that led to her house, but Maxie pointed on past it.

"Go on a bit farther," she suggested. "Alex mentioned that there was part of an old road where someone pulled off and parked a truck when Donny was killed—where they found his motorcycle down the hill in the brush. Let's take a quick look and be sure this person hasn't left another means of transportation there for an emergency getaway."

"Good idea."

Jessie drove on and turned into the short section of old road where she had called Alex's attention to the tracks and footprint she had found almost a week earlier.

By now, she thought, *they'd all be washed away.*

The two women sat staring at what confronted them in the headlight beams from the truck.

Pushed almost out of sight, facing out in the brush that had grown up on the old road, gleamed the chrome of another motorcycle, this one with black with green detailing—the colors of the Road Pirates.

"What now?" Maxie asked after a moment's silence.

"What now?" Jessie was suddenly furious. *"Now* I've really had it with people killing other people—on my property or off of it—with questions and no answers, with good people like Phil Becker getting hurt. In other words, with *all of it*!

"Now I make it impossible for anyone to get out of here on that thing."

Shoving the truck into low gear, she took her foot off the brake and stomped down on the gas. The truck lurched forward, Alex's extra-heavy bumper slammed into the front of the motorcycle, rotating its handlebars sideways, breaking off a mirror, propelling the machine to one side, tipping it over and off the edge of the old road into the brush below, where even with the windows up they could hear it crashing down the slope over rocks and through bushes.

The truck engine had died and everything grew very still.

"Well," remarked Maxie stoically, having had no time or opportunity to voice an opinion.

"That's one problem solved, isn't it?"

CHAPTER THIRTY

ALEX, ANGRY, FRUSTRATED, AND WINDED, HAD FINALLY reached the top of the hill over which the person he was chasing had disappeared. Panting, he stopped and stood still where the uphill trail joined the one at the top, holding his breath for a moment or two to listen, but heard nothing. There was also no sign of the light the climber ahead of him had used to gain the hill's summit and none on the slope below, where he had hoped to follow it down.

Gone to ground, he decided. *Or already halfway down and out of sight.* But he heard nothing to give him a clue.

As he debated which way to follow—through the woods where he and Becker had found the bit of fabric caught in the bark of a tree, or on the trail that led down to the house and dog yard—he suddenly remembered that in a pants pocket he had a Bic lighter that he used to light fires in the cast-iron stove in the house below. Pulling off a glove, he thrust a hand past the elastic waistband of his insulated ski pants, retrieved it from that pocket, crouched, shielded it with the other hand, and held its small flickering over the ground to the right, then the left. It provided just enough illumination to reveal a disturbance in the leaves that littered the frozen ground and vanished into the dark to the left.

Regretting the time this maneuver had cost him, he dropped the lighter into a jacket pocket and replaced his glove as he turned and stretched his long legs into a ground-covering lope on the familiar track.

Reaching the trail that went down to Jessie's, he took it and was finally headed downhill, though there was still no sign of the person he was trying to catch.

Uneasily aware that he could have left that person hiding somewhere above, halfway down he was reassured to see the yard light far below flash on. It told him that someone, or something, had activated the motion sensor on the driveway side of its tall pole, for the sensor was not set to respond to the movement of the dogs in the yard, only something near the house and the drive in front of it. The person he was after could have caused it to come on, but not necessarily. He considered this uneasily, remembering that halfway up the hill from the cabin he had heard the sound of his truck starting and assumed that Jessie and Maxie, having seen what transpired after his fall on the ice and the pursuit that resulted, would believe he would continue it and so must have intended to drive back home to meet him on the other side.

He had not heard the truck pull into the driveway below, however, and there was nothing he could do about the situation until he reached it. So he continued down the hill as rapidly as possible, hoping he was chasing the person from the cabin, whom he supposed was Robin Fenneli. But if it was, he could be chasing her straight into the two women in his truck. If she was carrying any weapon but the flashlight, that meeting could turn into real trouble.

* * *

From where she had pulled into the old road, through the bare trunks of the birch Jessie also saw the light come on in her yard, and heard the dogs in her kennel begin to bark in response to a stranger in the area.

Quickly restarting the truck's engine, she backed out onto Knik Road, headed for her own drive.

"Hold on," she told Maxie, and made a quick left turn into it.

The dogs she could see were tugging hard at their tethers and barking at something, or someone, near the house, but she could see nothing moving as she sped up the drive.

If it was Alex, she calculated, he would have come to meet them. So it must be the person he had been chasing over the hill from the other side.

Braking hard on the gravel, she slid the truck to a stop that slewed it slightly sideways behind her pickup and turned off the engine, effectively blocking in that vehicle.

For a long minute the two women sat looking carefully around for the source of whatever—whoever—had caused the yard light to come on.

Nothing moved.

Then Jessie reached under the driver's seat and retrieved a crowbar she knew Alex kept there.

Taking it with her, she opened the door, slid out onto the ground, and turned to Maxie.

"Stay here and lock the doors after me," she told her.

"I really don't think—" Maxie began.

But the slam of the door cut off her protest in midsentence.

After locking the door on the passenger side, she slid across under the wheel to lock the driver's door, then watched Jessie move, slowly and carefully, along that side of the truck.

"Shut up, you mutts," she heard her yell at her dogs, and, well trained and hearing the serious tone of her voice, except for a young laggard or two at the back of the yard near the woods, they abruptly did.

The stillness that resulted was so complete that with the window down an inch, for the first time Maxie could faintly hear not-so-well-trained Stretch yapping from inside the house, where they had left him with Tank. She could also hear the crunch and echo of gravel under Jessie's heavy boots as she tried to move quietly toward the front of the truck. A moment later she realized that it was not an echo she was hearing. It was another person walking somewhere out of sight between them and the house. From inside the cab she couldn't tell exactly where, but it must be somewhere on the other side of Jessie's pickup.

Where she was half crouched beside the left front wheel, Jessie had heard it too and, keeping her head below the level of the truck's hood and her body very close to the fender, she waited attentively.

The sound of other footsteps stopped, with an odd sort of scuffle.

In the minutes of long, listening silence that ensued, nothing could be heard moving. Stretch had stopped barking in the house, and, lacking motion, the yard light suddenly blinked out, leaving her temporarily blind in the dark.

She didn't move, but stayed where she was and considered her options until her ability to see in the dark gradually returned.

Then, as suddenly as it had gone out, the light came on again as someone else moved, out of sight, but in range of the sensor.

There was a slight click as a pebble rattled against another behind her. Abruptly she straightened to a standing position, but before she could whirl to confront whoever it was that stood behind her, someone spoke.

"Don't even think about it," a voice warned in a low, quiet voice. "I have a gun in my hand, so stay just as you are and drop the crowbar."

Inside the truck, Maxie was startled to find herself looking down at a dark figure that had moved into view so close to the window that had it been open she could have reached out and laid a hand on its shoulder. Alex's truck was not new, but it was new enough that lowering a window was as simple as pressing a button located in the door handle. Knowing that doing so would make a small but unmistakable sound, she did not attempt it. Instead, she sat still and quiet, wishing she had the crowbar Jessie had just dropped to the ground as instructed, and that the window was open, so she could have hit the person over the head with it from her perfect angle. Instead she sat silently to avoid attracting attention. Perhaps there would be something she could do later.

Looking down from her seat in the truck it was impossible to see who the person was for a generous hood attached to a dark coat hid the face of the wearer, extending far enough forward to also shield it from the illumination of the yard light on its pole high overhead.

"Now," that person said to Jessie, "toss back the keys to this truck."

"I don't have the keys," she said. "They're still inside."

Watching Jessie closely, the person, turning slightly toward the truck, reached out with their right hand and tried the door, allowing Maxie to see that in the left hand was, not a gun, but the flashlight they had used to light the way up the hill from the cabin on the other side.

"It's locked. Give me the keys or—"

The reach for the door handle had also given Maxie an opportunity she had been wishing for—not the same chance, but chance enough. Unlocking the door with one hand as she opened it with the other, she shoved it outward as hard as she could, slamming it into the figure standing there, sending it to its knees, then over onto its back.

"Now, Jessie—now," Maxie called out.

Scooping up the crowbar as she ducked and whirled around, Jessie took a couple of long steps forward to stand over the figure on the ground and take in the flashlight in lieu of a firearm.

Keeping the crowbar raised in threat, she looked down into the face of the woman on the ground.

"I know you," she said. "I recognize your voice—even though you tried to disguise it then, and are trying now. You were on the hill last Monday, weren't you? You made me give you the handgun I found next to where Donny Thompson was killed—by you? Who the hell are you?"

At that point Alex finally made it down the hill and into the yard. He came loping past the equipment sheds, around the house into the circle cast by the yard light, and up to the three women—two of them standing over the one on the ground, who was now sitting up, her hood fallen back onto her shoulders to expose long dark hair.

"Robin Fenneli, I presume?" he said to her, offering a hand to help her up.

She nodded, but said nothing as she brushed herself off after pocketing the flashlight.

"I see you've got things pretty well in hand here," he

said to Jessie. "Guess I shouldn't have been in such a rush when you're doing my work for me."

"You can thank Maxie," Jessie told him. "It was Maxie who knocked her down."

CHAPTER THIRTY-ONE

"Thank you, Maxie," Alex said with a smile and a nod. "You have good timing."

He reached in to remove the keys from the ignition of his truck, then closed the door and locked it.

"It's cold out here. Let's go inside where it's warm," he suggested, turning to guide Fenneli toward the house with a hand on her arm.

She said nothing in response, but went without protest, the other two women following closely.

"And, if you've had time to notice, Jessie," he tossed back over a shoulder, "it's starting to snow."

Jessie looked up to see a few large flakes drifting down like pale feathers in the illumination of the yard light.

A satisfied grin spread itself across her face.

"About time," she said. "But we'll see in the morning."

They had made it almost to the steps that led up to the porch when a voice from the darkness near the far side of the house, outside the circle of yard light, stopped them.

"Let her go, Jensen. She may not have had a gun, but I do, so just step away and let her go."

Alex turned quickly, shoving Fenneli behind him.

"Malone?" he questioned, recognizing the voice of the

man who stood, feet braced wide, holding a handgun that reflected enough ambient light to define its shape. "You know I can't do that. This won't work."

"Maybe you think you can't," came the reply. "But you're wrong. It's what will work for now. Come here, Robin. You've been avoiding me for days."

Fenneli spoke for the first time.

"No," she said, stepping halfway from behind Alex so she could see and be seen. "It's time this was over, Jeff. Give it up."

"Not a chance. Get over here before I use this thing."

He moved the gun so it was pointed at Maxie, who was nearest. "The old lady'll be first," he said, his voice rising. "Then Jessie. Do it! *Now!*"

Fenneli took another step toward him, but Alex threw out an arm to stop her.

Malone fired a shot that hit the ground directly in front of Maxie.

"Let me go," Fenneli begged Alex, pushing against his arm. "I've already been responsible for one death. I don't want to make it more."

"You didn't kill Donny Thompson."

"I didn't shoot him, no. I loved him. But if it hadn't been for me, he wouldn't have been killed. That makes me responsible, doesn't it?"

"How?"

"Donny came up the hill that night from this side, heading for Chuck Landers's old cabin on the other side, where I was supposed to be waiting for him. But I didn't wait. I climbed the hill and was at the top to meet him when he came up. We were going back there—to be together and decide what to do about our relationship. It just happened—us loving each other—neither of us intended it.

But we both knew that Jeff was crazy jealous and already suspected that something was up.

"He showed up before we could go down. He'd found Donny's bike across the road, where he'd parked it. He didn't say a word, just shot Donny in the head, and went back down this side of the hill and back to the bar, I guess. Donny was dead before he fell."

"You lying bitch," Malone shouted, taking a step forward into the light. Before anyone else could move, he leveled the handgun at her, and fired.

The bullet hit her in the left shoulder below the collarbone. Before Alex could catch her, she took one sharp breath and crumpled to the ground where he had been standing.

But he was not standing there anymore. With more people in the line of fire, before Malone could aim and pull the trigger again, Jensen was on him, shoving the gun wide and wresting it away with one hand, while he directed a solid blow to the man's midsection with the other. It left him rolling on the ground as he tried to regain his breath.

Flinging the gun out of reach, Jensen turned him over facedown, put a knee in the middle of his back, and held him there.

"Jess," he called. "Call 911 for an ambulance ASAP. Then get my handcuffs out of my duty coat in the house, toss 'em out here, and call the detachment for assistance—in that order. Tell them I've got it covered, but need backup on a shooting here. They'll know who to send."

Jessie sprang up, moving fast to do what he asked.

"Then bring some towels, a blanket, and ice in plastic for Fenneli," he called after her.

He turned to Maxie, who was on her knees beside

Fenneli, holding pressure on the damage in the woman's shoulder with the winter scarf she had been wearing.

"How's she doing?"

He was surprised to hear the wounded woman herself answer in a weak voice. "It's starting to hurt a lot, but I can breathe okay."

"She's okay for the moment, I think," Maxie assured him. "How long will that ambulance take? She's bleeding a fair amount."

"Just keep solid pressure on it. Jessie'll be back quick. She knows. Lying on frozen ground won't hurt her for a little bit, but as soon as I get Malone secured we'll move her inside if the medics aren't here yet."

They showed up in record time and the driveway was soon busy with an ambulance and a pair of medics, who were then gone with Robin Fenneli on her way to the hospital in good hands. All the law enforcement Alex could wish for showed up, sirens screaming, to take Jeff Malone to a holding cell in Palmer, where the investigation would proceed, eventually to trial and, hopefully, conviction.

Finally left alone, Alex, Jessie, and Maxie proceeded into the house, where they reviewed the events of the evening over hot coffee and much appreciated shots of Jameson.

"Well," observed Jessie, peering out the window for perhaps the dozenth time. "It's still snowing and there's over an inch on the ground out there and it doesn't look like stopping. Want to go for a dog sled ride tomorrow, Maxie?"

"Sure. But then I think I'd better arrange to get on back to Homer and make sure my own nest is still as cozy as I left it. If it's snowing here, the way the weather pattern's been going the last few years, it's undoubtedly snowing there too."

"Bet you're glad you're flying and won't have to drive on slick roads this time," Alex said, coming back from the kitchen, where he had taken their used glasses.

"You bet."

She stood up, drained the last swallow of her Jameson.

"Good night, all. I'm for bed," she said, heading for the stairs that led up to the guest room. "I've had more exercise in the last couple of days than in a week at home. And you two really do know how to entertain your guests with unusual events like those of this evening, don't you? Haven't had so much excitement since Jessie and I came up the Alaska Highway together."

"If I'd only had a light I would have got up it faster," Alex said the next evening, recalling his aggravating struggle to make it up the hill in the dark. "It's amazing how one small thing can alter the outcome of an action."

Then, with a grin, he gave those assembled a literary scrap memorized in childhood, as he often did: "For want of a nail a shoe was lost. For want of a shoe a horse was lost. For want of a horse the rider was lost. For want of a rider the battle was lost. For want of a battle the kingdom was lost. And all for the want of a horseshoe nail."

"My Daniel always said it was 'tup-ney nail,'" Maxie said. "But that may have just been the way Aussies say it."

"According to my mother, it's 'two-penny,'" he agreed. "But I looked it up once online and couldn't find two-penny used anywhere. Did you know that Benjamin Franklin used the verse in *Poor Richard's Almanac*?"

"Where do you get all that stuff, Alex?" Becker teased him.

"Oh, here and there. We were big readers. My folks both encouraged it."

They were five around the big round table for Maxie's Friday night send-off dinner, which had been appreciated, and dessert had now taken its place—a peach cobbler that had been keeping warm in the oven and was served with a side of vanilla ice cream, much to Alex's approval.

Jessie sat with her back to the kitchen and to her right around the table were Maxie, Phil Becker, his sister, Alvina, and Alex, who completed the circle of friends, old and new.

Tank and Stretch, also well fed, were, as usual, snoozing on the rug in front of the sofa and kitty-corner from the stove.

"How's your arm, Phil?" Jessie asked.

"Doc says it's doing better than he expected," came the answer. "But I'd still like to know who cut my seat belt and ran me off the road out there."

"So would I—and I intend to find out. I think the key is in the Road Pirates, if we can convince someone to talk.

"There are some other loose ends I'd like to tidy up," Alex added, and contributed one that was still on his list of things to investigate. "I want to know who sabotaged the brakes and steering on Sharon Parker's motorcycle—and why. But I've a feeling it has nothing to do with Donny Thompson's death, so I'll have to look elsewhere. First, I'm going to have a serious sit-down with Pete at the Alpine Inn in Sutton tomorrow. There's been enough of him *keeping his own counsel*."

"You going out for the funeral?" Becker asked.

"Yes. I think it's the least I can do—that and explain to the family exactly what happened, as well as I know it. Jessie and I went to see Robin Fenneli today and she laid it all out pretty clearly for me, and I believe her. Jessie's volunteered to go to Sutton with me and has an errand of her own. Robin asked her to deliver flowers, since she'll be in the hospital a few more days."

"Malone?"

"Will be in jail from now till next Tishah-b'Ab, if I have anything to say about it."

The next morning Jessie drove Maxie back into Anchorage to catch her short flight to Homer at the far end of the Kenai Peninsula, hugged her good-bye, and sent her on her way.

"And thanks again for the ride with your sled and dogs yesterday," Maxie told her. "I've always wanted to do that. It was great."

Jessie watched her walk away and wave before she disappeared onto the tarmac to board the small plane for the flight home.

She felt singularly lonely all the way back to the Mat-Su Valley, but very glad to have such a dear friend.

"I'm glad we went to the funeral," she said to Alex late that evening, laying down the day's paper and getting up to bank the fire in the cast-iron stove for the night.

"Me too," he agreed, unfolding himself from where he had been sprawled on the opposite end of the sofa with the editorial page. "It was good to be able to have a few answers for some of the Thompsons' questions, and though I'm not fond of funerals, it was a nice, short service."

Stepping up behind her, he waited until she finished with the fire, stood up, and turned around into his arms, where he held her close for a moment or two before leaning back to look down and say, "Hey. You know that thing about degrees of separation?"

"Uh-huh."

"I'm glad I don't have to search through five or six people for the one person I'd want most to find."

"Oh, really?" Jessie gave him an impish grin.

"Yeah, really."

"How many degrees, then?"

"None, love," he told her. "No separation at all, okay?"

"Works for me, Trooper."

Also Available

Murder at Five Finger Light
A Jessie Arnold Mystery
by
Sue Henry

Jessie's friends, Laurie and Jim, have acquired their dream—an old lighthouse on the Alaskan Inside Passage—and invited everyone they know for a party. This is a weekend Jessie won't soon forget—especially when one of the guests ends up dead.

At first the death seems accidental. But when someone cuts the telephone and the radio connections, Jessie realizes there's a killer loose on the island.

Available wherever books are sold or at penguin.com

NEW IN HARDCOVER

The End of the Road

A Maxie and Stretch Mystery

by
Sue Henry

Maxie McNabb and her miniature dachshund,
Stretch, are just back from their latest
adventure when a murder shatters the quiet in
their hometown of Homer, Alaska. Now it's up
to Maxie to find the killer—a search that leads
her to a place called "the end of the road."

Available wherever books are sold or at
penguin.com